Praise for the Men of Mercy Series

"Lindsay Cross delivers high-powered action, alpha heroes and an exciting conclusion!"

- ELLE JAMES
New York Times and USA Today bestselling author

"This is one of those books that the phrase sit down, shut up and hang on would be used because it's a wild ride from page one to the end."

- **5 Star Goodreads Review**, Redemption River

"This book was wall to wall action. Once the danger hit, it never slowed down. I was late leaving my house because there was no way I could stop reading."

- **5 Star NetGalley Review**, Redemption River

BOOKS BY LINDSAY CROSS

MEN OF MERCY NOVELS
REDEMPTION RIVER
RESURRECTION RIVER
RECKLESS RIVER
RAVAGED RIVER
ETHAN'S PROMISE – MAY 2016
AARON'S HONOR – JULY 2016
MERC'S STORY – FALL 2016
SHERIFF LAWSON'S STORY – FALL 2016
ANTICIPATION - 2015

Reckless River

Men of Mercy, Book 3

Lindsay Cross

Copyright Warning

Published by Cypress Bend Publishing LLC

Cover Design by Kari March

Reckless River
All Rights Are Reserved. Copyright 2015 by Lindsay Cross.

First electronic publication: October 2015
First print publication: October 2015

Digital ISBN: 978-0-9968360-2-9
Print ISBN: 978-0-9968360-5-0

To my family and friends whose unwavering support saw me through the tough spots.

DOSSIER

TASK FORCE SCORPION (TF-S)

A branch of Joint Special Operations Command (JSOC)
Ft. Grenada, MS

MACK GREY: Detachment Commander, Captain
  ➤ Recruited from the 75th Ranger Regiment, Ft. Benning, GA
  ➤ Specialized Skills: direct action, unconventional warfare, special reconnaissance, interrogations specialist, psychological warfare
  ➤ First in Command. Responsible for ensuring and maintaining operational readiness.
  ➤ Height: 6'
  ➤ Weight: 195lbs
  ➤ Combat Experience: Operation Gothic Serpent, Somalia. Operation Desert Storm, Operation Iraqi Freedom, Operation Crescent Wind, Operation Rhino, Operation Anaconda, Operation Jacan, Operation Mountain Viper, Operation Eagle Fury, Operation Condor, Operation Summit, Operation Volcano, Operation Achilles

HUNTER JAMES: Warrant Officer, Detachment Commander
- Recruited from the 75th Ranger Regiment, Ft. Benning, GA
- Specialized Skills: direct action, unconventional warfare, special reconnaissance, psychological warfare
- Responsible for overseeing all Team ops. Commands in absence of detachment commander.
- Height: 6'3"
- Weight: 230lbs
- Combat Experience: Operation Enduring Freedom, Operation Crescent Wind, Operation Anaconda, Operation Jacana, Operation Mountain Viper, Operation Eagle Fury

RANGER JAMES: Team Daddy/Team Sergeant, Master Sgt.
- Recruited from the 75th Ranger Regiment, Ft. Benning, GA
- Specialized Skills: direct action, unconventional warfare, special reconnaissance
- Plans, coordinates & directs Team intelligence, analysis and dissemination.
- Height: 6'2"
- Weight: 225lbs
- Combat Experience: Operation Enduring Freedom, Operation Crescent Wind, Operation Anaconda, Operation Jacana, Operation Mountain Viper, Operation Eagle Fur

JARED CROWE: Weapons Sergeant, Sgt. 1st Class
  - Recruited from Delta Force, Ft. Bragg, NC
  - Specialized Skills: direct action, unconventional warfare, special reconnaissance, Sniper
  - Weapons expert. Capable of firing and employing all small arm and crew served weapons
  - Height: 6'0"
  - Weight: 220lbs
  - Combat Experience: Operation Enduring Freedom, Operation Crescent Wind, Operation Anaconda, Operation Jacana, Operation Condor, Operation Summit, Operation Volcano, Operation Achilles

HOYT CROWE: Asst. Weapons Sergeant, Staff Sgt.
  - Recruited from Delta Force, Ft. Bragg, NC
  - Specialized Skills: direct action, unconventional warfare, special reconnaissance, Sniper
  - Weapons expert. Capable of firing and employing all small arm and crew served weapons
  - Height: 6'0"
  - Weight: 210lbs
  - Combat Experience: Operation Enduring Freedom, Operation Crescent Wind, Operation Anaconda, Operation Jacana, Operation Condor, Operation Summit, Operation Volcano, Operation Achilles

AARON SPEIRS: Medical Sergeant, Sgt. 1st Class
- ➢ Recruited from Delta Force, Ft. Bragg, NC
- ➢ Specialized Skills: direct action, unconventional warfare, special reconnaissance, medic
- ➢ The life-saver. Employs the latest field medical technology and limited surgical procedures
- ➢ Height: 6'1"
- ➢ Weight: 195lbs
- ➢ Combat Experience: Operation Anaconda, Operation Jacana, Operation Condor, Operation Summit, Operation Volcano,

RISER MALLON: Asst. Medical Sergeant, Staff Sgt.
- ➢ Recruited from Delta Force, Ft. Bragg, NC
- ➢ Specialized Skills: direct action, unconventional warfare, special reconnaissance, medic
- ➢ The life-saver. Employs the latest field medical technology and limited surgical procedures
- ➢ Height: 6'2"
- ➢ Weight: 215lbs
- ➢ Combat Experience: Operation Anaconda, Operation Jacana, Operation Condor, Operation Summit, Operation Volcano, Operation Achilles

MERC: Engineer Sergeant, Sgt. 1st Class
- ➢ Recruited from Special Operations Group (SOG) of the Central Intelligence Agency (CIA)
- ➢ Specialized Skills: direct action, unconventional warfare, special reconnaissance, Demolitions, psychological operations
- ➢ Demolition expert. Trained in psychological warfare, conducts field interrogations.
- ➢ Height: 6'5"
- ➢ Weight: 250lbs
- ➢ Combat Experience: Classified

ETHAN SLADE: Communications Sergeant/Commo Guy, Sgt. 1st Class
> Recruited from the 75th Ranger Regiment, Ft. Benning, GA
> Specialized Skills: direct action, unconventional warfare, special reconnaissance, communications
> Communications expert. Employ latest FM, multi-channel, and satellite communication devices.
> Height: 6'0"
> Weight: 200lbs
> Combat Experience: Operation Condor, Operation Summit, Operation Volcano, Operation Achilles

SHANE CARTER: Weapons Sergeant, Staff Sgt.
> Recruited from the Marine Corps Forces Special Operations Command (MARSOC), Camp Lejeune, NC
> Specialized Skills: direct action, unconventional warfare, special reconnaissance, weapons expert/sniper
> Weapons expert. Capable of firing and employing all small arm and crew served weapons
> Height: 5'11"
> Weight: 180lbs
> Combat Experience: Operation Iraqi Freedom, Operation Condor, Operation Summit, Operation Volcano, Operation Achilles

CORD CARTER: Weapons Sergeant, Staff Sgt.
- ➤ Recruited from the Marine Corps Forces Special Operations Command (MARSOC), Camp Lejeune, NC
- ➤ Specialized Skills: direct action, unconventional warfare, special reconnaissance, weapons expert/sniper
- ➤ Weapons expert. Capable of firing and employing all small arm and crew served weapons
- ➤ Height: 6'1"
- ➤ Weight: 210lbs
- ➤ Combat Experience: Operation Iraqi Freedom, Operation Condor, Operation Summit, Operation Volcano, Operation Achilles

MR J: CIA Liaison, Embedded with ISA
- ➤ Special Activities Division (SAD) of the Central Intelligence Agency (CIA)
- ➤ Specialized Skills: Classified
- ➤ Training: Classified
- ➤ Height: 5'10"
- ➤ Weight: 170lbs
- ➤ Combat Experience: Classified

Prologue

"Remind me why we're here again." Hoyt tossed the fresh-caught fish from the river down on the log at their campsite and pulled his fillet knife from his belt.

"You know why we're here." Jared's curt reply left much to be desired by way of explanation.

"I know why, but what I don't know is *why*." Hoyt grabbed the first fish off the stringer and cleaned it, using the overturned log as a makeshift table.

Jared continued to stoke the campfire, the river rushing by twenty feet away. The sun dropped low on the horizon, hiding behind the tall Tennessee Mountains. Tennessee...God, how he hated this place.

"I heard there's movement at Crowe Camp, you know this may be our chance for long overdue revenge." Jared threw the last log on the fire, the loud crash sending sparks flying into the air.

Katlyn Crowe, a.k.a. Miss Kay, was Hoyt and Jared's aunt. She was also the woman who had single handedly tried to kill them when they were children, and would have succeeded if it not for a scared little girl with the biggest golden eyes. She'd helped the brothers escape from Kay and Crowe Mountain.

"You really think Kay doesn't know someone is trying to overthrow her? She owns that mountain and all the people on it. One whiff of treason and she'd have the whole county reporting," Hoyt said.

Just thinking about Kay had Jared clenching his hands

into fists. She was the reason for his nightmares. The reason he had to flee his home. "I think any chance to get our revenge is worth a shot."

"And what if it's a trap?" Hoyt brought the fish filets over, laid them in a cast-iron skillet and placed it on the grate over the fire.

"Either we take the chance at getting even or we puss out. I think we made the right decision." The smell of cooking fish filled the air, but Jared doubted he could eat with his stomach crammed this full of revulsion.

Hoyt shook his head, the tired lines around his eyes deepening. The glow from the fire branding his skin a golden tan and his curly blond hair almost honey. Hoyt didn't possess the deep-seated hatred for the Crowes that Jared did. But Hoyt was younger than him, enough so that he didn't remember the pain, the starvation, the beatings Jared had taken to protect him.

Jared did though. He remembered every single one.

"I love you, brother. And you know I'll follow you anywhere," Hoyt hedged.

"But what? Finish what you wanted to say."

"But I think you've let this hatred eat at you for too long. I thought you were moving past it. But now I find out you've been keeping tabs on that place, after all these years. You're obsessed. If you're not careful, you'll spend your whole life hating and miss out on all the good." Hoyt's voice was quiet but dead on. His brother had always been the kind one, the happy-go-lucky ladies' man, but he didn't shirk from the shit either.

"How can you be so damn optimistic? You've seen the same crap I have on missions. You've seen the genocide, the rape, the murder. Hell, worse even than that. Not sure where you've been, but all I've seen is plenty of evidence that the human race is fucking evil." The last mission the brothers' Special Forces team had been on was a case in point. They'd tracked the terrorist, Al Seriq, to his compound in Pakistan to find hundreds of dead bodies, and to boot, they'd lost their teammate. There'd been nothing but death. And their team,

Task Force Scorpion, had lost track of the terrorist. Fuck.

"What about back home? There's a lot of good there." Hoyt flipped the fish over and uncapped a bottle of water.

"Home? We don't have a home. If you're talking about Mercy, Mississippi, that's where Hunter and Ranger are from. Not us. You think they want us staying around there?" After escaping Crowe Mountain, the brothers had quickly learned how hard it was to survive on their own. They'd seen the military as a light at the end of the tunnel. It provided three meals a day, a place to live, and a way to earn a living. Something the brothers had never had. Jared had joined up the day of his eighteenth birthday and Hoyt followed suit. "You think they want a couple of white trash orphans hanging around their family?"

Hoyt removed the fish from the heat and split it between two paper plates. He remained silent as he handed one to Jared and then took his spot on the ground, sitting cross-legged near the fire. The chilly fall air had a stiff bite tonight and Jared found himself hugging the fire, too.

They ate in silence. Had he been too harsh? Was Jared slowly murdering his brother's hope for no reason?

Or was he protecting him from heartbreak?

"I really like it there."

Jared was jerked from his thoughts by Hoyt's soft response. "I know you like it in Mercy, but you know better. You never get attached. Attachments are weaknesses. Next thing you know you'll be trying to get married and settle down. But you and I both know that's not in either of our cards." What did they have to offer? Nothing but white trash DNA and a past so screwed up even the SF psychologist steered clear.

Hoyt jumped to his feet and clenched his hands at his sides, his blue eyes burning as bright as the campfire. "Dammit, I'm sick of never being good enough. When will it end? When do we get to settle down and live out our lives without our past hanging over our every move?"

Jared stayed down, knowing Hoyt needed to get this out and come to terms. "When have I ever steered you wrong, little brother?"

Jared had devoted his life to raising Hoyt and protecting him. When the military tried to separate them into two different SF Teams, Jared had simply refused. After multiple fights and demerits, he'd succeeded. And now the Crowe brothers were the most decorated snipers in the whole Special Forces.

"You've never steered me wrong, but you've never let me live either. And now look where we are. We're back on this fucking Godforsaken mountain, probably walking straight into a trap, and for what? All because you need revenge for something someone did to us when we were little kids!"

Anger coursed through Jared's veins and he surged to his feet. "You might not remember what she did to us, but I do! I have to live with it every time I close my goddamn eyes. Of course I want revenge! I have to put these demons to bed." *Before I lose my mind.*

"I hope you're right this time, brother. I really do, because this is the last time I'll come back here. I intend to move on from this. I will make Mercy my home and I will find someone to have a real relationship with. I'm sick of being homeless and I'm sick of being married to the military. I want more!" Hoyt threw his plate into the fire and stomped off into the woods. He stopped at the tree line and turned around. "Don't follow me. I'll be back for second watch."

Jared collapsed back onto the ground, the fight draining from him. Had he been so wrapped up in his demons that he'd tried to drag Hoyt down with him?

Chapter One

Jared Crowe had felt the press of cold steel against his skin before, but he had never expected to feel it here, at his home. A place he hated.

"Lookee here, I done caught me a rat." Her voice had that hill folk lilt to it. An accent he normally found revolting, but for some reason he couldn't define, hers sounded nice.

Familiar.

Jared lowered his binoculars and placed them on the ground. The cold mountain air swirled through the mist that had not yet been dispelled by the early morning sun. Dry autumn leaves crackled, stirred up every now and then by a chilled breeze. A mockingbird let out a harsh caw down in the valley below, signaling a threat to his nest.

"Now, you keep them hands above your head and get up real nice and slow like. Don't make me blow a hole in your head." Okay, even if her voice was sexy, she was starting to piss him off.

Homegrown or terrorist he didn't care—Jared didn't like it when gun barrels were pressed to his head.

She stepped back and Jared pushed off the hard rocky dirt, careful to keep his arms away from his body. No need to alert her. He had time. She would look away. Blink. And then it would be over.

"All right, you're doing good. Now turn around."

Jared turned, just as slow and methodical as he had risen. Steam from his breath puffed in front of his face, but he didn't feel the cold. And even if he had felt it, he wouldn't have allowed it to affect him. His family had beaten any softness out of him long ago.

They'd beaten everything out of him.

He didn't experience normal emotions. He knew he was broken, but he didn't care enough to try and fix himself. It wasn't like he had a family or wife in need of his emotional support. The only people who needed him were his brother and his unit, and a sensitive weakling would be of no use to any of them.

Maybe that's why he found it so easy to smile at the woman in front of him, who was holding a shotgun as long as she was tall. "You fire that gun and it'll knock you on your ass, girl."

A wide-brimmed floppy leather hat obscured half her features, and damned if her clothes gave away any indication of her actual age. She looked like a little girl playing dress-up in her daddy's clothes. Loose baggy jeans, baggy shirt, and a worn-out leather vest. He'd died and gone to hillbilly hell.

But her lush, tempting lips were all woman. Then she lifted her chin and he saw her eyes. Awareness sucker punched him and he drew in a small breath. Her eyes, the amber color of pure mountain whiskey. He'd known one girl—one person in his entire life—with those exotic gold eyes. "Sparrow."

She blinked and steadied the butt of her shotgun against her shoulder, keeping a safe distance from him. "How do you know my name? What are you? You ain't no cop and you ain't no DEA. Them boys don't wear the camo like you got on."

Camouflage paint completely covered his face, and a black do rag was tied tight and flat against his head. She wouldn't be able to recognize him in his war paint, not after all these years, and maybe that was for the best. He could reveal his identity later, take her by surprise and rip that gun out of her hands before she shot herself with it.

"You're right, I'm not any type of law enforcement. If I were, you'd be a lot safer than you are right now." Jared made his voice menacing. Even allowed a little bit of his old accent to slip in. Let her know she wasn't dealing with some yuppie from the city who didn't know his way around the back woods.

"Who are you?"

"I'll keep that information to myself for now." While he figured out the best course of action. He had no intention of harming this girl. She'd been the only one to show him kindness after his parents' death all those years ago. But that didn't mean he couldn't use her to get into his aunt and uncle's compound.

"If you won't tell me, you'll have to tell them." She gestured past his shoulder. Jared glanced in that direction and spied two very large armed men.

A normal man would probably be scared.

But Jared hadn't felt fear in over a decade. He turned back to face Sparrow and gave her a wink. "Too bad, I was looking forward to getting to know you better."

Her eyes widened, her lips parted. She ducked her head, quickly obscuring her features with that monstrosity of a hat. But not before he'd seen the surprise. The fear.

Jared waited, calm and patient. He knew what it was to be feared. He waited for her hands to shake and tremble. Waited for her to back up a step and realize how close to danger she really was. But she didn't. She lifted her chin once more and those warm amber eyes flashed cold. "Jimbo, Bob, I caught me a spy."

As if to dare him, she stepped forward and placed her gun within his reach. If they'd been alone, he would have yanked it away from her. But not with two more guns pointed at his back.

"You're going to get to know me. Real, real good."

***

Sparrow's heart raced faster than a damn jackrabbit running from a fox. So much so that all she could hear was a buzz in her ears instead of individual heartbeats. Something about this man tugged at her memory.

How did he know her name? Sparrow gave a quick glance back at her adopted brothers, but their expressions gave away nothing. Not that they'd tell her anyway. Something was brewing between those two, something that boded ill for the mountain, and Sparrow couldn't figure out what. She'd been spying and quietly questioning everyone she could trust, but had failed to turn up anything other than a bad feeling.

Maybe now she'd gotten the break she'd been waiting on.

Then he smiled, and her heart had stopped its furious pace altogether. That wasn't a smile of warmth. It wasn't even a smile of acknowledgment. No, that was a precursor of death. Hard flat black eyes did nothing but reflect her own image back at her.

Her survival instinct kicked into overdrive, but she smashed it down. She couldn't afford to give herself over to fear. Not here. Not ever.

When Sparrow was eight years old, her mama, Tootsie, had finally overdosed on painkillers. Sparrow was the one who'd found her, naked and cold in their trailer. Tootsie's day trade had been her body. Her night trade had been the pills. Always the pills. From a young age, Sparrow had learned that in order to survive she needed to take care of herself.

Then Miss Kay Crowe had taken her in, and Sparrow found herself a turn-key family. One ready for her to move in with for good. One with a mother who wasn't a whore and a druggie. And even two real live older brothers. Even then Sparrow knew Kay wasn't a good woman, but she had to be better than Tootsie. And if she was willing to take in a whore's daughter, she had to be good deep down.

That innocent daydream quickly vanished. Her new brothers saw her as nothing more than a brat in need of a good beating, and they relished telling her the real reason why Miss Kay had taken Sparrow under her wing.

Miss Kay had made Tootsie a promise to watch out for Sparrow, and Tootsie had been Miss Kay's top-selling whore.

"Better turn him over to someone who can handle him." Jimbo's words yanked Sparrow back to the present.

"Well, then I guess he better be staying with me, seein' as how you lost the last one." Sparrow let the words drip from her lips slow like molasses. Jimbo Crowe, her oldest adopted brother, had turned out to be the very opposite of a protective family member. He used to cuff her and slap her around when no one was looking. The abuse hadn't ended until old man Squirrel taught Sparrow how to throw a knife. The next time Jimbo tried to corner Sparrow, she used her newfound skill to bury her knife into her adoptive brother's hand.

Bob Crowe burst out laughing, his tall skinny stature the exact opposite of Jimbo's big hulking one. "That girl don't take shit from nobody."

Jimbo's eyes would've turned red with rage if he had possessed that ability. Instead, his meaty hand shot out and wrapped around his little brother's throat, easily lifting the man off the ground. "You were saying?"

Bob kicked like a runaway chicken about to get his head chopped off. Even made the gurgling sounds to go with it, before Jimbo dropped him to the ground.

Sparrow had to move fast or she was going to lose her prize to her brother. This was her chance to find out what was really going on, and for some reason, she didn't want to see the camo man tortured by Jimbo. Torture was her brother's specialty. "I stake my claim."

She could feel the man's eyes on her, and there was the creeping sensation he was seeing more than she wanted. But she couldn't pay attention to him. Not yet.

Jimbo looked her up and down, and then spit a large wad of tobacco on the ground by his feet. "We'll see how long that lasts."

Then Jimbo turned and lumbered back toward home. Bob was a little lap dog at his heels.

"Tweedledee and Tweedledum," the camo man said.

"Come again?" *Tweedle what?*

"You know, Tweedledee and Tweedledum, off the cartoon," he said it like she was supposed to know what the hell he was talking about.

"Whatever. Now let's me and you get something straight." Sparrow took a small step back, her instincts warning her not to get too close. She could sniff a pig out a mile away, but this man wasn't a cop. Which meant he couldn't be bribed. Which was dangerous.

"I'm waiting." That small smile was back on his face.

Sparrow wanted to rip it right off, but she held her peace.

"You belong to me now. You do what I say. When I say it." Sparrow steadied the rifle against her shoulder, but he didn't look the least bit worried.

"Or what?"

"Or I'll turn you over to him." She nodded at her retreating brother's back.

He threw a hand up over his heart and stumbled back a step, "You'd just leave me like that? And here I thought we were making progress." His words teased, but his black eyes were still as empty as a bar pit.

Her threats weren't working against him, probably because he'd never seen what Jimbo could do with a hunting knife. But Sparrow had been forced to watch as her brother flayed a man's back. She swallowed and looked up at the stranger through her thick lashes, careful to keep her thoughts hidden. "Turn around. We're going home."

"And what if I don't?" He stepped forward and closed the distance between them, forcing her to tilt her head back to get a good look at him.

Her heart kicked up that furious pace again. What could she do?

"I can see your pulse racing. You're scared. That's smart."

She'd spent years perfecting her front of indifference, but he saw right through her. And if he could see, so could her family. Sparrow gritted her teeth and put the end of the barrel underneath his chin. "If you don't do as I say, then your brains are fixing to feed the birds."

His smile disappeared and Sparrow felt a surge of dominance. For some reason, even though she held the rifle, she'd felt like he was the one in control of the situation.

"Careful, little girl. I don't take kindly to having guns pointed at my head."

"And I don't take kindly to strangers spying on my family." Sparrow held her breath, waiting on his reaction. If he so much as flinched, her over-itchy trigger finger might jerk. She'd never had to shoot a man before.

She studied him, trying to see the face beyond the camouflage paint, trying to get a read on his thoughts, but all she could make out was a strong square jaw. Full lips. Black soulless eyes.

Then his teeth flashed bright white against the black and green paint, the look on his face positively evil. "All right, I'll go along with you. Where to, sweet thing?"

He turned around and Sparrow slowly and quietly exhaled the breath she'd been holding. She wasn't stupid. She might be ignorant white trash, but she knew when death was staring her in the eyes.

And she had Satan himself at the end of her gun.

.

Chapter Two

Jared walked back to his old house with all the enthusiasm of an inmate walking down death row. He didn't feel the cold air, didn't hear the leaves crunch beneath his boots. His vision tunneled on the half-moon circle of dilapidated wood shacks in the clearing ahead.

There were ten in all, plus a trailer on the far right. The largest cabin, the one that sat in the middle, housed the head of the Crowe clan, Miss Kay. She was a direct descendant of the infamous Ma Barker and twice as deadly. This camp acted as her headquarters, with the rest of her people spread out all over the county.

But it was the house just to the right of the middle that held his focus. It was a little house, with an even smaller closet. A closet with a bolt in the floor to which he and Hoyt had once been chained.

Chills skittered across his skin and dread settled heavy in his chest, but the fear he'd felt for so long as a child was absent. A killing rage had taken its place instead.

Two glass pane windows, dirty and faded and covered in cobwebs, sat on each side of a broken front door. A cypress porch littered with trash and warped with age and weather held up the front, just like he remembered. Hell on Crowe Mountain.

Sparrow propelled Jared into the clearing with that gun of hers pressed to his back. People stopped to stare, people he did not recognize. And thank God he didn't, because if he saw his aunt and uncle right now, he'd be tempted to forget his entire guise and strangle them where they stood. No, the clothes and lean malnourished forms were the same, but the faces were unfamiliar. Jared took a deep calming breath. *Remember your brother.* He was here to rescue Hoyt. But later, once Hoyt was safe, Jared would return.

And he would demolish the Crowe family once and for all.

"Hang a right. We're headed to that trailer over yonder." Sparrow's hillbilly twang drew him out of the dark chamber prison of his past.

The trailer would have been considered run down in any other place, and that was being generous, but here it fit right in. Half the underpinning lay twisted on the ground. A set of rickety wooden steps with no handrail led up to the front door. Still, the windows were intact, and there weren't any gaping holes in the walls. That was about all he could say for this sorry excuse for a home. "Yours?"

"Yep. Bought and paid for."

Jared turned to catch a brief blush rise on her cheeks, but that stupid, oversized hat swooped down and covered her expression.

He wanted to ask her exactly how long she'd saved up for the piece of shit, but there'd been a note of pride in her voice. He suspected the girl had probably worked long and hard for the privilege of having her own place.

He just prayed she didn't work the way most women up here did—on her back, with her legs spread.

"Nice. I'm guessing that's where I'll be staying too?" Jared said.

"I know it probably ain't what you're used to, city boy. But yeah, that's exactly where you'll be staying." Sparrow's voice held a tinge of hurt and he regretted his tone.

"Good, it's the best looking place out here. Do I get my own bed, or do I get to sleep in yours?" Jared stopped at the bottom of the steps. Sparrow stumbled forward, stopping just short of crashing into him. She backed up, but her fresh spring scent lingered in the air.

"Hey sexy, you can sleep in my bed," someone said from behind him. "Hell, I'll let a brawny man like you in for free too."

Sparrow stiffened and Jared turned to see a woman, at least he thought she was a woman, approach. He barely checked a smile at her obvious attempt to swing her less than generous hips as she walked. Her hip bones poked out above a sagging mini skirt. Her crop top provided just enough material to cover an almost concave chest, revealing a starkly outlined ribcage. To top it all off, her smile showed two missing teeth. He suppressed a shiver.

"Back off Geraldine, he's mine." Sparrow swung her gun toward the woman. Geraldine stopped and scratched her tangled hair. *Probably lice.*

"Whatcha mean yours? You don't know what to do with any man, least of all a real man like that." Apparently the threat of Sparrow's gun was useless. Geraldine pushed the tip of the rifle aside and swaggered closer to Jared. "But I do. I got all kinds of tricks to please ya."

Geraldine laid a hand against his chest and Jared flinched back. Lice would be the least harmful thing he could catch from her. "Sorry, ma'am, but I'm afraid I'm already spoken for."

Before she could protest, a knife appeared around the front of her throat. Geraldine froze and lifted her chin. Jared grinned. His little mountain cat had sharp claws.

"You might not worry about my gun, but you know how good I am with a knife." Sparrow spoke low and Geraldine trembled.

"I was just wantin' a touch. We ain't got no menfolk like him up here." Her words were cut off when Sparrow eased the blade a little deeper into her neck. Not enough to draw blood, but more than enough to get the point across.

"You remember what we did to Jack Wideman?"

Jared watched, fascinated, as every single ounce of blood drained from Geraldine's face. Sparrow's answering

smile was feral. "Yeah, I see you do. If I see you waggin'
your scrawny butt near this man again, I'll give you a
personal lesson, just like I did with Jack."

"No. No…I…I won't touch him. Never."

Sparrow thrust the woman away from the trailer and
Jared side-stepped to avoid further contact. Geraldine
wrapped a bony hand around her throat and took off.

"Dang it, I'll have to disinfect my knife after touching
that trash." Sparrow wiped the blade on her pants and tucked
it into a hidden sheath at her side.

"You were awfully rough on her."

"You want her touching you?" Sparrow asked.

Not with a hundred-foot pole. He recognized walking
syphilis. "No. But she didn't mean any harm."

Sparrow scanned the clearing behind them and picked
her rifle up off the ground. The few people still walking
around quickly made their way inside. Interesting. This little
scrawny girl seemed to invoke some fear in these folk.

"City boy. You wanna get her STD? Get in the trailer
before you draw more attention."

Jared took a moment to consider the benefits of
letting her continue to boss him around versus taking control
now. It would be better to let this play out a while, he
decided. Let her think she'd won. Jared lifted his hands in
surrender and entered the trailer.

Multiple pairs of dead eyes stared back at him from
stuffed heads. Squirrel. Deer. A bear's head? He turned and
shot her a questioning look. No way she'd taken down all
these animals herself. "You buy these already stuffed?"

"Let's get something straight. I'm not a sissy girl. And
just because I'm small don't mean I can't do that to you."
Sparrow indicated one really screwed up deer head—
evidently she'd shot that particular animal in the face instead
of the body. Then she reached into a wooden chest next to the
door and pulled out a rope. "Now go on through that door."

Sparrow indicated the only door on the right of the
combined living room and kitchen area. The living room was
sparse, containing a couple of wood chests, a faded blue

couch, and multiple travel magazines lying around.
Interesting. The hillbilly wanted to see the world. Go figure.

Jared obliged, curious to see where she was planning
to keep him, as if this cardboard box could truly contain him.
He turned a loose brass knob on the hollow wooden door to
reveal a tiny room that contained a bed, broken dresser and a
bedside table. That was it. The bedframe, while once white,
had rusted and faded in so many spots he couldn't describe
the color anymore. "If you want me to get naked all you have
to do is ask."

"Lay down, put your arms up, and hold on to the
headboard." Sparrow prodded him with the rifle and his
curiosity took a turn to irritation.

"You wanna keep that rifle, you better get it out of
my back." He stopped in the middle of the room and waited
for the pressure to be removed before continuing. Jared sat,
testing the dilapidated bed to see if it would hold under his
weight. When he felt sure it wouldn't crack in two, he laid
down to the tune of a loud creak and the feeling of a hundred
springs stabbing him in the back.

Sparrow pulled the rope off her arm and approached,
stopping just out of his reach. "Are you going to stay still or
do I have to go get one of my stepbrothers to hold you
down?"

"Yours to command. I promise I won't bite unless
you're into that kind of thing." Another blush stole across her
cheeks and Jared found he was enjoying her discomfort
immensely. Most of the women he'd dated were fake, but
Sparrow wasn't like that. Maybe she hadn't earned her keep
on her back after all.

"Grab the headboard."

Jared once again obliged, curious to see what she had
planned for after she tied him to her bed. He didn't bother
resisting—yet. It would be quick work for him to get out of
the bonds. His Special Forces training had taught him every
escape-and-evade trick in the United States government's
arsenal. He could lull the girl into false comfort, wait until
night fell, and use the darkness as cover to go off in search of

his brother. And he could finagle information out of the girl without her even realizing it.

Jared was first and foremost a sniper, but he could interrogate just as well. He'd just never interrogated someone like her.

Sparrow propped her rifle against the wall next to the bed. Her first mistake. How easy it would be for him to grab it and turn the tables. Or the ropes, so to speak. But he would let her get comfortable for now.

It had been nearly twenty years since he'd seen her, but Jared could never forget those golden eyes. Eyes that had haunted his dreams ever since. Had she joined up with Kay? Or was she simply one of those poor souls struggling to survive?

The thought of Sparrow slowly starving filled him with a sense of guilt. He should have made her leave with them. Even though they'd been children when she'd freed them, Jared had been big enough to drag her out, whether she'd wanted to go or not.

She leaned over him, reaching for his hands. Her floppy hat fell down, blinding her, and she ripped it off and tossed it across the room. Long caramel-colored hair, full of sun-kissed highlights, waterfalled down the sides of her face and tickled his nose. Her scent surrounded him now, flooding his senses. Honeysuckle and wildflowers. His cock swelled in an instant. Jared gnashed his teeth together, trying to quell his intense reaction to her nearness.

Sparrow leaned down further and her loose tank top gaped open, treating him to a glorious view of surprisingly plump breasts cupped in a plain sports bra. His gaze locked onto her beaded nipples through the cotton. Fuck he wanted to rip that bra down and reveal what was hidden beneath. The loose manly clothes she wore made her look stick thin, but womanly curves were concealed beneath them.

Sparrow sighed and sat up straight, leaving rope dangling uselessly on his wrists. Jared gripped the metal headboard with his hands, waiting for her next move. She stood there for a moment and studied him, trying to decide what to do. Well, he wasn't going to help her out one little bit.

"Keep your hands right there, got it?" Her voice was stern.

"Yes ma'am." He had no intention of acting up. Yet.

She placed a knee on the mattress, and in one swift movement straddled him, settling on his belly. Jared groaned and closed his eyes thankful she hadn't sat down lower on his body; otherwise, she would have gotten her own surprise. She leaned over him spreading her knees wider up his chest. His eyes popped open, unable to resist another view of her bare skin.

"You can stop with the theatrics right now; I know I'm not big enough to crush you."

If only that were his problem. Her shirt dipped down even more and he fixated on the pale mounds of her breasts straining against the material of her sports bra. It was a crime to lock those beauties up in serviceable cotton.

She should wear nothing but pure silk and lace, perfect for him to rip off her body.

Her hair curtained around him again, and her soft lips parted in concentration as she worked. He was aware of every inch of exposed skin—from the graceful hollow of her neck to her supple forearms peeking out from the rolled up sleeves of her checkered work shirt. Even more aware of the intense heat radiating from her core, pressed so intimately to his chest.

"There. All done." She sat back, a satisfied smile on her lips.

Jared tugged on the rope. He'd completely zoned out on anything other than her straddling him. It didn't give an inch—the knot she'd tied was worthy of a professional. A small ounce of foreboding seeped into him. "Where did you learn to tie knots?"

"Trapping. Working snares. Been doing it since I was a kid." Her words were so matter-of-fact, he had no doubt she spoke the truth. Holy shit. He yanked on the ropes, but they didn't move.

"Impressive." Jared wriggled his fingers and wrists, testing for any weakness. He found none.

"Might as well stop struggling. Nobody's ever been able to get out of one of my knots. And I used my new rope too, so it wouldn't snap easy." She made a snapping motion with her fingers, the emphasis driving in just how stupid his plan had been. He should have used that easy opening she'd given him with the gun.

His foreboding turned to real worry. He had to get out of here to rescue his brother. Hoyt's life depended on him. If he couldn't get free… "Nice, now what?"

"Now you tell me who you are and why you're here." Sparrow sat back on her heels, the curve of her ass grazing the tip of his cock. He clenched his muscles, fighting to free himself from the pull of lust.

Remember, you're the soldier trained in interrogation techniques. Now he just had to stop thinking with his dick for long enough to find out where Hoyt was being held. "My name is Jake."

She tapped her chin, staring down at him. Once again he was enthralled by the intense color of her eyes. They were golden, almost like a cat's, with a darker brown ring around the edges. "Jake. You don't look like a Jake."

He enjoyed hearing the name on her lips. Would enjoy hearing his real name even better. Her soft accent and long vowels stretched it out slow. Sensual. "And what do I look like?"

"I don't know. Killer? Tiger?"

"That's what people name their cats."

"True. Why are you here?"

"Why did you take me hostage?" he countered.

"You were spying on my family. Only our enemies do that." She shifted, brushing against his tip again. Fuck he wanted to rip free of these bonds and throw her down beneath him. Where was his detached logic now? Something about her was making him lose control.

"I have no interest in you. I was looking for a family member who went missing, know anything about that?" He studied her reaction intently, watching for any flash of awareness, but she didn't give away anything.

"Haven't seen anybody new around here in a long time, and I would know. Sorry, but you plopped down on the wrong piece of land."

"He told me he was coming here." Not really, but Jared knew without the slightest shred of doubt that Hoyt had been taken by the Crowes. Miss Kay wanted to finish what she had started all those years ago, even if Jared didn't know why. It was bad enough his parents had died when Jared was only nine, Hoyt six, but to have his aunt try to murder them....

Jared yanked on the bonds again, testing the bed frame. It screeched but held firm. Shit.

"What does he look like?" Every time Sparrow moved or shifted he felt her. Desire was holding him hostage as much as the damn ropes. *Got to get free. Got to find Hoyt.*

"What do I get if I tell you?"

"What do you get? You get to live." Her brows shot down as if confused.

"You won't kill me."

"Try me."

"How about we make a little trade—you give me something, I give you something."

"Give? What do you want?" She laid her palms on her thighs, kneeling over his body, the position incredibly erotic.

Blushing aside, maybe she wasn't so innocent after all. He had a plan and she was part of it. He knew he could get more information out of Sparrow than her giant ass brother. And he'd find it a hell of a lot more enjoyable too. "Kiss me."

She stopped moving all together and her eyes narrowed in on his mouth.

"Give me a kiss and I'll sing like a bird."

Chapter Three

Sparrow stared down at him in shock. He wanted a kiss? From *her*? Power emanated from the man's body, and she'd actually worried he would bend the bed frame by yanking on the rope. Even though his features were masked by the paint, there was no denying his strong square jaw or full lips. He was gorgeous. Gorgeous men never asked for kisses from Sparrow.

And she had no intention of giving away her first kiss to a man covered in war paint.

"No. No kisses." Why wasn't she moving? She should be interrogating him, threatening him with sharp knives and other wicked devices she wouldn't ever really use on another human being. But a delicious tingle had started down low her belly, something she'd never really felt before, and she wanted to feel it more.

"No kiss?" The first flicker of real emotion in his eyes, and it was disappointment.

He was disappointed she wouldn't kiss him? She chanced a quick peek down at herself. Still the same Sparrow—all bones and no curves. He was playing with her, teasing her. Anger built up inside her. He was doing it again. Even though he was the one tied to the bed, he was taking control.

She wracked her mind, trying to come up with a way to wrest it back from him. Sparrow had a feeling holding a knife to the man's throat would be useless. Pressing her gun into his belly hadn't even made him blink.

Then she noticed that his crystal-hard gaze was locked on her chest. "Then take off that over shirt," he said, his voice husky.

Undress? The most she'd ever undressed was to go swimming, and even then she wore a T-shirt and shorts. Unbidden, her mama's voice whispered through her mind. *"All men can be controlled. Show him a little skin, give him a slap and tickle, and he's putty in your hands."*

Sparrow hadn't understood back then, but as she got older and listened to the other girls around camp she came to realize exactly what her mama had been talking about. And she vowed to stay completely clear of men. That trap was way too easy to fall into. One time was all it took to get pregnant and end up shackled to some cabin in the woods, popping out babies every year. No life, no money, no future. Just a broodmare. The other path—the one her mother had taken—was even worse.

But until now, it had been easy to stay away from men. None of the others had made her feel this way. Hell, she hadn't even known men like this one existed. He lifted his hips, pressing against the growing ache between her legs, and she found herself caving. Just a little skin wouldn't hurt anything…

Besides, if she didn't fully interrogate him, Sparrow would lose all the gains she'd made with the Crowe family. She was so close to being moved up in the chain of command. If she sealed this deal, she was as good as promoted. No more worrying about where her next meal would come from. No more worrying about her best friend, Squirrel. No more worrying about being forced to whore. Sparrow would run her own section of the county, collecting the money from the girls and making sure to keep them in line.

She knew the price of failure all too well. She would be demoted, and in the Crowe camp that meant one thing for

a woman—she'd find herself on her back or on her knees.
Just like Tootsie, her mother.

A shudder worked through her. No matter how scared
she was to bare her body for Jared, she didn't have much of a
choice. She could play with him, hopefully enjoy it a little,
and get his information, or she could play the whore for the
rest of her life.

But she didn't have a choice. She'd never make it off
the mountain, no matter how much she dreamed of exploring
the world outside these hills. She had no education. No job
skills outside of collecting money for Miss Kay. And she
couldn't leave Squirrel behind. The old man was even less
likely to survive in the real world. He'd been born and bred
here, lived and trapped his whole life in the woods. Even if
Sparrow had a shot at making it out there, she couldn't leave
him behind. Jimbo had already told her what he'd do to
Squirrel if she left…

No. No way she could turn him over to that fate, no
matter how much she wanted to leave.

Besides, she sensed the man tied to her bed knew
exactly what was going on with her brothers and if Sparrow's
instincts were right, if they were planning to take their
mother down and take over the mountain, the whole
community was at stake. No matter how deadly Miss Kay
was, her brothers were worse. So much worse.

Sparrow had never used her body as a weapon. But if
that's what it took, she'd do it.

She swallowed down the knot of fear blocking her
throat. *You're not like your mother. This is your choice.*
Besides, he was gorgeous, and he was trussed up to the bed,
unable to do anything. She would be in control. She would
take and he would give. Those were odds she could handle.

"All right, Rambo. I'll play." She worked hard to keep
her voice steely and commanding, praying with each second
that he wouldn't see the fear lurking inside of her. She lifted
shaking hands to the top button of her loose cotton over shirt.
They were pearl snap, and like all of her clothes, the shirt had
come secondhand—heck, maybe third-hand—from the thrift

store. She popped the first one loose, the sound exploding in the room.

His eyes stayed fixated on her fingers. Maybe he really did want her. If he wasn't interested, he sure wouldn't be staring this hard at her chest. The next button came undone a little bit easier and by the time she hit the bottom button, she felt like a pro.

She shrugged the shirt off her shoulders, letting it slide down her arms real slow before tossing it on the floor. Something wanton overtook her—that was her only excuse. She shifted her fingers through her hair and tilted her head provocatively, letting her hair slide down around her shoulder on one side.

"All right, why are you really here?" she asked.

He took a deep breath and the movement expanding his chest so much that her knees almost lifted off the bed. "I told you. I'm looking for someone. A relative."

"And?" she demanded, frustration tingeing her words.

"Now the other shirt." His voice turned husky and deep. Sensual. Chills raced down her arms and she shifted, trying to ease some of the tension building down below. His stomach muscles flexed, which made the burning in her belly turn up a notch instead.

"You still haven't told me why you're here." She crossed her arms, pushing her breasts up a little higher. But her movements felt awkward and disjointed. She'd never given much thought to men and seduction.

"I told you, I'm looking for a relative."

"You know I'm asking more than that," she said.

His eyes finally lifted from her chest, only they weren't dead and cold anymore, they were full of heat. For her. Sparrow licked her suddenly dry lips and he fixated there next. Should she kiss him? How could she be this attracted to a man she'd never seen before? Let alone a man who could be here to do her family harm.

Miss Kay's words drifted through her mind, *How far are you willing to go for your family?*

Her stomach tightened.

"Maybe you should work on being more specific with your questions. I've already answered that one. If you want more, you've got to give more." His voice rasped across her sensitive skin, yet it carried the hint of a command.

Anticipation and anxiety warred within her. Undressing in front of him felt so…naughty. But this might be her only chance to experiment with a real man. Explore at her own pace.

And no one would ever have to know.

"I've only got so many articles of clothing left."

His smile was full of enjoyment. "I know."

What did she need to ask? *Smart questions*, she reminded herself.

"You're thinking awfully hard," Jared said, throwing down the challenge. Sparrow had never been one to back down from a dare.

"Who is it?"

He nodded to her shirt. Her heart fluttered in her chest, wild and crazy and out-of-control as she slipped her fingers under the hem and lifted it over her head. By the time she tossed the shirt on the floor, she was breathing hard and fast.

His gaze locked on her chest and embarrassment heated her body. She wanted to groan in frustration. Her sports bra covered her completely, but she felt so…exposed.

"You're gorgeous." His voice dropped even deeper and her nipples tightened in response to his words. He groaned and pushed his head back into the pillow, his body straining upwards. The sudden movement threw her off-balance and she barely caught herself on his chest. Their faces were only inches apart. She could smell him. Raw. Masculine. Delicious.

What was wrong with her? She had to keep her head on straight and stay away from his sinfully sexy lips.

"Kiss me. I'll die if you don't." His words were so sincere, so aching. He lifted his mouth to hers, but she held herself just out of reach.

Her own lips tingled and throbbed. Could she give him her first kiss? Should she? Her body screamed yes. *Yes.* "Tell me. Why are you really here?" Was that soft breathy whisper really her voice?

His neck muscles strained and bulged, but the rope held fast. "Because I tracked him here."

"Who?"

"My brother." He shook his head, as if he'd said more than intended, but she barely noticed. His chest was expanding and pressing into her aching body, and she wanted to rub her breasts across his chest to feel the friction. "God, I can feel your tight little nipples. Let me see them. Let me taste them."

Sparrow had to bite back a moan. This man was erotic beyond words, talking to her like that, so…dirty.

Sparrow forced herself to sit up, but she couldn't help the slight thrust her hips gave. His eyes darkened instantly.

"Tell me your brother's name."

"The bra. Take it off." Any soft teasing had completely disappeared—his command was harsh, and her body reacted like whiplash.

All inhibitions gone, Sparrow pulled her bra over her head, eager to see his response. To see him wanting her. She let the material drop and crossed her arms over her chest, holding the material in place.

He growled, deep in his throat. The sound reminded her of a giant grizzly bear.

"Tell me," Sparrow said.

"Your arms. Need to see."

Sparrow shifted, the uncomfortable tightness between her legs growing every time he spoke. Even more, when he looked at her like that, he looked like he wanted to eat her alive.

Brazen and bold, she uncrossed her arms. Before she could think, he bucked hips high, tossing her forward. Sparrow landed flat on his chest. The instant her naked breasts pressed against his hard muscles she tensed, the sensation almost more exquisite than she could tolerate.

"Let me see. Bring them to me."

As if some foreign being possessed her, Sparrow dragged herself up his chest, until her breasts hovered just out of his reach. Chills beaded across her skin. She could feel his hot breath on her. Feel the urge to dip down. His lips closed over her nipple and instant white, hot heat shot straight down her core. Her body lit on fire, tight and needy at the same time. She moaned, her hips moving of their own accord, and *still* he didn't let go. He hadn't taken her lips yet, but he was kissing her more intimately than she'd dreamed possible.

When he let go, she whimpered, but he quickly lavished attention on her other breast. Licking and biting, driving her wild. She locked her fingers behind his head, holding him to her, lost in his caress.

"Untie me. I need to touch you, to feel you," he leaned back into the pillow.

Sparrow shook her head, "No." She was out of breath. Losing her mind.

"Then kiss me," he commanded.

She shook her head again. "No kissing."

He snarled, his frustration evident, and she pulled him to her, wanting him to resume where he'd left off. Greedily, he sucked her nipple into his mouth. The tension inside her grew to near explosion. She rocked her hips harder against him.

"That's it, honey, ride me just like that. I'll take care of you."

"You feel good. Really good." Breathless and craving more, Sparrow lay against him, enjoying the feel of her body pressed to his.

"You're so beautiful. Perfect. Untie me, let me pleasure you."

"I can't untie you." Sparrow couldn't stop touching him. She traced his neck, his chest, his corded arms.

"I can't keep going like this. Neither can you. You have to give me at least one arm. I promise you won't regret it." His voice was rough with desire.

Sparrow chewed on her bottom lip, giving the thought serious consideration. Could she risk it? He'd already given her pleasure, but she knew there was so much more to be had. Her body craved for something else, something deeper. She lay on top of him, her head beside his, her aching breasts pressed to his chest. He kissed her shoulder, her neck, anywhere she maneuvered for him to reach. She couldn't think when he was touching her.

"That was only a teaser. Untie me."

She lifted up on her elbows, wondering at the man panting beneath her. "A teaser?"

His smile was feral. "I almost made you come just from sucking on those pretty nipples, and dammit, I want your mouth so bad."

His words had her panting with need. She had almost…come? That was what all the whores talked about? No wonder they gabbed so much about it, cause that had been freaking amazing. "What about you? Did you almost…"

He ground his hips up again and she became very aware of the hardness pressed between her legs. "Does it feel like I came? I'm hard as a rock for you. Fuck, I need you. Touch me. Please." Sparrow shifted so she could see the huge tent lifting up the front of his pants. She wasn't so naïve that she didn't know his dick was hard. And that in order for him to get off she would have to…touch it.

Tentatively, she leaned back and let her fingers trace its length. It jumped beneath her hand as if it was seeking her touch.

"That's it."

"What do you need me to do?" Curious, she cupped his length, learning his shape. He bucked into her hand. Seeing him like this was intoxicating. This incredibly powerful male tied up beneath her, desperate for her to touch him.

"Wrap your fingers around me." She knelt beside him on the bed and unbuttoned his pants, slowly inching the zipper down to reveal his hardness. Jesus almighty, he was just as big down there as the rest of him.

Her fingers grazed the bare skin of his shaft, watching in fascination as a small bead of moisture collected on the tip. He sucked in a breath and she stifled a gasp as he grew even bigger. Longer. He was huge. She'd never seen one before now, but she didn't think they were all made so perfectly.

"Put your hand on me," he pleaded. His brow was covered in sweat. Whatever she was doing, he seemed to really like it. Emboldened, Sparrow traced the bulging veins running down his length. Another drop moistened on his tip and she moved as if in a trance, smearing the small bead of wetness over his crown.

"Jesus, you feel so good. Now, stroke me."

She focused on the task, wrapping her fingers around his girth and beginning to move her hand up and down, light and slow and unsure. His hips thrust up to meet her every move.

"Harder, Sparrow. Squeeze harder." His harsh command sent a surge of fire through her veins. She felt alive, powerful. She wanted him. Wanted to please him, as he had pleased her. So she gripped him tighter, pumping him faster.

"That's it baby. That's it. Almost there, don't stop."

Sparrow concentrated, timing her movements with the rhythm of his hips as he thrust up into her hand.

"Yes, baby that's it. So close." He strained into her.

Unashamedly, she felt that now familiar ache between her legs. Knew what it meant and the hint of where it could lead. She squirmed and rubbed her thighs together, wanting him to touch her.

"Open up, Sparrow. I know you're in there." Miss Kay banged on her front door. Sparrow froze, her hand unmoving on his dick.

"Don't stop, ignore it," he commanded.

"Unlock the door." Miss Kay wouldn't wait long. Dammit, she was so close. Sparrow couldn't stop touching and cupping him now. He thrust up into her hand.

He held Sparrow's gaze. "Finish. Just ignore them." Miss Kay banged on the door again. If she caught Sparrow like this, Sparrow might as well kiss her future goodbye.

Chapter Four

As if struck by lightning, Sparrow bolted from the bed and threw on her muscle shirt, hiding those magnificent breasts. Next came the button up.

Agony such as Jared had never known coursed through his body. He'd been so close. Now she was going to leave him, literally, with blue balls.

"Dammit, Sparrow, you can't leave me like this. Untie my hands."

Every muscle in his body tensed. He watched as she finished buttoning her shirt with trembling fingers. Sparrow's cheeks, flushed with pleasure a moment ago, were now pale. "Can't. She'll come in if I don't go out."

Whoever was at the front door banged again and Sparrow jumped. It was obvious she was afraid of the woman.

"Untie me. At least let me take care of myself." God, his cock was so hard he couldn't think. Couldn't form a single thought outside of Sparrow's hands. Her breasts. Her silky soft skin in his mouth.

"No. I'll be back. Just…just stay here." With that, she yanked up his pants. Jared didn't lift his hips to help her this time. Frustration and anger mixed, morphing into some emotion he couldn't name.

Jared gave a merciless laugh and yanked on the ropes binding his hands to the bed. "I don't really have a choice, do I?"

She buttoned his pants and yanked his shirt down. Her gaze was no longer focused on him. She kept stealing anxious little glances over her shoulder. "I'll be back, I promise I won't leave you like this, but I have to go."

His last glimpse of her before she ran out the door was an expression of regret and longing. But that didn't stop her from slamming the door behind her or leaving him on the edge of what would have been one of the most intense orgasms of his entire life.

No. Whoever was outside scared the girl so much she hadn't even wasted a breath before shooting up from the bed to get dressed. Jared lay back, his muscles straining, and squeezed his eyes shut. Think of cold rivers. Dead puppies. Nuns. But nothing worked. His dick was so hard it hurt.

Fuck, she'd been so sexy. The sexiest woman he had ever seen. And yet her movements had been hesitant, like she didn't know what she was doing. Like she'd never touched a man before. The thought sent blood coursing to his cock again, stretching him to near exploding.

Dead puppies. Dead puppies. Dead puppies. But the image and the taste and smell of Sparrow surrounded him. Fuck. Someone could dump a truckload of dead puppies on top of him right now and it wouldn't matter. The only person that could ease this pain was that wisp of a girl. A girl who'd run out of the room and left him here with his hands tied.

Jared had never known such agony. His attempts to ignore the pressure did nothing. He tried to rip the rope that held him, but the rough material just sawed into his skin. Even if he could focus on escape techniques, he probably wouldn't succeed given his state of mind. The humiliation of his position sliced through him like serrated knives. He was the one in control, always. Yet this…this…innocent girl-woman had him in a position of submissiveness. His hands had been bound of his own accord. A cold sweat formed on his brow. After being tied up in that dark closet, he'd vowed never to be bound again. Ever. The ropes binding his hands seemed to tighten. The air grew thick and heavy.

She'd left him like this. Straining and helpless. He vowed right then and there that he would turn the tables. He would tie her up, drive her wild enough to beg, then leave her hanging. Still, he couldn't wait to explore her sweet depths— he'd only gotten a sample of her, and it wasn't near enough.

The bedroom door cracked open and he yanked his head from the pillow. Only this time it wasn't Sparrow. A large woman filled the door, her shoulder-length black hair matted and tangled. Her sallow sagging skin a perfect background for her dull brown eyes. Uncaring eyes that belonged on a pit bull, not a woman.

Recognition slammed into him like a wrecking ball, obliterating his lingering lust and desire to make way for a cold blast of killing rage.

His aunt, Miss Kaitlyn Crowe, also known as Miss Kay, stared at him with curiosity but no recognition. Jared waited for her to realize who he was, but that didn't happen. "I see my Sparrow done good. Caught herself a grunt. What's your name, boy?"

Her voice sent cold dread down his spine. That voice had once haunted his days and terrorized his nights. He lunged up against the rope so hard blood trailed down his arms. The room shrank. Grew darker, more sinister. The closet...

"Can't speak? Well, my boys can fix that problem real quick." Kay snapped her fingers. Her oversized faded floral dress a mockery of the monster inside.

"I staked my claim. He's mine to interrogate." Jared heard Sparrow, but he couldn't see her.

Kay wasn't nearly as huge as he remembered, probably because he'd left this place at age ten, but she was a big woman. Much bigger than Sparrow. "Girl, you don't know what to do with no man. Never have. Best you let Jimbo see to this."

"You can't break the code," Sparrow said. Mountain code, even he remembered that from his youth. His mom and dad had lived and died by the code. Jared curled his fingers in a tight fist, the only movement he allowed. He hadn't planned on seeing his nemesis for the first time in this position. But he wouldn't be tied up for long, and once he got free...

"And just what do you think you can do?" Kay stepped fully into the room, allowing Sparrow to slip past. Their difference in size and stature was so great it was almost comical. But nothing was funny now. Not when the woman who'd tortured him all those years ago stood not five feet away.

"I have a plan. I was working on it when you interrupted. You know you can't break code. He's mine." Sparrow argued, her hands on her hips. His little bird had claws. Ones she wasn't scared to show.

Code was more sacred than the law around these parts. Mountain folk might be backwards hillbillies who could give a shit about secular laws, but they had their own system. And if you broke that system, the punishment was swift and severe.

Jared watched the war going on behind his girl's eyes as Kay wagged a finger in her face. Sparrow wanted to fight back, but she was holding herself in check. Interesting. Maybe she wasn't so solid in the Crowe clan after all.

"I'll give you two days. If you ain't broke him by then, I'm giving him to Jimbo. Got that? You know what'll happen if you don't get it done." Kay turned to him then, the curious look replaced with a gleam he remembered all too well from his youth. "You better sing to my Sparrow, boy, because Jimbo don't play. You'll do well to remember that."

Without another word, Kay lumbered from the room and slammed the front door of the trailer. Silence surrounded them, but the older woman's presence still hung heavy in the room.

"Why would you work for a woman like her?" Jared bit out between clenched teeth.

Sparrow shook her head. "You wouldn't understand."

"You're right. I don't understand, explain it to me."

If possible, Sparrow's face went even paler. "She owns this mountain and everyone on it."

Chapter Five

If only he knew. Miss Kay didn't just own the people on this mountain, she owned the entire county. She owned the land. Grew the pot. Sold the drugs and alcohol. Controlled the prostitutes.

Now that the mines had shut down, the only way for mountain folks to earn a living around here was through her adoptive family. Whether they wanted to or not didn't matter—those who disobeyed disappeared.

Sparrow hadn't scrimped and saved her entire life to throw away the meager existence she'd foraged for herself. Especially not for this man who'd brought her close to her first orgasm only minutes ago, but was now looking at her like she was covered in the maggots that had infested the corn crop.

Sparrow lifted her chin. She was a survivor. And she sure as hell wasn't going to follow in her mother's footsteps because she was too scared to take risks. It was time for her to take the bull by the horns, or the man by the cock, so to speak.

She had two days. Two days before Jimbo took over. Two days to solidify her position in management or end up on her back. Literally. Miss Kay had always made it perfectly clear to her what failure would mean. As soon as she made a mistake, she'd be forced to turn to her mama's old profession—even if Jimbo had to tie her to the bed to make sure she followed orders.

God, what she wouldn't give to be out of this mess. Miss Kay's methods of maintaining control were decisive and brutal, but at least they were logical. If you stole or tried to double cross her, you would be punished or killed. Pretty simple way to keep folks in line.

But Jimbo – he was a loose cannon of destruction. He didn't need a reason to torture other than the simple fact he liked it. He liked to hurt people. He liked it when they screamed and begged.

She barely held the shudder in check. Jimbo had always tormented her. Teased her. Hurt her. But recently his glances had turned darker, more sinister. He had other thoughts about Sparrow, and she had no interest in finding out what they were.

No way in hell would she let that happen. Sparrow studied the man on her bed. The paint on his face camouflaged his features and helped to conceal his expression, but not even a blind person could miss the loathing in his gaze right now.

As inexperienced as Sparrow was with men it was pretty obvious that the giant erection tenting his pants had completely wilted. She never backed down from a challenge, even one as big as the man tied to her bed. Sparrow approached him. "Where were we?"

He stared her down and she fought the instinct to cringe. Yes, the lust and desire from earlier had been replaced by revulsion. "We were in the middle of your pathetic attempt to seduce information out of me using your scrawny little body."

His words pierced an arrow through her heart. The torments and teases from the local whores sprang up in her mind. Scrawny Sparrow, the virgin spinster. All because she hadn't given it up by the age of twelve.

Yes, she was used to being called scrawny—she'd always been the smallest and the skinniest in her adopted family. But that only meant she'd learned to scrap harder, and if he thought he could scare her away with those few words he had no idea just how scrappy she could get. Sparrow tapped a finger on her chin, as if contemplating what to do next. "My scrawny little body didn't seem to disgust you so much before. Especially when you latched on to my titties like a baby calf sucking at her mama's teat."

He dug his head down into the pillow, yanking and pulling against the rope. She didn't bother telling him it was a useless endeavor, that old man Squirrel had taught her to tie a knot so sturdy that not even a bear could rip itself free. But there was no reason she couldn't enjoy the show of those giant muscles flexing and straining.

"Girl, any man would suck on a pair of boobs if you shoved them in his face." He yanked again, so hard the iron bed frame bent forward.

Sparrow smiled, because despite his words, that tent in his pants was rising again. She stayed right where she stood and shrugged out of the over shirt once more. He tracked her movements like a wild animal caught in a trap.

"I'm sure curious to see that face of yours." Sparrow ran to the bathroom, soaped a wash cloth, and returned. There was something about him that was familiar and she wanted to find out. Problem was, she had a feeling he might bite her if she got too close right now.

Whatever Miss Kay had done to him—and she was sure the older woman had done something; that hadn't been empty dislike in his eyes, but the black hatred that came of knowing a bad woman well—had been enough to set this man on fire. But regardless of that, regardless of whatever lay in his past, she would break him. And she would turn over whatever information he gave her to Miss Kay. Sparrow took a deep breath, stealing herself against any pity for him. It was either her or him, and she'd sure as shit choose herself any day of the week.

"I'm gonna wash that pretty face. I want you to hold real still, you hear?"

He snarled. Wounded animal? More like a rabid wolf. The direct approach definitely wouldn't work. Maybe if she caressed him again, he'd calm down. Sparrow congratulated herself on the bright idea and tossed the washcloth to the floor. She approached him from the foot of the bed. His leg shot out with a sudden jerk, and she barely avoided being knocked down by his ferocious kick.

Holy shit. The man was deadly. Everywhere.

"Come close, I dare you." Veins bulged is his neck and his eyes glowed with menace. He truly was a beast. A lump formed in Sparrow's throat and she tried to swallow. Maybe the sexy, teasing man from before had all been the act. Maybe Miss Kay had simply set the beast free.

If her plan had any chance of working, he would have to cooperate. Or at least not try and kill her with his feet. She realized she would have to tie his feet to the bed, too, but each of his tree-trunk legs was bigger than she was. Even if she threw her whole body on top of him to pin down his legs, she'd be just as likely to get knocked out as she would to succeed. She needed help.

"Tell you what, I'll give you a few minutes to calm down. You sit tight now, okay?" Sparrow blew him a quick kiss, confident her rope would hold him in place. She ran from the room to tune out his shouting and eased out of her back door.

Sparrow headed straight out from her trailer into the woods, and then hooked a sharp right. She would know the path to Squirrel's cabin with her eyes closed and walking backwards, but she needed to stay out of sight of the rest of the camp. Even if Miss Kay didn't have eyes on her, Jimbo would. She could practically feel his creepy gaze crawling up her spine. He wouldn't hesitate to strike if he sensed the least bit of weakness.

Miss Kay's threats were legitimate, and she would most certainly carry them out if tested, but deep down Sparrow knew the older woman loved her. She'd protected Sparrow on many occasions and given her the chance to succeed in her business like one of the blood family. For which all of her adopted brothers hated her.

Too bad for them, Sparrow had flourished, learning to steal, cheat, and deal just like they did. She'd constructed her armor as the meanest and most accurate knife thrower in the state, and when tested, she'd backed it up on more than one occasion. But that didn't mean she didn't long for peace. She wanted to get her toe hold high up, above Jimbo's reach, so she could garner the opportunity to take care of old Squirrel and herself.

Sparrow approached the old cabin out in the woods, making as much noise as possible to alert Squirrel to her approach. He should be taking a nap right about now, but he'd been known, in his less sober moments, to fire off a few rounds at anyone who trespassed on his property. And just because the sun hadn't set, didn't mean the old man wasn't wasted.

"Squirrel, you up?" Sparrow hollered from the edge of the clearing, careful to stay tucked up close to a giant pine tree. Rough bark scratched her arm, but she ignored it. She would need the protection of the trunk if Squirrel was in one of his moods.

"What you hidin' out there in them woods for girl? Get your ass out here, you know I can't see that good no more." The familiar gravelly voice calmed Sparrow's nerves, and she stepped clear from the tree line just as Squirrel emerged from the old shack, a bottle of homemade brew in his hand.

"What you up to today?" Sparrow walked up onto the front porch, yanked the bottle from his hand, and took a swig. Sweet fire traced a burning trail down to her stomach, but she needed the liquid gold to help calm her nerves. She'd always had a steady hand, but having Jared tied up to her bed made her as nervous as a tom cat in a dog pen.

Squirrel's black eyes almost disappeared in his weathered face from the way he narrowed them at her. His grey beard hung low, almost to his belly, and his hair looked like it hadn't been brushed in days. She would have to tread lightly, make sure he was on one of his lucid days. She couldn't take the risk of him accidentally putting a bullet in her captive's head because he'd gone into one of his spells.

"You know good and well what I've been doing. Same thing I do every day. Now why don't you tell me what you want? You know old Squirrel'll help ya out." Squirrel took the bottle from her and downed a couple of gulps, then wiped his mouth with his arm. He'd once told her that whiskey was like lifeblood to him, and he could get mighty rowdy if someone tried to take it away.

Sparrow joined him on the front porch and ducked her head, her bravado gone now that she was with this man who had become her surrogate father. Squirrel knew everything about her. If she told him she needed help killing a man and hiding the body, he wouldn't flinch. But telling him she needed help seducing a man? That was an entirely different story.

"I came here because I need your help. But you can't tell nobody." She chanced a quick peek up. Squirrel stood with one arm braced on a beam of the twisted wood porch, staring out into the woods. His loose long sleeve shirt fell back, revealing a bony arm covered with scars. What she wouldn't do to be able to give him a better life. He was the only father she'd ever known. And if she managed to make it to the top and start earning that cash steady, she'd make sure he never had to work another day in his life. Never had to go out hunting and trapping from dusk to dawn.

"You done finally killed Jimbo?" Squirrel looked at her again, but the only emotion on his face was curiosity.

"If only."

"You ain't gone and stole from Miss Kay now have you?"

"Nope." *I've got something even better*. Her stomach fluttered like a thousand moths around a lantern at midnight.

"Lookee here, I ain't got all day. I got to be checking my traps soon, so you'd best go on and spit it out so I can fix whatever problem you done created."

"I got me a man tied up to my bed." The words rushed from her lips, and she slapped a hand over her mouth, wishing she could push them back inside.

Squirrel's bushy brows shot straight up into his hairline and he gave a good long whistle. "Well, you shouldn't have a problem with that. You're pretty enough."

Sparrow resisted the urge to stomp her foot and instead took a deep breath and let the whole story spill out. She finished by telling him she had two days to get the information—or else. "So I figured I could use his body against him."

"Or I could let you use my Bowie knife. Peeling some skin will usually get a fella to talk right quick."

The thought sent bile rushing to her mouth. She couldn't stand the thought of hurting someone like that. She could handle threatening, some mild violence, but she'd never drawn blood. "I'm telling you, he ain't a normal man. Physical threats don't scare him."

Squirrel took a step back, and a board creaked and then broke beneath his feet. Sparrow barely managed to snag his shirt to keep him from toppling into the yard. This old shack was scarcely held up by patched tin and rusted nails.

"I got it now, you can let go." Squirrel brushed off her hands and carefully eased around the newest hole in the porch. "Guess I gotta get some more wood."

"I got some under the trailer. I'll bring it by for you later." He shouldn't have to live in this dump. She wanted something better for them both, and now she might have the means to get it. "Back to my idea."

Squirrel studied her from head to toe. ""Well, you ain't got them curves most men like, but ya got perty eyes and hair."

Sparrow crossed her arms over her chest. "What? Do I need to be fat like old Bertha to get a man's attention?"

Squirrel took a step back and threw his hands up. "No, girl. You women sure know how to twist a man's words." He sighed. "All right, I'll help you get fixed up, but the rest is up to you."

Sparrow nodded, not trusting her voice. "Listen, I need your help to hold him down while I get him tied up tight."

"Hold on, let me get something." Squirrel ran back into the shack. When he re-emerged, his Bowie knife was strapped to his leg and there was a pistol at his hip. "Lead the way."

They made it back to Sparrow's trailer in record time, easing around the perimeter of Crowe camp to avoid being seen. She led the way into her bedroom. As soon as she walked over the threshold the man's gaze shot to hers, those midnight eyes darkened with fury. A predator's grin stretched his full lips tight. "Couldn't handle me on your own, little girl?"

"He sure is a big'un," Squirrel said.

"That's why I needed your help." Sparrow completely ignored his remarks. *Remember, it's him or you.*

"Looks like you did a good job on the knot. You got some more rope ready?"

"All the rope in the world isn't it going to keep me tied to this bed, old man." His fake smile disappeared altogether and he lunged hard against the rope. The bed frame groaned under his animalistic power, but it held. Barely.

"Yeah, it's on the floor." She had to fight the instinct to turn tail and run from the room. He didn't look mad—he looked furious. But all she had to do was keep it together. He'd wanted her. His body couldn't deny it. She just had to figure out a way to rekindle that flame before he figured out a way to break free and strangle her.

Chapter Six

Jared watched in growing shock as one of the ugliest, scrawniest old men he'd ever seen pulled out a giant pistol and a knife so long it stretched from his hipbone almost to his knee. Problem was, as comical as the old man looked holding those big old weapons, he held them with an easy familiarity. The same kind of ease with which Jared held his sniper rifle.

Squirrel cocked the pistol and took aim at Jared's head before approaching the bed. "Now, I want you to hold real still for my girl."

He placed the knife right between Jared's legs and a cold sweat broke across Jared's lip. If either of them so much as flinched, he'd lose his balls to that razor-sharp weapon.

"That's right, boy. You move and them family jewels will be the next thing hanging on my wall."

"You can threaten to cut off anything you want, but you and I both know I'm not gonna lie here and let her tie my feet to the bed." Jared forced his heart rate to slow and focused on his enemy's weakness. Weak wrist, probably brittle bones all over. If Jared managed to aim a kick just right, he could take out the old man out. Then he'd only have to contend with Sparrow.

Not only had she left him with a raging hard-on, but she was obviously tied as tight as twine with Kay. Shit. He'd considered telling her the truth and possibly enlisting her help, but now that wasn't going to happen.

Sparrow fidgeted with the extra rope, staying a good two feet out of Jared's reach. *Smart girl.* He was ready to take them both out any chance he got. "You get close to me and you know what will happen."

She paled. "Squirrel?"

Squirrel removed the knife and sheathed it, watching Jared close all the while. "I reckon you're right, young fella. I ain't seen your kind around here in a long time. I don't know who you are." Squirrel leaned in until his face was only a few inches from Jared's. "But I recognize you for what you are."

"Squirrel!"

***

Squirrel tossed the gun in the air, caught the nozzle, and slammed the butt of the pistol into the man's temple before he could so much as flinch. Sparrow gasped and dropped the rope as his head lolled to the side, unconscious. Squirrel whistled, flipped the gun in the air once more, caught it by the butt, and tucked it into the back of his pants. Easy as pie.

"What did you do?" Sparrow squealed. She'd never made that sound before in her life, but she hadn't expected him to practically kill her hostage. How the hell was she supposed to seduce the man now?

Squirrel slapped his hands over his ears. "Quiet down, girl, no need to yell. That fella woulda cut himself clean through to keep you from tying him down. I could see it in his eyes. You better hurry and get them feet tied up quick like, and make sure you pull them knots extra tight. You can only hold back a bear for so long."

"How am I supposed to seduce him if he's unconscious?" Sparrow cried.

"He ain't going to be unconscious for long. Pass me some of that rope, I want to make sure you do it right."

Sparrow stared at him dumbfounded. She'd pictured this going a lot more smoothly. Squirrel gave an exasperated sigh and picked the rope up off the floor. He gave her a once over, and Sparrow resisted the urge to cross her arms over her chest.

"I ain't had me a woman in a while, and I might be an old fool, but you ain't going to get nowhere dressed in them man's clothes. You need something girly."

She yanked the rope out of his hands and tied it to the first bed post, her movements jerky. "And just where am I supposed to get something like that?"

Squirrel took over, his old gnarled fingers tying the rope with a speed born of decades of experience. "I reckon I'll have to go steal you some clothes."

Squirrel finished the knot securing the man's second leg and placed his hands on *her* hips. "What the hell are you doing?" she asked, yanking back out of his grip.

"What do you think? I got to figure out what size you need." Still holding his hands the same width apart as her hips, Squirrel lifted them up to eye level. "I just got to go find you something about this size."

"Jesus Christ, what are you going to do? Walk up to every girl you see and ask if you can squeeze her hips?"

Squirrel chuckled, "Not a bad idea, but no, we got to keep this secret."

"You can't just walk up to somebody and ask them for clothes, you know. They'll guess something's up."

Squirrel scratched his beard, his small frame putting him at eye level with Sparrow. "Hadn't thought of that. Well what about Geraldine? She's scrawny like you. I could steal something from her clothesline outback."

Sparrow flinched back in horror. Geraldine was the nastiest prostitute on Crowe Mountain. That girl would spread her legs for anybody and anything. "I ain't going to wear nothing that whore has worn."

"Well, there ain't no other whore here that's as little as you. You want me to go get you something just as baggy as what you're wearing right now? Aren't you trying to seduce him?"

Sparrow backed up until she hit the wall. She'd always thought her trailer was large and luxurious, but the

room seemed to be growing smaller and smaller. Her heart
thundered in her ears as her mind raced to search for any
other solution. Anything.

She came up with nothing.

"If you're having second thoughts, I can leave you my
knife. You already know how to use it." Squirrel pinned her
to the wall with his steady gaze.

Sparrow shook her head, the horrific thought of
slicing into that man's flesh making her stomach turn "No. I'll
do it."

Squirrel nodded. "Stay put, I'll be back in a couple of
minutes." He cast his gaze at the man, still unconscious on
the bed. "You might want to take his clothes off if you're
planning on using your women's wiles. It'll be easier if you
do it while he's out cold."

After he left, Sparrow turned to survey her captive.
Dear Lord, his broad chest took up nearly the entire width of
her bed. Curiosity urged her feet forward. She slid a finger
beneath the hem of his shirt, lifting the cotton inch by
glorious inch. So this was what washboard abs meant. There
was not one single spare ounce of fat on him. She could trace
the outline of each little square, counting a full eight pack.
Ten if she was generous. And Christ if those muscles didn't
dive into a V and disappear into his black pants.

She recognized the now familiar ache growing hot in
her body. Sparrow moved as if under some spell, pushing his
shirt higher and higher, then lifting it over his head and
leaving it to dangle at his wrists. The stark line of camouflage
face paint stopped just below his collar bone and smooth tan
skin took over the rest of the way down. Reminded of her
previous mission to see his face, she dove for the wash cloth.
Careful not to touch the swelling bump on his temple, she
washed the paint away. Then she removed his black beanie
and took a step back to get a good look at him.

Her mouth felt liable to fall straight to the floor. Black
as midnight hair neither too short, nor too long, full and thick
and begging her fingers to sift through it. A shadow of a

beard darkened his jaw line. But his lips were even more sinful. Full and sensual, drawing her in for a kiss.

He moaned and her heart shot into her throat. He shifted once and then settled. *Finish the job. He's just a man. Just a man.*

She repeated the mantra over and over in her mind, but that didn't stop her hands from trembling as she reached forward to unsnap the button of his pants free.

Just a man. Just the most mouth-watering, sexy man imaginable.

She had to straddle him to slide his pants down, but the way Squirrel had tied each leg to a separate bed post, she was only able to pull them partway down his thighs. Massive thighs. Thighs as big around as her entire waist.

But his thighs weren't what garnered her attention. The thick shaft lying on his belly was what had her biting her lip. Even limp, he was huge.

The front door squeaked open and banged shut. Sparrow hastily re-zipped his pants, knowing instinctively that the proud man would hate her if he awoke completely nude and restrained.

Squirrel stumbled into the room. "I hit the jackpot, girly. You sure you're up for this?"

She stiffened and jumped from the bed. It always got her back up when someone questioned her abilities. She could do this. She would do it, even if her insides quaked at the sight of him. Squaring her shoulders and lifting her chin, Sparrow said, "Just give me the damn clothes. I want to inspect them for ticks."

"I always wanted something better for you than this place. Ain't right, a girl like you being stuck out here." Squirrel extended an alarmingly small bundle and Sparrow snatched it from him. She didn't have a choice. The information he might have was the only thing that could save her and Squirrel, and she wouldn't hurt him for it.

"Yeah, well I want something better for you too, and if I take care of this problem, I might just get the break we need." And hopefully not lose herself in the god tied to her bed.

Squirrel approached the bed and leaned in for a closer look. "Something about that face is familiar." Squinting down at the man, he scratched the corner of his mouth. "I know I've seen it before."

Sparrow rolled her eyes. "You didn't hear him talking enough. He ain't from these parts. The accent ain't right."

"I'm going to think on it for a spell. Get me a sweet dram to help clear my thoughts." Sparrow almost snorted, but she held quiet. Squirrel clearly believed what he was saying, and when had he ever lied to her?

"You really think you've seen him before?"

The way the man's expression had altered from sweet and sexy to psycho-killer the moment he saw Miss Kay had been unmistakable. Yes, he definitely knew the Crowe matriarch, but maybe she wasn't the only person up here he knew. "He changed when he saw Miss Kay. I could tell he wanted to kill her."

Squirrel scratched his grizzly beard, the deep grooves on his forehead wrinkling in thought. "I knew it. That boy's been here before, sure enough, I just have to figure out when. And why." He reached into his pocket and pulled out a small vial of clear liquid. "This here's my own special brew. If he don't cooperate, or you get scared, sprinkle a little bit of this into some whiskey and give him a drink."

Sparrow took the small vial and held it up for inspection. The glass tube was about the length and diameter of her pinky finger. "What is it? Will it hurt him?"

"Might make him a tad groggy, but it'll loosen them lips up enough that he'll sing louder than a damn whippoorwill. It's my own truth serum." Squirrel waggled his bushy brows, obviously proud of his invention. "And he won't remember a thing afterwards."

Drugging him seemed underhanded, dirty, and perfect. If she couldn't get him to give her answers straight on, she wouldn't hesitate to use the serum. "My thanks."

Squirrel's expression turned serious once more. "I know you ain't never been with no man."

Sparrow tried to interrupt him, embarrassed, but he held up a calloused hand. "And I know you're also the most stubborn creature on this entire mountain. Just be careful. A man like this is experienced. Don't let him get into your head, and I sure as hell wouldn't tell him you're a virgin."

Heat didn't just rush to her face, it exploded across her skin in an instant. Even her chest felt scalded with embarrassment. "How the hell do you know that I'm a virgin? You don't know everything about me."

"And just what boy around here did you let touch you?"

The names and faces of every male she could think of flooded her mind, but she wouldn't have let one of them within ten feet of her person. "None of your damn business."

"Just like I thought. I'm serious, girl, a man like him will take advantage of your innocence. Don't you let on that you ain't never been with a man. You seen how them whores act around camp. Just do what they do and you should be fine."

Sparrow stood there in shock, unable to form a coherent thought. Squirrel, old enough to be her grandpa— her only real father figure—was urging her to act like a prostitute after a hundred-dollar bill.

He pressed his Bowie knife into her hands. "I don't care what happens. If you fear for your life, you slit his throat. I can hide the body where nobody will find it. Got it?"

Sparrow couldn't speak, so she just stood there nodding and clutching the whore's clothes and the knife to her chest.

"Good, now get yourself changed, cause your fella ain't gonna stay out much longer. You better be ready for a bear when he wakes up."

Chapter Seven

Jared came to consciousness in an instant, and was greeted by a pounding head. Rage ripped through him as he remembered how the old man had knocked him out. But they were talking over him—Sparrow and the grizzled guy—so Jared kept quiet and listened to their conversation. If he'd learned one thing in his years in Special Ops, it was that knowledge was power.

So Kay was still here, running the show. Running Sparrow, too, it seemed. He barely registered the dim glow of the lamp on the bedside table through his slitted eyes. He was too focused on the conversation going on around him.

They were sending in a virgin to tame him. It was like sending a sheep to tame a wolf. He'd been with plenty of women, and seducing them had never been a problem. Women seemed to gravitate toward him, drawn to his darkness.

Sparrow would be easy prey. He simply had to lay the bait and spring the trap. He remained motionless, his eyes closed, until he heard the door shut behind them. *His shirt was gone.*

Jared's eyes shot open to survey his body—she'd stripped him except for his pants. Bound his feet to the bed too. Fuck all. The now familiar anger pulsed through is veins, and he bowed up completely from the bed in an attempt to break free, disregarding the pain at his wrists.

He hated being restricted. That's why he preferred to sleep outside on missions, why he didn't have a permanent home to go to between jobs. He didn't like to be tied down to anything after what he'd survived. Even the thought of it was too constrictive. And yet he'd willingly let her tie him to her bed. *Why?*

He didn't like that his own behavior didn't make sense to him. He liked clear. Concise. Black and white. Not the unyielding gold of Sparrow's eyes.

Remember your mission. Remember Hoyt. He had to get free. And it seemed the only way he could do this was to turn this innocent's game against her—seduce her and use her to find Hoyt.

Jared listened to her move about the trailer, the paper thin walls doing nothing to mute her movements. The shower cut on and the image of her naked, steaming hot water running down her body, sent a fresh wave of lust straight to his cock. Shit, those were not the thoughts of a man bent on escape and rescue.

He'd have to move fast. Hoyt had been missing for way too long. Images from Jared's past, of the dark closet with the rusted bolt in the floor flashed through his mind. They'd been held there together with no food or water, left to starve to death in their own piss. And fucking Kay Crowe, his own flesh and blood, had put them there.

Sparrow was the one who set you free.

Jared tried to ignore the memory of her small hands and frightened eyes as she cut through the ropes holding them to the floor. She'd risked her life to save theirs.

And now she worked for the very woman who'd nearly killed them.

A few minutes later he heard a thump, followed by a shriek and a loud bang. She had to have thrown something. He couldn't help the smile tugging at his lips. Her reactions were quick and honest. Her eyes were a mirror to her thoughts. Her taste was as sweet as the honeysuckle growing in the hills. God, her taste had nearly taken him hostage. But now he was prepared. He was focused. Kay had ensured he'd remembered who he was and why he was here. His brother. Hoyt was being held prisoner somewhere in this compound and Jared would do whatever it took to find and rescue him. But when Hoyt was safe and sound, Jared would return to mete out his revenge, and he wouldn't leave a single Crowe standing.

The floor creaked in the hall and Jared sucked in a breath, the anticipation of seeing her again nearly mastering his logic. Then he heard her long indrawn breath, like she was preparing for battle. Hell, he might have to coax *her* into the bed. If he could get her to straddle him again, he'd get those nipples between his lips and…

The door creaked open on rusted hinges that hung slightly off-balance, and its weight sent it banging against the wall. Sparrow stood unmoving, her fists clenched at her sides. Jared's breath caught as he took in her appearance. She was clearly embarrassed, but she was far from laughable. She was smoking hot. A short white crop top barely skimmed her ribcage, dipping down low enough he could almost make out the top of her nipples. Nipples that would be visible through the near transparent material of her top if not for the bold black words, "Insert Slot A," with an arrow pointing straight up to her mouth. The thought of her on her knees flooded his mind with desire. *Jesus Christ.*

Her trim waist and belly button were fully exposed over the top of a pair of low slung cut-offs. He could only imagine how sexy her ass looked in those jeans. Her hair hung long and loose. Damn, his cock was already hard and she hadn't even summoned the nerve to look at him yet.

She finally lifted her gaze, starting at his feet and stalling at his waist. His cock jumped in response when her lips parted. Fuck all if he couldn't get that image of her on her knees, taking him between her lips, out of his mind. He had to do something to distract himself before his plan flew straight out the window, and he succumbed to pure lust.

"That is a definite improvement," Jared said.

Sparrow's golden gaze jerked up to his and a slight tremor ran through her body. It reminded him of how she'd been as a little girl—those same huge eyes wide with fright. He couldn't help but feel the tiniest bit guilty for planning to twist this encounter to his own ends, but he wouldn't harm her, emotionally or physically. Jared let his head fall back to the pillow and released a weary sigh.

Maybe he should lie and tell her she was scrawny and ugly, but the words wouldn't leave his mouth. She was beautiful and precious. And from the way she'd acted around Miss Kay, he could tell she was scared of the older woman. Could Kay be forcing her to do this? Using her like she loved using everyone under her power? Maybe he should rescue Sparrow from this nightmare when he left with his brother.

"Come here, sit beside me." Jared kept his voice gentle and silky smooth.

Sparrow walked across the room, her steps tentative but graceful. *How could something so pure exist in a hellhole like this?*

The mattress barely dipped under her weight as she sat down near his waist. When she sucked that full bottom lip between her teeth, he barely managed to hold back a groan. She might be pure and innocent and he might have good intentions, but he wasn't a saint. He fully intended to sample just a little bit of her wares before he convinced her to free him.

"How would you like to begin?" Jared asked.

Sparrow's arched eyebrows dipped down in deep thought. She seemed to come to a decision, her face hardening with it, and she grabbed him between the legs. Jared gasped as pain shot straight up from his injured balls and nausea twisted at his stomach. "Shit."

Sparrow yanked her hand back like she'd been bitten by a snake. "I didn't mean to."

Before Jared could gather enough breath to tell her to give him a minute, she ran from the room. He focused on his breathing, getting through that first rolling wave of nausea. Had he thought her innocent? She was fucking deadly.

Dammit, she was probably halfway across camp right now. What a royal clusterfuck. How long would he have to

lay here until someone was sent in here to interrogate him
with a knife now that the sweet way hadn't worked. He could
only pray it wouldn't be Jimbo. That big son of a bitch
looked brutal.

But Sparrow returned a few minutes later. She
hovered in the doorway and he could tell she was still
shaken. But then she surprised him. She lifted her chin and
re-entered the room. It wasn't until she clunked down the two
glasses on the nightstand that he noticed the bottle of
whiskey clutched in her hand. She poured herself a shot,
downed it, and then took one more.

"I'm gonna do this." She replaced her glass on the
table, then knelt on the bed and straddled him, settling her
core right on top of his cock. Blood flooded that part of his
anatomy, making it even harder.

"I'm ready, darlin'."

She reached for his face and palmed his cheek. The
sensation of that small touch was pure electricity. Jared
kissed her palm. "I've been waiting all night to kiss you."
Sparrow bit her lip and he groaned. "Every time you do that
it drives me wild."

She released her lip instantly. "That?"

Jared nodded, wishing his hands were free so he
could yank her to him. "I can only imagine how soft they are,
how sweet you taste. Come here."

She dropped down onto her elbows, her lips hovering
just above his. The sweet smell of honeyed whiskey filled his
nostrils. He forced himself to hold perfectly still as she
lowered her head, gently pressed her lips to his and gave him
a stiff, closed mouth kiss. And then she sat up with a look of
satisfaction. "How was that?"

"I felt like I was kissing my grandma," Jared said.

Her cheeks flashed bright red and fire sparked in her
gaze. "And just how exactly do you want to be kissed?"

"You've got to put some feeling into it. Open your
mouth, let me have your tongue," Jared ground out the
words. He'd always made it a rule to steer completely clear
of innocents. He preferred a woman, hot-blooded and lusty—

one who knew how to handle a man. But for some reason, instructing her like this had him nearly dripping with pre-cum. And damn if that look of angry determination on her face wasn't sexy as hell.

She pressed her lips to his again and Jared held as still as he could, letting her learn. When her lips parted and sucked his lower lip between hers, his hips shot up off the bed. She continued exploring, moving her hands to his shoulders, her soft fingertips tickling his skin. Jared's resolve to let her go at her own pace melted away. He rose as much as he could, biting her lower lip and pulling her down to him. When he felt her resistance cave, he slanted his head and plunged his tongue into her mouth. Her response was immediate and passionate. Quickly learning, she met him head on. By the time they parted, they were both panting. His cock was harder than a fucking piece of granite and they'd only kissed.

"I want to touch you," Jared growled, driving his hips against her core.

"No, I'm the one who's gonna touch you." Her eyes were wide with wonder as she traced his chest with her palms. Her innocent touch made his balls tighten up nearly inside his body.

"You told me your name is Jake. You're here looking for your brother. You know Miss Kay—and you hate her." Sparrow continued to rub circles on his chest, finding his nipples and brushing her thumbs back and forth over the tender peaks.

Had he thought she would be so easy to play? She'd inferred quite a bit from his reaction to Kay. He would have to hold his cards closer from here on out. "Well, I guess you know everything now."

"What is your problem with Kay?"

"We played this game before. You want something from me I want something from you." Remembering the taste of her nipples, Jared let his gaze fall to that tiny white shirt.

"Tell me why first." Sparrow's delicate fingers lifted to her rib cage and held on to the bottom of the tiny shirt, arms crossed, ready to yank it over her head. Her hips moved forward and back and the sensation of her crotch rubbing against the length of his cock was nearly enough to make him come undone.

She was driving him wild, so he decided to give her what she thought she wanted to know. But he wouldn't tell her the truth. "I'm here because my brother made a deal with Kay, and now he is missing."

"What kind of deal?"

"No, sweetheart, that's not *our* deal." Jared dropped his gaze. If she didn't take that shirt off right now, he was going to detonate. She yanked the sexy material off. His mouth went completely dry. Had he thought her breasts were sexy before? They were full, heavy, and her nipples were rock hard and begging for his mouth. "Lie down. Let me taste those pretty nipples again."

She lifted her hands, cupping their fullness as if in offering. "Tell me."

"If you don't stop humping my dick, I'm going to cum in my pants."

She fell onto his chest. "Tell me what I want. What does he look like? What did he want from Kay?"

Jared was having to fight harder to fabricate plausible lies—those tight little nipples were driving him crazy pressed against his own. Her entire body mimicked the movement of her hips as she rubbed up and down him, slow, sensual, and sizzling.

"He told me he was coming here, but he never came back. I haven't been able to get in touch with him, and I think something bad might have happened."

Please don't stop. Just don't stop. She rewarded him by pressing her sweet lips to his, this time without an ounce of hesitation. Her tongue plunged into his mouth, her kiss demanding. There was no hint of awkwardness. His tigress.

Where was this feeling of possessiveness coming from? He'd never kept a woman longer than one night, never thought of a woman as his…

"Untie me. I've got to touch you." Jared rasped, his

oxygen all but gone.

"I can't. I can't risk it."

"You can," Jared commanded. But the little minx sat back, riding his cock, the rough material of her jean shorts pressing hard against his engorged flesh. "I told you what you wanted to know, now it's your turn. Take those shorts off." He couldn't help the harsh authority in his voice this time. He was losing his mind, needing to touch her, to be inside her. Needing to take her.

Sparrow stood up right there on the bed, her feet straddling his hips. She unsnapped the button, slowly slid the zipper down, and then hooked her thumbs into the top of the cut offs and slid them down her long lean legs, torturing him with every inch of flesh revealed. When her shorts were to her ankles, she kicked them off and stood proud and naked, except for her panties.

They were white cotton with black lettering to match her barely-there top. There was a black arrow pointing straight at her crotch, and the words "Insert Slot B" were stamped across the top.

Jesus fucking Christ.

She dropped to her knees and straddled him again, falling forward onto her arms, her long, silky hair trailing across his chest. Her tight nipples and flushed skin spoke to her arousal as much as the small moans coming from her lips. He could just imagine how wet her panties would be, if only he could get his hands untied to touch her. Right this minute he'd be willing to say anything to get inside her.

"I can't wait to touch you, to put my hands on you. Run my fingers through your hair. Hold your head to mine as I take your lips, and my kiss won't be gentle this time, Sparrow, it will be hard. I want to show you how a kiss should be."

Her eyes went even more heavy-lidded, but she still held herself aloft over him.

"And when I'm through with your mouth, I'm going to cup your beautiful breasts. I'm going to squeeze them and roll your nipples between my fingers until you're moaning with pleasure."

She bucked against him, her tight nipples grazing his chest.

"Show me Sparrow, cup yourself for me, let me imagine what my hands would look like on your soft skin."

Chapter Eight

Sparrow's body was on fire, her skin so sensitive just the brush of his chest against her drove her wild. Never had she experienced so many sensations at one time. His voice rasped over her skin. Sexy. Commanding. Hot. She wanted so badly for him to touch her.

It was like someone else had taken over her body. Some wanton. She sat back on her heels, savoring his hard length pressed against her panties. Unable to resist, although she didn't understand why, her hips rocked forward and back. The pressure was building in intensity with each movement.

Unbidden, her fingertips grazed her thighs, skimmed her belly, and then cupped her breasts, squeezing them for the man beneath her. They felt heavy and swollen, aching for his touch.

"That's it. Now pinch your nipples." He locked his gaze on her, commanding her even as he was bound to her bed.

Sparrow felt like she would die if she didn't follow his instruction. She'd never touched herself before, never explored her own body or anyone else's. Following his lead, she took her thumb and finger and squeezed each nipple, pulling and twisting. Intense pleasure combined with pain pulled a sharp cry from her lips.

"That's it sweetheart. That's it. Harder."

She tugged and didn't try to hold in her cry of pleasure. She watched, her lids heavy, as he yanked at the rope over his head, and right at that moment she would have given anything to feel him touching her. She knew instinctively that while her hands might feel good, his would drive her absolutely wild. "Hank."

"Free me." She let her head fall back while riding his cock. Tension built inside her and she knew it had to lead to something, but she had no idea where.

"God, I can feel how wet you are. You're soaking those panties. You need me to touch you. To take care of you. To give you sweet pleasure. All I need is one hand, Sparrow, that's it. Let me show you."

Sparrow was a woman possessed. She didn't need to understand what would happen, she just knew he would take care of her. She rode him faster, moaning with each thrust and before she even realized what was happening, her hands were skimming up his huge arms and tangling in the rope.

"Almost there, baby."

He bit down on her nipple and she cried out, bringer her hand back down to cup his head, her body buckling under the intense pleasure.

When he released her, she wanted to weep. "Untie me and let me make you scream."

Her fingers shook so bad she couldn't get a firm grip on the knot. Frustrated, she yanked, and the rough rope burned her flesh.

What are you doing? Had she lost her mind? Suddenly she was just as desperate for release as he was.

Her head dropped and she let her arms fall to her sides. She couldn't risk it, no matter how much her body screamed for his.

"Get the knife and cut the goddamn rope." He bucked beneath her, but instead of scaring her, it only made her hotter. Wetter.

Squirrel had been right. He was too much for her. The sexual eminence flowing from his body controlled her. She wanted to do as he asked. She wanted what he could give her like she'd never wanted anything in her entire life.

She knew what she had to do and she wanted to weep from despair. She reached over to the bedside table where Squirrel's knife rested beside the two shot glasses, one laced with truth serum.

"That's it baby, use the knife to cut the rope. I swear to God, I'll give you pleasure like you've never dreamed." His raspy voice sent goose bumps racing across her flesh. Her heart tripped and her fingers fumbled over the handle of the Bowie knife.

That's all that stood between her and ultimate pleasure. Or—her worst nightmare.

Sparrow steeled herself and reached a little further, grabbing the bottle of whiskey and pouring a shot in each glass.

She downed hers first, praying the liquid would give her courage to finish her task. She'd never in her life had a problem with being deceitful and devious, that's how she rolled—it was the only way to survive up here—but something about this man pulled at her soul and she found herself wanting to save him instead of use him.

Self-preservation kicked in, though, and as much as she wanted to be his savior, she wanted to live more. Sparrow lifted the glass to his lips. "Drink. Let me think on this a spell."

He drank without question. "More. Give me another shot." Sweat beaded along his brow and she obliged, pouring him another whiskey. He downed it like a man dying of thirst. How much longer could she hold out? They both needed release.

"I want to cut you free. I want to real bad. But I can't risk it. I'm asking you nicely, so please tell me the truth. What do you want with my family?"

"Right now all I want to do is to bury myself between your thighs."

He might as well have struck a match and set her ablaze.

Desperation edged through her veins. How long

would it take for the drugs to kick in? Freaking hell, this man was sex incarnate. She wanted to enjoy him longer, even if she meant to ultimately destroy him. After tonight, she might never get to kiss him again. And after him, no man would ever measure up.

Sparrow pressed her lips to his, seeking solace in his touch, wanting to lose herself for just one more minute.

He met her full force, lifting his head from the pillow and going at her aggressively. Possessively. She'd always imagined sweet little kisses and loving words. But Hank, even bound to the bed, dominated her.

As his kiss grew lazy, she realized the drugs had started working. Still, she clasped him to her for a while longer, unwilling to give up their connection. No matter how hard she held him, though, he slipped away, and she let his head drop to the bed. "Hank?"

"Hmmm?" His lids lay heavy and low, and his grin was languid.

"Why are you here?" Sparrow forced the guilt down. He might look innocent right now, but this man was deadly.

"Hoping to get laid." She couldn't help but smile at his groggy words.

"I want you too. But if you want me, you'll tell me why you're here, why you came to my mountain."

"My mountain," he echoed.

Had she given him too much? If he was going to do nothing but repeat everything she said, this would be useless. "Jake, why are you here on my property?"

He closed his eyes and his black brows dipped down in frustration. "Not Jake. Not your mountain. *My* mountain."

Sparrow sat back on her heels, crushing her crotch onto his still hard cock, Jared answered by pressing into her.

"Who are you?"

His eyes opened and she was swallowed whole by their blackness. "I'm the boy who got away."

His words tugged at her, pulling forth an inkling of premonition, like she should know exactly who he was—and she had the sinking sensation that she did know. Sparrow braced her arms on the mattress, watching the expression on his face. "Tell me your full name."

"Jared Crowe."

Sparrow fell backwards off the bed and shoved her fist in her mouth to keep her scream inside. The boy from her dreams. One of the two she'd found tied and beaten like dogs, stuffed in a closet to starve to death. Her young heart had been unable to stand their torture a moment longer, so she'd snuck into their shack one night and set them both free. Jared and Hoyt Crowe.

The heirs to Crowe Mountain. Miss Kay had held them hostage after their parents' sudden death, holding on to them to secure the land deed to the mountain and surrounding land. After the boys' disappearance, Miss Kay had told everyone they were dead, leaving her with an indisputable claim to Crowe Mountain.

If Miss Kay found out the identity of Sparrow's captive, she'd kill him. Slit his throat and burn the body. Had Sparrow set him free as a child only to trap him as an adult?

She approached the bed on trembling legs.

"Why would you ever come back here?"

"She took him. She took my brother. Have to get him back. He can't stand the dark."

Sparrow nearly doubled over. He'd been telling a partial truth earlier. But why would Miss Kay go after the Crowe brothers after all these years?

Sparrow sank to the bed, elbows braced on her knees, and let her head fall into her hands. A memory she'd buried long ago whispered to her from her subconscious. *"Come with us. I'll find a way to take care of you. Get you out of this place."*

Even then, beaten and starved, he'd tried to save her. But that was before Tootsie's overdose, and Sparrow hadn't had the heart to leave her mother to fend for herself. Tootsie could barely get out of bed most days, let alone manage the trailer. And now the tortured boy she'd set free had come home, and if Sparrow carried through with her plan and used him to ensure her position with Miss Kay, it would all but ensure his death.

"Have you seen him, Sparrow. Have they got him in the closet?" Jared's voice dropped to that of a child in pain, hurt and questioning. Unbidden, tears rose to her eyes and she shook her head because she couldn't force words through the tight cinch around her throat. "I wish you would've came with us, Sparrow."

His words shook her tears free. "I wanted to. I wanted to more than anything."

"Where's my brother? Where is he? I have to find him before they hurt him."

This was no longer the strong, dominating man from minutes ago; this was the little boy she'd saved all those years ago.

The last rays of sunlight streaming through the broken window blinds faded, leaving the room in a strange sort of dark twilight. The old lamp on her nightstand was too dim to light much beyond the table on which it sat.

Jared strained against his bonds. "No, not the dark. Please not the dark."

His pleas ripped her from her thoughts. His skin had turned pale and sweaty, and his pupils were huge and unfocused. Her heart ripped in two, straight down the middle. No. She could never turn him over to be murdered, not even if it meant her own death. She would save him and his brother again. Just like when they were little kids. It felt a bit like fate.

"Sparrow, please untie me. I can't take it. Too much. Have to protect him. Have to protect you," Jared was rambling now, turning his head from side to side on the pillow.

Sparrow caressed Jared's face with one hand and reached for the knife with the other. Yes, she would help them escape, but maybe she would go with them this time. If she could convince Squirrel to leave, Jared could help them start a new life. A life somewhere far away from this place that ran on drugs and booze and whoring.

Chapter Nine

When Jared came back to consciousness, his head was heavy and throbbing. He reached up to clasp his temples between his palms, trying to rub some of the grogginess away. Memories of Sparrow naked and riding him flitted through his mind. Her sweet smile, the taste of honey whiskey, and then…nothing. Just darkness.

Darkness made lighter as soon as he realized she'd set him free. Jared shot upright, the sudden motion setting off such a pounding sensation in his head he nearly fell off the bed.

"Whoa, slow down." Sparrow appeared in front of him, the skimpy outfit from before back in place.

"What did we do?" His voice was rough and gravelly, like he hadn't spoken in a while and needed practice.

"Nothing. You passed out." He remembered nearly losing control. He remembered the feel of her skin on his. He remembered wanting her as he had never wanted anything in his entire life. Why couldn't he remember the rest?

"What do you remember?" Sparrow asked.

Jared searched through the haze in his mind, but came up with nothing but fuzzy cobwebs. No sunlight showed through the blinds, and the room was dark except for a crappy lamp. "Did I sleep the whole day?"

Sparrow followed his gaze. "No, it's after midnight now. You slept for a few hours."

"What happened?"

Her cheeks flushed pink and she avoided his gaze. He grabbed her hand, gently wrapped his fingers around her wrist, and pulled her to him. "What happened?"

"I, I got scared. I got scared that I was losing control of the situation. So I gave you just a wee bit of something special in your whiskey, something to knock you out."

"You drugged me?"

That tempting pink blush turned to dark red, and instead of the anger he'd expected to feel, he found himself wanting to comfort her. He gave a tug and she fell into his lap, simply enjoying the sensation of her skin against his. "It's okay. I'm not mad, you can tell me."

It was true. He should be furious. He should tie her to the bed and leave her there so he could go out looking for his brother. Instead, he eased his fingers up and down her arm in an effort to soothe her.

Sparrow blew her hair out of her face and turned the full force of her amber eyes on him, causing his breath to hitch. He knew this wasn't a normal reaction. Maybe the explanation was simple. Maybe memories from the past were the only link between them. But his instincts told him it was something more. And years of Special Forces training had taught him to trust his instincts.

"Jared, it was really stupid of me to try and seduce you to get information. But I didn't count on feeling this way. Having these reactions. And I got scared. That's why I drugged you."

His gut tightened as the first shimmer of anger edged its way into his psyche. He hated the thought that he'd spent the day tied down. If a man had done it to him, he would've killed him.

Then she clasped his hand between her two tiny ones and held it up between them, her gaze fraught. "I remember who you are now. You're the boy from my dreams. I…I thought you died. Miss Kay told everyone you and Hoyt were dead."

So much for the element of surprise. Jared tilted his

forehead to hers. "I remembered you the minute I saw you."

She pulled back, the shock clear on her face. "Why didn't you say anything?"

"How was I to know that you hadn't turned into one of them? I mean, you stayed here. This place is evil." Before she could say anything he continued, "Look at who owns it. Miss Kay chained and tortured her two orphaned nephews, her own flesh and blood, for no reason whatsoever."

Her mouth fell open. "You don't know?"

"Know what?"

"You're the true heirs to the mountain. Your mama and daddy had the land deed, so when they died you would have inherited half the county."

All those years of wondering why. The not knowing had left scars on his soul far deeper than any physical injury. Scars that bled tension into his veins. Scars that tormented him in his sleep. Now the same girl who had saved him all those years ago was easing his suffering once more.

"Jared, say something. You're scaring me." Sparrow cupped his cheek, her fingers soft and healing against his rough skin.

Jared laughed, but even he could tell there was no humor in the sound. No, this was the type of laugh that landed someone in a psych ward.

"Oh, Lord. I shouldn't have told you that."

Jared reeled in his emotions. After having spent so many years pushing them down and containing them, it was almost easy. Grabbing her wrist, he pulled her to him. "Don't you see, Sparrow? You've given me my freedom again. All these years...I couldn't understand why our only kin would have done that to us."

"Oh Jared, I'm so sorry."

"How did you know?"

Her smile, just as broken and scarred as his own, twisted sideways. "Nobody pays attention to the whores' kids. I was invisible. I was sitting out back, making mud pies underneath Miss Kay's porch, when I heard her and Carl talking." Sparrow paused, her eyes welling with sadness.

"That's when I heard about you and Hoyt. They wanted to kill you both for the land."

"So you risked your life to save mine?" Jared felt an odd tightness form in his chest. He'd gone so long on autopilot, not caring about anything, that he couldn't even process his own reaction to what Sparrow had done for them.

Sparrow nodded, "I'd always thought my life was so bad, you know, living with a druggie prostitute mama, but at least she loved me in her own way. She never beat me. Never hurt me."

"What if Miss Kay had caught you? Do you know what she would have done?" Jared's heart stopped, the tension in his chest growing.

Her broken smile stayed in place as she caressed his cheek, and Jared felt himself leaning in to her touch. "Remember what I said? I was invisible. They never even suspected me. And since Miss Kay had kept it such a big secret that they were hiding you, she couldn't question anyone. Not long after you disappeared, they started spreading the word that y'all had drowned down in Blue Hole Lake."

The story was almost too crazy to be true. Almost. But in the most twisted fucked up way he could imagine, it made sense.

"I haven't heard about your brother being held here, but I don't think Miss Kay knows. I think Jimbo and Bob have him." Sparrow's words brought him back to the present. *My reason for being here in the first place.* Even if Miss Kay wasn't involved, Hoyt was being held against his will. Jared swallowed the huge lump of guilt. Hoyt had tried to tell him his thirst for revenge would result in regret and Jared had made Hoyt come here. He was responsible for Hoyt's capture.

"I need your help," Jared said. "I don't remember much outside the closet. Where would they keep him?" Jared could barely remember his own parents' faces. All his memories seemed to start in that closet.

Sparrow bit her lip and fell silent. Then she nearly

jumped off his lap, her feet slapping the floor. "The only place strong enough to hold a grown man would be the old shack in the woods. Nobody goes out there anymore. If they kept him in camp, people would be talking."

"Can you take me there?" Jared's feet hit the floor with urgency. He buttoned his black pants and searched for his shirt. Sparrow pulled it out of the rumpled sheets on the bed and handed it to him.

It was still dark outside. If he could get Hoyt out before the sun rose, then he could summon his team for extraction before Kay figured out she had both Crowe brothers in her clutches. Jared winced inwardly; he and Hoyt had pretty much gone AWOL. They'd informed their commander they were taking leave for a week, but that had been two weeks ago. He could only imagine how pissed off the rest of the team would be. But no matter how pissed, they would come. Task Force Scorpion wouldn't leave their men to die.

"Absolutely." Sparrow snatched the knife from the nightstand and strapped it around her waist.

Jared paused, unable to look away from the sight she presented. That skimpy white top which showed off her stomach, cut offs that could give Daisy Duke a run for her money, and fucking sexy legs with a huge bowie knife strapped to her hip. Damned if she wasn't the sexiest creature he'd ever laid eyes on. "You know how to handle that thing?"

"I learned how to skin a deer when I was just a kid. What do you think?"

He didn't doubt her abilities with that knife. Anyone who could survive up here for this long would have to be able to take care of herself. Speaking of, his gun and supplies were hidden in the woods near where Sparrow had originally found him. "I need a gun."

"Follow me. I've got some choices. You want a handgun or a shot gun?" Sparrow headed to the living room, Jared hot on her heels. She stopped before a chest that sat directly beneath the wall of animal heads.

"Do you mount all the ones you kill?" Jared asked.

Sparrow paused in what she was doing and looked up at the wall. "Nah, just the ones with a story behind them. The rest I usually sell the skins and keep the meat. I don't waste anything if possible."

The deer with the rearranged face drew his attention again. "And that one, what's his story?"

She cringed. "My first kill. Squirrel forgot to tell me where to aim the gun." Then she bent over the wooden chest and Jared forgot all about the deer. Her shorts showed off her ass to a spectacular degree, stealing his breath. When they got out of here and his brother was free and clear, Jared had every intention of finishing what she'd started. Only this time, he wouldn't be the one tied to the bed.

"Will this work?" Sparrow thrust a surprisingly nice nine-millimeter pistol and KA-BAR knife in his direction.

Jared raised a brow, even though he knew he shouldn't be surprised at the collection. He'd have to remember Sparrow wasn't like the primped and prissy girls he'd dated in the past. He hadn't figured out all of the intricacies of what she was like yet, but he wanted to. "Perfect, what else you got in there?"

She passed him a couple of extra clips of bullets. Jared tucked the pistol and knife into his waistband, and the extra ammo went into his cargo pocket. Sparrow proceeded to pull out a rifle and a rolled leather bag about the size of his arm.

"What's in the bag?"

Sparrow didn't pause, "My throwing knives. Never go anywhere without them."

"You weren't kidding about being good with a knife, were you?"

Sparrow's gaze turned confident, her smile saucy. "Honey, there ain't no one on this mountain better with a knife than I am."

He could only imagine. "What else you got in that chest?"

"A couple of hand grenades, a few more pistols and

shot guns, and some extra ammo. You know, the regular stuff." She shrugged and closed the lid. "But this should get us out of here just fine."

"Do I want to know why you have grenades?"

"Nope. Better off if you don't. Now, are you ready to head out? Night time is burning and we gotta move." Sparrow headed toward the back door, slinging her rifle over her shoulder as she went.

He'd left something important behind the last time he ran from this mountain, and he had no intention of repeating that mistake. "Pack your bag. I'm not leaving you behind the second time."

Sparrow stopped in her journey to the door. "I…I don't think I can leave, Jared. This is my home."

Jared crossed the room to her and took her arms in his hands. His stomach tensed just thinking about leaving her here to rot in this place. And when Kay found out he'd escaped…. "What do you think Kay will do when she discovers that you let me go?"

She paled and he felt a small tremor run through her. "Miss Kay is the only mother I've known; she won't hurt me."

Jared leaned in close, holding her gaze. "Then why are you trembling?"

Sparrow ripped away from him and paced the confines of the small kitchen/living room area. "You are asking me to walk away from my life." But the words were delivered in a shaking voice, as if she already realized that the life she was talking about was no kind of life.

"Yes. I am. And I'm asking you to start a new one with me." Jared stopped breathing the moment the words were out of his mouth. He'd never come this close to declaring any sort of intentions toward a woman, but Sparrow was as different from the other women he knew as lava was from ice. Something about her drew him in, made him lose control and *like* it. He wanted her.

She stopped pacing. *What was she thinking?* He really didn't want to have to drag her out of here, though he would if she continued to resist. Still, for some reason, he wanted her to want to come with him.

"What about my family?" Her words were whisper thin and Jared found himself drawn to her again.

"Kaitlyn Crowe is no one's family. She might have given you the means to support yourself, but what else has she done? Did she put you to bed at night? Cook your meals? Did she take care of you when you were hurt?" From the look on her face, Jared already knew the answer.

"I know what she did to you and your brother wasn't right, but she gave me a home. Me, a whore's kid. She gave me a chance when no one else cared."

"She took you in because she owed your momma. Do you really think she won't punish you for this?" He wanted to shake some sense into her. Get the stubbornness out of the girl.

"I don't know." But the way she said it told him she *did* know.

"I think we both know it won't be pretty. I won't leave you behind, Sparrow. Not again."

Sparrow didn't answer. Instead she studied him with those huge golden eyes, as if searching for something. It seemed like an hour before she answered. "Give me five minutes. You better get your boots out of the bedroom."

Sparrow disappeared into a different bedroom this time. Jared retrieved his boots and do rag from the bedroom floor, and quickly put them on. By the time he sat down on the living room couch to wait, Sparrow marched into the room, knee-high snake boots strapped up her legs. A small bag, one that couldn't hold more than a couple sets of clothes, was slung over her back.

"I mean it Sparrow, we're never coming back here. You need to take anything that you want. I can even carry something." He had the feeling he would be carrying his brother out of these woods, but a bag of clothes wouldn't add much to his load.

"Got everything I need right here, sugar. I travel light." Her tone was so matter of fact, he had no doubt she meant it. Her lifetime of belongings amounted to less than what most women would bring for an overnight stay at a hotel.

Sparrow carried more weapons than she did clothes.

Heck, she'd only been back in his life for a day, and she was already challenging his understanding of women.

"I gotta make a quick stop on the way out. Squirrel's cabin isn't too far out of the way."

Jared grabbed her arm. "We don't have time. Plus, I can't risk him alerting anybody."

Sparrow yanked her arm free and lifted her chin. "I ain't leaving without telling him goodbye. Out of this whole place, he's the only one who ever really cared about me. He was willing to kill you and hide you from Miss Kay just for me. Believe me, he won't tell a soul."

"I'm putting my foot down. My answer is no." Frustration welled inside him. Grown men followed his commands. This little scrap of a girl would have to do the same.

"Well, good luck finding your brother when you don't know shit about this place." Sparrow crossed her arms over her chest, the movement pushing her full breasts up, mounding over the top of the low-cut shirt.

"Shit. Fine. Lead the way. But I'm telling you right now, if I even suspect Squirrel's going to alert anyone, I'll silence him." Damn stubborn woman.

"Good thing you won't have to worry about that. Now follow me. Keep quiet and keep low." He followed Sparrow to the back door. Rather than just swing it open, she cracked it, listened for a spell, and peeked out. Then, apparently satisfied that no one was watching, she opened and stepped down.

Jared's breaths puffed in the cold air. The night would provide plenty of camouflage for their movements; the moons spare light filtered through the trees in a kaleidoscope of dark and light. Jared quietly closed the door and turned just in time to see Sparrow all but disappear into the woods.

She was silent, and would've been completely

invisible if not for her white shirt. Jared felt a small twinge of guilt for asking her to leave her home. She moved like she belonged here, like she was part of these woods.

The pine trees grew thick and their needles carpeted the ground, masking the sound of their footsteps. Jared stayed close to Sparrow, but he continued to cover their exit. The cabins behind them were dark and silent, most of their inhabitants passed out drunk or high. Still, Jared didn't relax even after the camp disappeared from sight. His instincts were pulling tight inside him, warning him to stay alert.

A few minutes later, they arrived at what Sparrow had referred to as Squirrel's cabin. To Jared, it looked a sight more like a shack barely held up by rotting wood. She held up her hand for them to stop just inside the tree line. "Keep watch out here. I don't want you to scare him."

Jared grabbed her arm. "Don't be long."

Sparrow nodded and he let her go, watching her disappear into the shack before he turned to scan the surrounding area. He tried to imagine what it must've been like growing up here in poverty, forced to work in the mines or deal drugs to survive.

For the first time Jared counted himself lucky to have come back. He'd escaped once, and he would do it again. Only this time he had Sparrow, and for some reason, she made him think about the future instead of the past.

Chapter Ten

Squirrel slept on a narrow cot against the far wall of his cabin. He probably wouldn't know how to sleep on a real bed even if it was all he had. She took the moment to study him. Memorize his features. The long scraggly gray beard. The deep weathered lines carved into his tanned face. His old gnarled hands that had always been gentle with her.

Her heart ached, but she knew deep in her soul that her time on the mountain was over. Just like she knew that Squirrel was an old man, set in his ways, and would never survive anywhere but at his home. She shook him, but he only snorted and then resumed snoring. Sparrow shook him harder until he finally cracked open one eye. "You done lost your mind, girl?"

His gravelly voice made Sparrow smile through the tears pricking her eyes. "No, Squirrel. I got to talk to you, though. I need you to wake up."

She half expected him to tell her to go away and come back in the morning, but he sat up and rubbed the sleep from his eyes, moving a sight slower than he once did. "I figured out who he was," she said. "He's Jared Crowe. He's the heir to Crowe Mountain."

Any traces of sleep disappeared from Squirrel's eyes completely and he slapped a hand on his bony knee. "I knew it. Knew I'd seen that boy before."

"We think Miss Kay has his brother hidden away

somewhere. I'm going to help Jared find him."

Squirrel stood up and grabbed his shotgun from beside the bed "I'm coming with you."

Sparrow placed a hand on his shoulder, urging him to sit back down. "No, you're going to stay right here. You're gonna go back to sleep. Because…because I'm leaving with them."

Squirrel's weathered face looked sad, but there was understanding in his eyes. "I knew you weren't for this life, girl." He grabbed her hand, his rough calluses soothing instead of scratching her skin. "I'm sure gonna miss you."

Sparrow swallowed back tears. She'd known he would understand. He always did. She threw her arms around him and hugged him tight, his bony shoulders pressing into hers. "I'm gonna come back for you as soon as I can. I'm not leaving you in this place."

Squirrel sighed and she felt it all the way down to her toes. For the first time in a long time, his weathered face reflected his age. "I can't leave this place. Don't know nothing else but these woods. Don't you worry, old Squirrel was surviving long before you was born, I'll continue to after you're gone."

Tears pricked her eyes, burning like the acid they were. "I'll miss you. You're the only person I ever loved."

"Don't be going all sentimental." Squirrel pulled away, but she saw the sheen of tears in his eyes. Her heart squeezed and the pain spread out over her ribs.

He lifted his leather necklace with the bear claw hanging from the center over his head and handed it to her. Squirrel called it his good luck talisman, and she'd never seen him take it off. That claw was from the first bear he'd ever killed.

"You take this," he said. "You take this and remember old Squirrel."

Sparrow reverently placed the leather thong around her own head, not bothering to try and hold in the tears any longer. The bear claw hung down between her breasts, over her heart.

"I'll never take it off," she vowed.

Squirrel nodded, "And don't you forget the things I taught you. Just cause you ain't living in the mountains no more don't mean you ain't gonna have to fight to survive."

Sparrow pulled him to her for one last hug, knowing it would probably be last time she'd ever see him. "I'll never forget you. I love you."

"You better go on. Daylight's coming, and if you're gonna get out of here, you're gonna have to move it."

"You take my trailer, move out of this old cabin as soon as the shit settles, okay?" Sparrow pulled away, her chest aching with grief, and wiped the tears from her eyes.

"You bet. Been waiting for my big break." He winked at her and all the lines on his forehead disappeared for the moment. She could see the spirit still strong in his eyes. She wrapped her hand around the bear claw and left, leaving a giant chunk of her heart behind in that cabin.

Jared stood waiting for her at the edge of the clearing, his back to her. "Let's go." She knew her voice was raw with tears, but she didn't care. She would force herself to look to the future, but she would never forget where she came from.

She would never forget her past.

***

Sparrow had been crying. He could see the sorrow on her face plain as the moonlight spotting the ground. But he kept his mouth shut. He would comfort her later, when they were safe. Right now he had to focus on finding Hoyt and getting them all off Crowe Mountain alive. Before the sun rose. "Which way?"

Sparrow pointed east. "Follow me, it's not far."

She took off at a brisk jog and Jared followed, trusting her sense of direction. She ducked and dodged and swerved between trees, and he followed in her footsteps, thankful for her fast pace. Now that he finally had an idea of where his brother was, he couldn't stand to wait another minute. He wanted to full out run, but knew he'd more than likely injure himself if he tried to make his way through the dark forest like that.

They emerged into a small clearing around a shack not much better than Squirrel's. Sparrow took another step forward, but Jared jerked her back into the cover of the trees. "Wait. Watch. If he's in there, there could be someone keeping guard."

Once Jared was sure no one was walking sentry in the yard, he crept around the perimeter of the trees, Sparrow fast on his heels. The shack was almost completely submerged in the dark woods. There was barely enough room on the sides to walk, and the small yard had maybe a ten-foot clearance out front. He crossed to the side of the shack, backing up to the wall and ducking low. There were no windows. Jared checked the back—no door. The only entry was in the front.

Jared inched his way to the front and peeked around the corner. The small porch stood empty. He took a deep breath, held up a hand for Sparrow to stay put, and stepped onto the porch. The roof listed to the side. Jared froze. A few heart-stopping seconds passed, but when nothing else happened, he crept carefully forward, trying to avoid the most rotted floorboards. When he got to the door, he paused and listened. There were no sounds from inside. He leaned against the wall next to the door and sucked in a breath, fighting the chill creeping up his spine.

Silence could mean his brother wasn't even in there. Or that he was asleep. Or unconscious. Or dead.

Please let him be okay.

"Hey, I've got your back." Sparrow appeared beside him, her voice a hushed whisper.

"I'm going in first. You stay out here until I clear the room."

Not waiting to see if she agreed with his orders, Jared raised his pistol and gently nudged the door with his free hand. There was no resistance; the door swung open without a hitch.

A sense of foreboding stole across his shoulders, tightening the muscles there. His senses went on heightened alert. If they were holding his brother captive here, they would have posted a guard. At least locked the door. *Something.* Which meant the cabin was either empty or his brother was already dead. Fervently praying for the first, Jared stepped inside, sweeping his pistol around the one room shack. A barrel topped with an extinguished lantern and a coil of rope rested in the corner of the room. A chair with a table in the back. Then he allowed his gaze to lock onto the object in the center of the room.

There was just enough illumination from the moon to highlight the figure of a body suspended from the ceiling. Jared shoved his gun into his waistband and ran forward, his stomach rolling with fear. He knew before seeing Hoyt's face that he was the one hanging there. Limp.

Jared quickly felt for a pulse, a heartbeat, anything, but his hands were shaking so bad all he did was scrape against bare skin. "Dammit."

Without warning, a light flared from the back corner and Jared jerked his gaze up, ready to attack, only to see Sparrow flicking on a battery powered lantern. Jared turned his attention back to his brother and the sight before him stole his ability to breathe. To think.

He knew it was Hoyt. He had the right blond hair, size, and stature, but the blood and swelling covering his body made him almost unrecognizable. A long deep cut sliced down his left cheek from temple to jaw. Strips of flesh hung from his back as if he'd been…skinned.

"What did they do to you?" Rage expanded inside him until he felt like a pressure bomb about to explode. His baby brother. He'd failed to protect him. Failed to save him.

"Oh. My. God." Sparrow approached Jared, but he barely recognized her presence.

Jared almost wished his brother were dead. He couldn't imagine the agony he had been through. The rage forked through his veins as he lifted his fingers once more to check for a pulse. He found one, weak and fast, but fucking real, and his knees almost gave out right then and there. "He's alive."

Blood dripped from Hoyt's body onto the floor.

"We have to cut him down." Sparrow pulled the knife from her hip. "Jared, you need to get behind him and brace him. I'll cut the rope."

Unable to form words, unable to do anything more than stare in horror at his little brother, Jared simply obeyed.

His brother shuddered and moaned, causing him to freeze in his tracks. Sparrow stood directly in front of Hoyt now, the knife clutched in her hand. Slowly lifting his head, opening the one eye that wasn't completely swollen shut, Hoyt mumbled, "No more. Don't let her do this to me anymore."

What had he said? Don't let *her* do this anymore? Jared's gaze shot to Sparrow in time to see the shocked expression on her face. Her nervous honey colored eyes cut to his.

Hoyt heaved and tried to struggle. "Oh God, not the knife."

Then someone else spoke from the doorway. Someone Jared had hoped to meet when he had his gun locked and loaded. Jimbo said, "Good job little sister. Now we got them both."

Realization dawned. It was a trap. It had been a trap all along. Jared felt disbelief and rage and hatred well up in his gut. "You did this?"

Everything she'd said to him had been a lie. Everything. And he had fallen for the oldest fucking trick in the book. "You little bitch. You're gonna regret this."

Sparrow flinched back. "Jared, I…"

Jimbo cut in, "You're smarter than I gave you credit for. When you came up with this plan, little sister, I didn't think it would work, but I'll be damned. Miss Kay is definitely going to promote you now."

"It's about time too." Bob appeared beside Jimbo, thumbs hooked in his oversized overalls.

Sparrow's gaze flipped wildly back and forth between the two men. Her innocent appearance was so disgusting now that he knew the truth. "No, I swear—"

"This is the big break you've been waiting for. Both Crowe brothers trapped together. Easy to make 'em disappear now." Bob took a step closer, as if the deal was done.

The monster inside Jared broke loose. Cold lethal calm settled over his body and he knew what he had to do. Sparrow knew about the gun tucked in his pants, but Jimbo didn't, and he was the bigger threat. Before either of them could prepare, Jared launched across the room, ripping the gun from his pants and pistol-whipping Jimbo across the face. The huge man fell hard and fast to the ground, unconscious, blood leaking from his temple. Jared reared back and kicked Bob in the jaw. The skinny man dropped to the ground, his lifeless body, giving an outlet to the rage eating at his guts.

Sparrow gasped and Jared aimed his pistol straight at her head. "Nothing but evil on this mountain. I trusted you, and you did this to my brother."

She held her hands out and he spied the roll of knives strapped to her waist. Awareness slapped him. She'd bragged about how good she was with a blade, and apparently she'd expertly cut off strips of his brother's back to prove her efficacy.

If he'd had the luxury, Jared would have vomited right then and there.

"Drop your gun. Now." Jared kept his pistol leveled right between her eyes.

"Jared, I don't know what he's talking about. I had nothing to do with this."

Her words cracked into him like a whip. Jared strode over to her, barely able to restrain himself from slapping her, and pressed the tip of his pistol to her forehead. The force of his brutal anger practically bent her backwards. "Drop your fucking gun now."

His hand shook, his control slipping, but he couldn't afford to lose it. Not yet. Not until he got his brother to safety.

Then he would mete out his revenge. Jared would extract his own pound of flesh, and he would start with

Sparrow.

She lifted the rifle strap over her head and lowered the gun to the floor beside her.

Jared nodded toward the coil of rope in the corner. "Since you're so good with a knife, cut some rope. Tie his hands behind his back and take off his shirt." Jimbo's shirt would be big enough to completely wrap around Hoyt, and it was the only thing close by that would provide any type of barrier between his brother's raw wounds and the environment.

"Jared, please, I didn't do this. I had no idea he was really in here."

Jared snarled, barely able to restrain himself from attacking her. "The next words out of your mouth will be your last. Get the fucking rope!"

She paled and pressed her lips together, turning to do as he commanded. It was a struggle for her to roll Jimbo's hulking body to the side and pull the shirt from his body, but Jared offered no help. If it were up to him, she would suffer for every second of every day for the rest of her short life.

Finally, she wrested the shirt from Jimbo, cut a length of rope, and tied his hands behind his back. She gagged him with a dirty discarded cloth and secured it with another piece of rope around his head.

"You're going to help me get that shirt on my brother, and so help me God, if you cause him one more ounce of pain, I'll slit your throat. Do you doubt me?" Jared had never spoken so harshly to a woman in his entire life, but when he looked at the blood dripping from the open wounds covering Hoyt's entire body, it was all he could do to keep from screaming.

Sparrow grabbed Jimbo's shirt from the floor and approached with caution. Without speaking, Jared yanked the knife from her grip. "I'm going to cut one arm loose. Feed it through the sleeve." He waited on Sparrow's nod and as gently as he could, he reached up and cut his brother's left hand free of the binding. Hoyt groaned again, then slumped over, losing consciousness.

Jared breathed a sigh of relief, knowing that any movement would cause his brother excruciating pain. Moving slowly and with obvious care, Sparrow eased the shirt up and hooked it around Hoyt's shoulders. Jared cut the other arm free, caught his brother beneath his arms, and held him up so that Sparrow could finish wrapping the shirt across his brother's exposed back.

As gently as he would handle a baby, Jared lowered Hoyt to his stomach on the floor, careful not to touch his destroyed back. When they were still just kids, Jared had vowed to protect his little brother. He'd always been the mature one in their relationship, the one responsible for watching out for younger Hoyt. Jared had wanted his brother to have the freedom to be wild and fun loving. To have happiness unshadowed by nightmares and memories. And up until tonight, Hoyt had been exactly as happy and bright and charming as Jared had hoped he'd be. Until Sparrow and Crowe Mountain. Reckless brutality took over his rational brain and Jared grabbed Sparrow around the neck. "You're going to suffer for what you did to him."

He ripped the rope from her grip and yanked her wrists together, violently binding her hands in front of her. The woman he'd thought so innocent, so pure, was nothing more than a liar. A murderous villain. Jared was determined to destroy this woman who had taken away his last bit of humanity.

Chapter Eleven

Sparrow thrust her hands forward, holding her wrists together so that Jared could easily bind her. Once he was done tying the rough rope, he attached a lead rope to his belt, effectively leashing her to him.

The anguish she saw in his face ripped apart her soul. More than anything in the world she wanted to comfort him. She couldn't imagine what a nightmare this must be for him.

But if she spoke again, he might very well kill her. Especially after what Jimbo had said. She'd known for a long time that he viewed her as a threat. He'd snuck behind her back to screw up her alcohol shipments and other minor things, trying to make her look bad in front of Miss Kay, but he'd never pulled anything like this before. He'd intentionally tried to have her killed. His words had sealed her fate with the Crowe brothers.

And Bob...they'd always had a careful peace between them, as if each understood the need to keep Jimbo at bay. She didn't know what to think about his presence.

The small ounce of hope Sparrow had held onto since she was a little girl died, weighing her to the floor like a huge oak tree had fallen on her shoulders. She would never have a loving family. She would never have a happy, fulfilling life.

She had to help Jared and Hoyt get as far from here as possible, whether he wanted to kill her or not, and as soon as they were at a safe distance, she would try and escape. Jared had no idea just how slippery she could be. As soon as a distraction presented itself, she would escape. Then she could make her way back to Crowe Mountain, stop Jimbo. If he took over, there would be nothing but misery for everyone in the county. And Squirrel wouldn't stand a chance.

"If I even feel you move in the wrong direction, I'll do to you what you did to him." Sparrow followed Jared's gaze to Hoyt's unconscious form on the floor. Never had she seen something so gruesome. So horrible. Nausea rolled through her stomach and up her throat, but she clamped her teeth shut. Vomiting would do nothing but piss Jared off even more. Unable to speak, she nodded and averted her gaze.

Jared grabbed her jaw, squeezing until she cried out, and forced her to face his brother. "Look at him. Don't turn your head from him. You did this. Enjoy your handiwork."

Her eyes watered with pain under his crushing grip. "Please, you're hurting me."

Her words only enraged him more. He yanked her head around like a puppet. "I'm not hurting you…yet."

He flung her head backward, and if not for the lead rope, she would've stumbled to the floor. Instead he grabbed the restraint and yanked her to him. Before she could react, he took her own knife and sliced a small band from the bottom of her shirt, baring even more of her rib cage. She hadn't realized how exposed she was in the revealing clothing until this very moment. When he was looking at her as if he wanted to kill her.

"Jared, please…"

He ripped the black do rag off his head and shoved it into her mouth, then tied the strip from her shirt around her head, effectively gagging her with her own clothes.

Sparrow tried to focus on breathing through her nose, but the gag felt suffocating. She wouldn't be able to make more than a muffled moan if she tried to speak or scream. Not that anyone would help her anyway.

"You try and slow me down, I'll kill everyone you know. Do you understand?" Jared's harsh voice pierced her. She could care less if he killed Jimbo. The man needed killing. Sparrow briefly considered struggling right then just to see if Jared would make good on his threat. But if he took care of Jimbo, she knew instinctively Squirrel would be next. Jared had seen how much the old man meant to her.

Jared scooped his brother into his arms and gently laid him over his shoulder. The position would ensure a hell of a headache for Hoyt when he awoke, but it was the only way his back would remain untouched. Hoyt was still out cold, and he didn't make a sound. That was good.

Jared stepped around Jimbo, unconscious on the floor. Sparrow stopped to kick him in the ribs, but the short length of rope between her and Jared didn't allow for much room.

She stumbled off the porch after Jared, barely managing to catch herself. *Get it together.* She focused on Jared's broad back, his fluid and lethal movements. The strength in him was apparent in the way he carried his brother, a man almost as big as he was, like he weighed nothing.

The moon had risen straight overhead by the time they reentered the woods, Jared carefully maneuvering through the trees. The smell of pine was strong in the freezing night air. October could be warm during the day, so much so that you didn't even need a jacket, but the nights were always colder on the mountain. Sparrow shivered, becoming more aware of her skimpy attire. Not that Jared would care. He'd only care if she got hypothermia. Then he'd probably be pissed at her for slowing them down. Might even kill her.

"Keep up." Jared's harsh command yanked her from her misery. They were headed straight toward Squirrel's cabin. Alarm shot through her. What if Jared planned to start his revenge right now, by taking out the one person she loved?

She immediately slowed, trying to delay him as her mind scrambled to figure out a way to change his mind. Jared kept walking like she hadn't put up any resistance. Her alarm turned to panic and she dug in her heels, pulling against him with all her might.

Jared stopped so abruptly she slammed into the solid tree of his body. When he turned to face her, she shrank back, her survival instincts kicking in.

"Do you want to die right now?" His hoarse voice was so different from before. All traces of the sweet sexy man with the haunted dreams were completely gone. Sparrow shook her head wildly, trying to indicate they should head down the mountain, not around toward Squirrel's cabin.

Jared smile was cold. "You think I'm going to listen to you? When you led me into a trap in the first place?"

Sparrow tried to speak, desperation clawing its way through her body, but all she managed was a muffled moan through her gag.

"You're worried about the old man? Good. You should be." Jared gave her his back once more and started walking, forcing her to stumble after him. The rough rope chafed her wrist, but the fear burning in her chest overrode any pain.

She tried to pull back once more, but he kept moving, as unstoppable as a fierce storm. She was nothing against the force of Jared Crowe.

All too soon they were back at Squirrel's cabin. Her heart beating wildly in her chest, Sparrow tried to think of anything she could do to save Squirrel. The man pulling her along wasn't the Jared she knew. He was a lethal killing machine bent on revenge. He believed she was guilty of the most unforgivable thing imaginable, and would harm anyone if he thought it would cause her pain.

Sparrow drew in a deep breath and screamed, but the sound came out as more of a muffled sob. Her lips burned from being pulled so tight. Jared turned in a flash, his free hand around her neck, and backed her up against the nearest tree.

His shoulders heaved and his look was menacing. Deadly. "You hurt what's mine, now I hurt what's yours."

***

Darkness enveloped him. Surrounded him. Filled him. And the girl standing before him was the reason.

He had thought she would be his light. His guide. A girl in need of rescue from an evil family, an evil mountain. He had been so blinded by her beauty and apparent innocence that he'd failed to see the evil that resided inside *her*.

If he hadn't been holding onto his brother right now, he wasn't entirely sure he could have stopped himself from strangling her. But the fear he saw in her gaze, the fear he'd put there, gave him a cruel sort of pleasure.

The girl was reckless, uncaring for her own life. How could she have played so innocent that he'd believed her? How could someone who'd saved his life destroy his brothers?

Jared shook off the confusion. He didn't have time to question her motives. He had to get the hell off the mountain, but she was coming with him and he knew exactly how to get her cooperation. No matter that he would never actually harm the old man, as long as she believed he would and Jared intended to use him against her. He wanted her to feel the same desperation she'd made him feel. "You do this to my brother. Why shouldn't I kill the old man?"

Sparrow's liquid gold eyes widened further as she jerked her head from side to side, her muffled moans a pitiful attempt to prick at his conscious. She could have saved herself the effort. His conscious had been snuffed out long ago.

"What's that? I can't hear you." Something inside him twisted his lips into a cruel smile. And whatever that something was twisted his insides into something dark and dangerous that skated the edge of control. He'd always been so calm, so reasonable. He'd needed to be to raise his little brother. But seeing Hoyt this broken, this damaged, had done something to him. "I bet you'd be willing to do anything to keep me from killing the old man."

Her nod was fast, delivered with no hesitation.

Jared shifted his hand, skimming it down her collar bone and around the neck line of her ruined shirt before grabbing her breast, squeezing it just enough to show his control. He knew what would hurt this woman the most. "You are mine. You will be my whore. You will do exactly as I say, when I say it."

She paled and shuddered. He knew she wanted to back away from him, but he'd trapped her against the tree. Jared continued his caresses, rubbing his thumb across her nipple until it hardened under his touch. Sparrow jerked to the side, trying to escape his grasp. And he let her. "You will willingly submit to me in all things, or I will go in there right now and slit that old man's throat."

Jared's stomach clenched into a tight fist of disgust. He was so disgusted by the words that he had to swallow the bile. He'd never treated a woman this harshly. Never.

But a woman had never tried to kill his family before either.

Dammit. It didn't matter. There was no way he could ever force her.

She moaned through the gag and closed her eyes. He forced down the guilt and let himself really feel the heavy weight of his brother, draped unconscious and bleeding over his shoulder. His guilt subsided. "So what's it going to be? You willingly give yourself to me or do I kill him now "

Her eyes opened, tears spilling down her cheeks. Shame punched him in the gut, but that just made him angrier. She didn't deserve his guilt or his shame. She only deserved his loathing.

She nodded one time. The sacrificial martyr.

A jolt of uncertainty slid into his conscious and he stepped back, needing to distance himself from her. The emotions rolling through him were so powerful he was about to snap. "Now, follow me. If you give me any trouble, so help me, I'll come back here and murder every last one of them."

Jared turned and strode away, feeling only one tug of resistance as Sparrow caught up with his longer stride. He would skirt back around the mountain to where he'd hidden his bag with the sat phone, medical supplies, and weapons. From there, he knew the fastest and easiest way down to his hidden boat near the river. Once he got a safe distance from the compound, he'd call for help and get his brother home

Hoyt shuddered in his arms and Jared reached back, feeling for his brother's arm. The feeling of Hoyt's cold skin made him stiffen. He knew he didn't have much time, and he didn't know the true extent Hoyt's injuries. Jared picked up the pace to a jog, careful to move his brother as little as possible.

He reached the spot where Sparrow had held a gun to his head and stopped. His duffel should be hidden beneath the nearby bush. "Feel beneath that bush, my bag should be there," he ordered.

Sparrow squatted and reached beneath the bush, pulling his bag free. Jared let out a small breath of relief. "Let's go."

He continued to head west down the mountain, slowing only when it was so treacherous he risked dropping his brother. The girl tugged on him from behind, having a hard time holding onto the heavy weight of his duffel bag with her tied hands, but he didn't care. Jared forged ahead, listening with relief to the growing roar of rushing water. As they neared the river, he turned south along the water. His arms ached. His back hurt. His muscles strained under his brother's weight. But he ignored all those things, his sole focus on getting to the boat and getting them to safety.

Chapter Twelve

Whore. Just like her mother. Bile rushed up her throat and Sparrow swallowed frantically, the gag suffocating her. Jared wanted to humiliate her, and he could not have picked a better way. Her worst nightmare had come true.

Jared increased his pace, roughly yanking her behind him, and she stumble-stepped to keep from hitting the dirt. The duffle bag clutched in her bound hands left her no choice but to carry it directly in front of her, dangling awkwardly and in the way. The handle scraped her fingers raw, the rope was cutting into her wrists, and her arms were steadily going numb. Muscles strained across her back and shoulders from the burden of the bag's weight and the constant pull forward.

A low hanging tree limb slapped her in the face and she cried out. Hot wet blood dripped down her cheek and her eye started to water. Jared didn't slow, didn't care; he was probably happy for her suffering. Given what he believed, she could hardly blame him.

She had to pay more attention to her surroundings. Sparrow forced herself out of her misery and quickly took stock of the situation. They'd descended the mountain to the river, turned south, and were now walking parallel to the bank. He must have a boat hidden somewhere. She had to escape before he got her on that boat. She could hide out in the mountains and make her way home. Then she would reveal Jimbo's true plan to Miss Kay before her brother managed to take her down. After his attempt to goad Jared into murdering her, she thirsted for revenge.

If Miss Kay didn't do anything about Jimbo, Sparrow would get Squirrel and head out. They could survive together. She would find a way to take care of him. They could run and run, as far away from any Crowe as she could get them.

Especially Jared Crowe.

He'd touched her intimately, against her wishes, and she'd *responded*. She'd felt her body arch toward him. Shame filled her at the thought, at the realization that she still wanted him. A shiver rolled down her body, and she shook it off, forcing herself to forget the feeling of his lips on her skin, forcing herself to forget the lazy grin on his face as he teased her.

Tears ruthlessly gathered in her eyes. She'd let herself hope and dream of a future with Jared. And now that dream had turned into a nightmare. *You should know better, Sparrow. White trash doesn't get to dream.*

"Keep up." Jared's harsh voice pulled her from her thoughts. She could clearly see his muscles straining under his shirt as he carried his brother. Her arms were exhausted from carrying the bag, so she could only imagine the exhaustion he must feel. But he didn't slow down, not once.

Sparrow had recognized Jimbo's handiwork the second she'd seen Hoyt's back. A few years ago he had forced her to watch as he skinned a man alive. But that man hadn't survived. Sparrow didn't know who is luckier. If Hoyt lived, the memories of his torture would haunt him forever.

The memory of witnessing it haunted her.

According to Jimbo, that man had been stealing from Miss Kay. So he'd made an example of him—an example of what would happen to anyone who went against the Crowes. When Jimbo finished, he hung the man's ruined body from a tree in the middle of the clearing to serve as a warning.

The Crowes owned the mountain and the people on it. The cops never showed. They were either too scared or already in Miss Kay's pocket. No one dared to talk openly about the body. The example had been swift and effective and gruesome, but it had ensured the honesty of everyone who dealt with Miss Kay.

The mountain dropped off suddenly to the right and they both stumbled. Jared's leg shot out straight, barely managing to catch himself, but the force of the momentum sent Sparrow sailing through the air. She didn't have the luxury of catching herself with her hands, not when they were bound. Her body impacted the ground, the duffel bag just barely saving her face from smashing into a rock. Pain crawled up her legs, but her momentum caused her to roll downhill. And she would have continued rolling if Jared hadn't planted his feet. The short length of rope pulled tight, yanking her back like a fish caught on a hook. Fire burned through her shoulders and arms.

"Get up." There was no concern in his voice. No emotion of any kind. Just bottomless black eyes staring at her with loathing.

She sympathized with him, really she did. She knew his anger was coming from his pain and concern for his brother, from his conviction that she'd done something unforgivable, but there was only so much a girl could take.

As much as she wanted to say, *Oh excuse me for falling, your highness*, the giant gag choking her mouth prevented her from issuing any sound. So Sparrow settled for a good glare and simply lay there on her stomach.

Which didn't exactly make Jared happy.

"I said, get up." Miss Kay's boys would've yelled at her, probably kicked her while she was down. But not Jared. His voice got quiet. Cold and deadly, kind of like the calm right before the tornado ripped through your house and destroyed your livelihood. She fought the instinct to shiver.

She had gotten so good at not being noticed. Her whole life, everything about her had been carefully chosen to be neutral. Her clothes. Her lifestyle. Her expressions. But this man pulled forth a range of reactions from her, all of which were anything but neutral. And right now the emotion he tugged on most was anger.

Thank God for the gag or she might've stuck her

tongue out at him in a childish tantrum. But she couldn't do that. So, hands bound, lying flat in the dirt in a shirt that showed more skin than a goddamn bikini, leaves and sticks snagged in hair, Sparrow lifted her bound hands and flipped him off.

Jared blinked, unmoving except for his clenched jaw and the veins bulging on his neck. She swore she saw a tremble move through him—not, not a tremble, more like tremors. Like his body was shaking in an attempt to contain his rage. "I warned you what would happen. The more you slow me down, the worse off you'll be. The old man will pay for everything you do."

Her anger deflated like a worn-out balloon. He wasn't just angry. He was deadly and she had every reason to fear him.

"I see you're beginning to understand that I'm serious. Good. This is my last warning." Jared squatted, his movements careful, and she watched his fingers curl around the handle of the duffel as he stood back up. She couldn't deny the small slip of relief inside her. A relief that disappeared when he turned and walked away, the short slack of her rope disappearing as he dragged her across the ground. The nearly nothing clothes she wore offered absolutely no protection from the rocks and sticks and thorns scattered across the forest floor.

Sparrow rolled from side to side, trying to avoid the more hazardous objects jutting out of the earth, but she had no protection against the elements of the Tennessee Mountains. And still Jared didn't slow. So she gritted her teeth and used all of her strength to yank her feet beneath her, staggering into a walk.

The bare skin of her stomach, knees, and thighs burned. *Why the hell didn't I change before I left?*

The answer taunted her. It was because of the way Jared had looked at her in these clothes—like she was a goddess walking the earth. That sexual power had made her heady. So instead of changing like any idiot would have done, she'd slapped on her snake boots, tucked in her knife, and sauntered around for him to drool over.

Her knife. She had completely forgotten about the knife stuffed in her boots.

Escape was possible.

***

Hoyt started shaking in his arms. The thin shirt draped around him was doing little to shield him from the elements. His body turned hot, then cold, then molten. The chance of infection was a real threat to his brother's life

For the hundredth time that night Jared gave thanks that he'd received field medical training in the Special Forces. After they got to the boat, he could patch his brother up. But even if he survived the physical wounds of what had happened, would he stand a chance at surviving the mental ones?

Ignoring his own pain and fatigue, Jared continue his steady pace forward, never stopping, never slowing. His only thought was for his brother. He burst through the edge of the trees at the riverbank and ground to a halt.

Sparrow didn't slam into him this time and Jared glanced back to see her gazing out at the water, her expression wary. Good. As soon as he got them on the boat he could relax. There'd be no chance of her escaping and he would be one step closer to getting Hoyt the serious medical attention he needed.

Jared surveyed the area, spying the fallen tree a few hundred feet downriver to his left. He'd tucked his boat beneath that tree, concealing it with camouflage netting. His brother groaned and the tremor that shook him was so fierce that Jared would've dropped him if he hadn't been holding on tight. Hoyt's fever seemed to be climbing at an alarming rate. Jared's heart raced at the very real threat to his brother's life and he took off toward the boat with renewed vigor.

A few minutes later he stood staring down in shock over his hiding place. The boat was gone. Jared shook his head. Must be the wrong tree. Maybe he'd come out of the woods too far upriver. Determined, Jared continued down the bank, steadily scanning the edge of the river, trying to ignore the sense of foreboding seeping down his spine.

After traveling several more feet, he was forced to stop when the riverbank fell off sharply. At that moment, any chance that the first spot he'd stopped at was the wrong one completely disappeared. Jared turned around, brushing past a startled Sparrow, and headed back to his starting point. He stopped at the fallen tree once more and stared down. There was nothing but leaves and water.

"Son of a bitch." Fucking hillbillies. Nothing was safe in these parts. Not even a fucking boat.

Sparrow made some type of moaning sound and Jared turned his furious gaze on her. She kept gesturing and nodding her head. Determined to ignore her, he turned back to face the empty spot, but for what? His only means of transportation was gone. And the threat to his brother's life had increased a thousand times over. Sparrow tapped him on the back, but Jared clenched his jaw and ignored her. Adrenaline pumped through his bloodstream, his heart rate increasing with each second. What was he going to do? There was no way he could carry his brother the next fifteen miles to the nearest town. Especially before sunrise.

Sparrow nudged him again, reminding him that this was all her fault, and he turned, ready to unleash the full force of his fury on her. "Touch me again and lose a finger, got it?"

Instead of backing up, she rolled her eyes. The freaking girl rolled her eyes at him. When he could snap her neck with a flick of his wrist and toss her lifeless body in the river.

She kept indicating some spot beyond him with her head and lifting her hands.

"You think I'm going to untie you?" As a matter fact, he had every intention of doubling up the rope as soon as he got her into a boat or truck or whatever the hell method of transportation he could find.

She shook her head no and indicated her gag. It was

obvious she wouldn't let up until he heard her out and his back was screaming for a break. Jared gently settled his brother onto his stomach on the ground and sat the duffel bag down next to him. The he yanked her to him, using the rope as a leash. Her chest slammed into his and physical awareness shot through his body. How could he still be physically attracted to such a monster? His reaction only made him angrier. "You that desperate you can't wait until we get out of here?"

Jared cupped her ass and lifted her against his hard cock, forcing her to feel his body. She moaned and shook her head, but he didn't release her. "As much as I look forward to it, too, sweetheart, we can't right now."

He thrust against her belly again and watched her eyelids grow heavy. Her nipples budded beneath the near see-through material of her cropped shirt. Fuck she was hot. And deadly. Jared forced himself to remember what she had done to his brother. He tangled a hand in her hair and yanked her head back, eliciting a grunt of pain from his captive. Jared nuzzled against her neck, up to her ear, savoring the shiver his touch evoked. Whether it was aversion or arousal or some combination of both, he didn't care, his body craved hers. But no matter how much he wanted her, he couldn't force her. "Don't worry, I promise to use your body as soon as possible."

She jerked against him, pushing against his chest with her bound hands, but her attempt was laughable.

When he pulled back, he fully expected to see tears in her fearful eyes, but she shocked him once more. Her golden gaze had turned molten with fury, and she reached up and started tugging at the gag, making noises like she was trying to talk. Fuck. He let go of her hair and yanked the gag down, pulling the wad of material out of her mouth.

Sparrow coughed and sucked in deep heaving breaths. He could only imagine how she must long for a drink of water. But had she given his brother the same courtesy?

"The boat." The words rasped out of her mouth and Jared stiffened.

"My boat? Where the fuck is it?" Before he knew what he was doing, Jared buried his hands in her hair once more, bending her backwards. She'd probably asked someone to move it while she was busy playing the innocent seductress and distracting him.

"Where the hell is my boat?" He was so close to pushing past reason. His vision didn't turn red. And it didn't turn black. It just hazed over from the force of the rage surging through his veins.

"Not me. I didn't take it."

Jared gave a tug on her hair again. "Of course not, you were too busy trying to get me naked. Miss Kay's boys, though, where did they stash it?"

"I don't know. I have no idea. I swear." She shook her head fervently, and he wound her hair around his fist, holding her immobile.

"Just like you swear you didn't set me up?" The rage beat at him, battering down his logic. The need to punish her rose fast and hot. He pushed her away from him, knowing the more he touched her, the closer he was to losing control.

"I know you don't believe me, but I had nothing to do with what happened to your brother. I could never hurt anybody like that."

"If you don't want me to gag you again, you'll shut your mouth right now. I'll never believe another word you say." She looked like she wanted to say something else, but she wisely chose to close her mouth. Good.

Focus. Think. He had to get as much distance between them and the Crowes as possible. Jared unzipped his duffel, grabbed his sat phone, and dialed headquarters. Merc, Task Force Scorpion's deadliest assassin, answered. "Where the fuck have you been?"

Shit. They were probably pissed. "No time. Need an evac pronto."

"Where?" His team might want to grill his ass when he got home, but they were efficient at their job, and Jared knew Merc would recognize that he meant business.

"Hold for location." Jared quickly ripped the

topographic map out of his bag and shined a small flashlight, locating the nearest feasible extraction point. After communicating the coordinates, Jared added, "Merc, make sure Aaron brings his medical kit. I also want the Doc prepped and ready to go as soon as we get back to Mercy."

"What the fuck happened? Are you hurt?"

"Not me. Hoyt."

The line went silent for a second then Merc asked, his voice deadly, "Who did it?"

Jared's gaze cut to Sparrow, who had sunk down to the ground and pulled her knees to her chest. With her forehead resting on her arms like that, she looked for all the world like a lost little girl. "Don't worry, I've got her. Just get here ASAP."

"Her?"

"Hurry."

"Okay, ETA twelve hours. Extraction Hoyt Romeo. We'll chopper in as close as we can, then send a boat to bring you back to the chopper. I'll have the medical team ready and waiting for your arrival back at the compound."

"Roger." Jared hung up the phone and stared at his captive. The sympathy he felt for her only pissed him off more.

"Get up. We have to move."

"Where?"

"Why do you care? Get the bag." Jared squatted down next to his brother and did a quick check. Hoyt's breathing was shallow, his pulse was weak and rapid, and his blond hair was drenched in sweat.

"I know this mountain better than anybody. They'll track us. We have to move fast."

"Isn't that what you want?" Jared snarled.

Chapter Thirteen

The damn man was infuriating. Hardheaded. And what she wouldn't give to place a well-aimed kick to his butt. But her muscles lagged in fatigue, so much so that the bag nearly dragged on the ground in front of her. She kicked it with each step, not on purpose, but because she didn't have the strength to heft it further up.

They stayed as close to the river as possible, using the moon to light the way. How had she ended up in this mess? And why had Jimbo said that about her? Why had he even known to say it? Thoughts swirled in a confusing tornado. Jimbo had known the real reason she had brought Jared to the cabin.

No one had told her about the brother.

A knot of fear started to grow in her belly. The more she thought about it, the more she knew they'd set her up. Used her to lull Jared into a sense of safety so they could ambush him. No way Miss Kay was involved. If she'd known, Jared and Hoyt would already be stiff in the dirt. But Jimbo, she could definitely see Jimbo pulling something like this. Only his plan backfired. Her stupid older stepbrother hadn't counted on the sheer power possessed by Jared Crowe. The attack he'd made on Jimbo had been so fast and brutal and efficient.

But the gentleness he'd used with his brother was the exact opposite. And her skin would never forget the sensation of his soft caresses. He was a man of extremes, Jared Crowe.

God, she really was like her mother. She needed to get her head on straight. Focus on the situation and not on her confusing feelings for Jared.

She couldn't abandon them yet, not until she knew they were safe. From the conversation she'd overheard, it sounded like they just had to make it through until the morning. Jared kept a fast pace heading downriver, which meant they were moving south.

An area Sparrow knew well. She had hunted and trapped here her whole life with Squirrel. She knew the ravines, the valleys, the steep climbs and eddies. The small caves where critters like to hide.

Ravines. Sparrow ground to a halt. "Stop."

Jared kept walking like she hadn't spoken at all. Sparrow dug her heels in and leaned backwards as far she could, resisting his momentum with all her might. "You've got to stop now and head east."

"East?"

Resisting the urge to stomp her foot, Sparrow said, "If you continue south along the river, you're going to hit a huge ravine and a drop off so steep there's no way you can cross it. Then you're gonna have to walk up the whole length of the ravine to go around it. You might not lose a day, but you'll definitely lose a few hours."

Jared studied her, his expression inscrutable. His brother moaned and shifted in his arms, still unconscious.

"Look, I know you don't believe me. I guess I wouldn't trust me either right now. But I swear, if you don't cut back east, you're going to lose hours. And he ain't got that many hours of travel left in him."

"Shit." Jared bit out the curse.

"Either way, we're still heading away from the Crowes. My way is faster."

His silence stretched out, grating along Sparrow's nerves. Finally, he spoke, "All right. You take lead, but I swear to God…"

"I know. You'll slit my throat and kill everyone I know." She tried to make light of the situation, but her attempt sounded pathetic even to her own ears.

A cold wind rushed across the river and swept up the side of the mountain and she couldn't help the shiver. She was dressed for midday August heat, not the crisp fall night air. But she wasn't going to give Jared even a moment to second-guess her idea. They took off once more, this time with Sparrow in the lead.

She did her best to keep the pace up, traveling the dark woods by memory. The farther away from the river they went, the thicker the big cedar and pine trees grew together. The dry sound of crunching leaves disappeared into the soft swish of old pine needles underfoot.

What she wouldn't give to be able to fall back behind them and cover their tracks, but the added luggage and added weight made it impossible. Their best hope was to get as far as possible before Jimbo had the chance to wake up and alert his brothers. Even if Miss Kay was somehow ignorant of his doings, Bob always followed Jimbo's lead.

They finally made it to the ravine that was spanned by an old rope bridge. Sparrow had made the crossing many times, but she'd always been alone. Now she had two full-grown men on her tail and a heavy duffle bag to weigh her down.

"You've got to cut the rope." Sparrow said. They'd never make it if all three of them went across together.

"Not a chance."

"This here ravine is nearly a hundred feet deep. That bridge was built when Squirrel was a little boy. You really think it can support all our weight at once?"

"You better pray it does. Cause I'm not cutting the rope."

Sparrow stepped closer to the edge and peered down into the deep dark hole. Moonlight was filtering through the trees in a speckled pattern, but she could just barely make out the bottom. Dread weighed heavy in her stomach. If they fell, they would all be dead.

"You're not making any sense. We're doing this to save your brother. If we all go across together, we will all die."

"And if you hadn't done this to my brother, none of us would be here in the first place."

A shiver worked down her body and it had nothing to do with the rickety bridge of death.

She weighed her options. There was a slim possibility of getting to her knife and cutting through the lead rope before Jared could stop her. His brother would slow him down, and if luck was on her side, she might make it across the bridge and escape. But she'd seen the speed with which Jared had moved against Jimbo.

"You're being stubborn." Sparrow eased one toe out onto the first wood plank and slowly leaned forward, carefully distributing her weight. Then she stepped fully onto the plank, tensing as she waited for the whole thing to collapse. Nothing. The bridge held.

But it had always held her. Her heartbeat sped to triple time. She only had a couple feet before Jared would be on the bridge too. And his brother. Sparrow glanced back and nearly screamed. He was standing right behind her. "What are you doing? Back up!"

Maybe if they stayed spaced out far enough...

"No way. For all I know, this is another one of your set ups."

"Set up, my ass. You're going to kill us."

"As long as you die too, I'll be happy."

God, she had to get away from him. Without picking up her foot, Sparrow slid forward onto the next plank. And then the next, repeating the process until she was about five or six planks out and the lead rope was pulled tight. The bridge shifted and she knew without looking that Jared had stepped onto it.

Sparrow sent up a prayer and grabbed the rails. She was shaking now, whether from the cold or fear, she didn't know. Probably it was both.

"Are you going to move or just stand here all night?"

Sparrow jumped and then chastised herself. The last thing this old bridge needed was her leaping around on it like a bunny. But Jared's voice had been so close she swore she felt his hot breath on the back of her neck.

Too scared to turn back and look, she began inching her way forward once more, barely lifting her foot enough to slide it onto the next plank. And the next. And the next.

The bridge screeched, long and loud, protesting the weight. Fear snaked up her legs. They were straight over the middle of the deepest part of the ravine.

Keep moving. Keep moving. Keep moving. Sparrow chanted the mantra over and over in her mind as she continued forward. Over halfway there. They were still in the air. Closer now. Just a couple of feet left.

Then she heard it. A loud crack followed by a whoosh and the sound of rope snapping.

"Move!" Jared shouted and Sparrow took off, gaining momentum even as she felt the ground dropping out from under her. With a last burst of adrenaline, she landed on the other side, panting and scrambling for secure footing.

She heard a grunt and then turned to see Jared perched on the edge of the drop off, his heels hanging over air, his toes on solid ground. Sparrow sucked in a breath and pulled with all her might, yanking him toward her.

***

Jared kept his expression carefully blank and glanced over his shoulder into the dark and seemingly bottomless ravine. That had been close. Too close.

He was letting his emotions control his actions— something he'd never done. And something that would result in their death if he didn't get his head on straight. But he sure as hell wasn't going to admit his mistake to Sparrow. "See, told you we'd make it."

Aggravation twisted her lovely features. "We almost died."

"Almost doesn't count."

She let out a frustrated little shriek and stomped her foot. And for some reason, Jared found that movement incredibly amusing and sexy. When she stomped her foot, her breasts bounced up and down, bare beneath the white shirt. Suddenly the memory of her taste assaulted his senses.

"You're crazy. We could've died."

"It's all part of the plan, sweetheart. Now Miss Kay's boys won't be able to follow us so easy, will they?" That had totally not even crossed his mind, but again, he liked to play his cards close.

Even closer after she'd saved his life. If Jared had been on the other end of that rope, he'd have cut it in a split second. But she'd saved him…again. Confusion painted his mind and filled his blood. Why couldn't she just be evil? She would be so much easier to hate, but with every passing hour he found more and more reasons to doubt his hasty judgment of guilt.

"If our bodies were at the bottom of that gorge, no one would find us either."

Jared shrugged, unable to combat that truth. Regardless, they had made it. Now they had to find shelter for the night. His arms were fast giving out and even though her chin was tilted at a defiant angle, the wariness etched into Sparrow's features was undeniable.

The fastest option would be to hug the river and set up somewhere closer to their extraction point. But Hoyt needed protection from the elements. His skin was hot to the touch and Jared's arms were drenched in sweat. He needed antibiotics and his wounds cleaned before he caught an infection. An infection that could kill him. "Head back to the river and look for shelter."

Sparrow dropped the bag and glared at him. "No. Not until you promise you won't do anything so foolish again."

Jared took an intimidating step, "Did you forget our little deal? You obey me without question."

The girl didn't even falter. "Yeah, I know. But it's awfully hard to obey you when you're acting like an idiot."

"An idiot, am I?" She couldn't be much more than five feet tall and about a buck ten soaking wet, and yet she continuously proved that she wasn't really scared of him.

"What's your suggestion?"

"I know of a small cave not far from here. It's close to the river, well hidden. And I know for a fact Miss Kay's boys don't know about it."

"And how do you know that?"

Sparrow looked away. "Because it's where I used to hide from them."

Jared swallowed the sharp spike of sympathy. She might've had a rough upbringing, but that didn't change the fact that she'd nearly killed his brother. *Hadn't she?* "Show me."

She nodded and headed straight south, away from the ravine. The mountain sloped steeply upward, and Jared's calf muscles burned and screamed in protest. He forced himself to ignore the pain and continue. It wasn't his life that was at stake—it was his brother's.

The ground leveled out slightly and Sparrow hung a right, curving around the side of the mountain.

"This is it." Sparrow stopped by a group of tall bushes and Jared looked around.

"I thought you said there was a cave."

Sparrow grinned, "I did. It's right here." Then she turned sideways and sliced her hand into the bushes, pulling them back to reveal a small cave, about as tall as Jared's chest.

"All kinds of critters like to hide out in here, mostly raccoons, squirrels, rabbits, no big deal. It's too small for the bear to get in here, but we can fit just fine."

This was perfect, but was it too perfect? "And who else knows about this cave?"

"No one. Not even Squirrel. This is my own place."

The cave was situated three quarters of the way up the mountain, well hidden, its small opening perfect for defense against intruders. He couldn't have picked a better spot himself. "I guess it will have to do for tonight."

Her expression of pride fell, but he ruthlessly ignored her and turned into the cave, clutching his brother, careful not to squeeze too tight as he bent at the waist and entered the cave. The pull on the lead rope gave Sparrow no choice but to follow him.

The cave narrowed, then widened out, the ceiling opening up enough so that he could stand fully. The small cavern made about a ten by ten room and stood just over six feet tall. There was no back exit. Yes, it was a good spot.

As gently as possible, he knelt on the ground and laid Hoyt on his stomach, carefully turning his head to the side so the cut on his cheek faced up. Hoyt moaned, and the sound sent an immediate rush of helpless anger through Jared.

"We can build a fire, give you some light to get him warmed up." Sparrow offered. Jared glanced up but couldn't make out her features in the darkness.

"No fire. Bring me the bag."

She shuffled over to him and place the bag to his right. Jared opened it and searched inside for his chem lights and headlamp. When he found the chem lights, he shook them until they lit up, filling the cave with a warm green glow. Next he snapped the head light on and shined it inside his bag, pulling out his medical kit and a blanket.

He stretched the blanket out on the ground and shifted his brother onto it. The sight of Hoyt's hollowed out cheeks, scruffy beard, and sweat-drenched hair made his heart hurt. Jared checked his pulse to find it racing.

He was malnourished and abused. Could Sparrow really have been responsible for these horrible injuries? A mass of conflicting emotions swirled out of control in his mind, making it impossible for him to focus. Jared peeled Hoyt's shirt back with shaking hands, revealing the mangled mess of his brother's back inch by inch, the urge to roar with fury growing each second. Pieces of Jared's skin had stuck to the shirt and he had to peel each one off individually. By the time he was through, Jared was a shaking mass of wrath.

"Can I help?" Sparrow knelt at his side, her voice gentle.

Jared stared at her, unable to determine what to say or do. *Snap the fuck out of it.*

"Stay away from him." Jared rolled Hoyt to his side, his alarm growing when he spied the hundreds of small cuts crisscrossing his torso and abdomen. They weren't as deep as the wounds on his back, but half of them oozed pus and blood. Rage like he'd never known overwhelmed him.

It was her. Her brother said it was...and she brought me right to that cabin. And now she had the audacity to gasp like she was horrified at the sight. But that didn't matter now. Jared didn't matter. Sparrow didn't matter. All that mattered was Hoyt.

Jared clenched his hands into fists, knowing that if he spoke he would lose control.

Surveying the cave, he found a large vertical rock jutting up out of the floor, maybe three feet away. The body of it was almost rectangular and nearly straight up and down. He needed to put as much distance between him and Sparrow as possible right now. Jared dug into his duffel and pulled out a small coil of rappelling rope. Then he stood and yanked her over to the rock.

"What are you doing?"

"Need to make sure you don't run away while I try to repair the damage you've done."

"I won't run away. Let me help you."

The fury hit him again, and before he knew what he was doing, his hand was around her throat. From somewhere in a distance, he realized what he was doing and knew he should stop. *Now.* But his brother, the one person in the entire world that he loved, had been tortured unto the brink of death.

"You think I'd let you touch him? Look at him. Look what you've done."

Sparrow made a choking sound.

"No, you're not going anywhere."

Jared forced his fingers loose and Sparrow dropped to her knees, gasping and grabbing at her throat. Uncaring of the pain he'd caused her, Jared yanked her up from the floor and pressed her to the rock, quickly winding rope around her entire body pinning her arms to the side. When he finished, rope banded from her chest to her waist, effectively locking her in place.

The red marks on her neck gave him a tinge of remorse, which only pissed him off more. How could he feel sympathy for her?

Because I want to believe she really didn't do it.

"Can you keep quiet or do I have to gag you again?" His question was met with silence.

Jared dropped to his knees beside his brother and ripped the field medical kit from his bag and laid it out beside him, surveying his brother's face, chest, and abdomen. He decided to clean the deepest cuts first. One large one gaped open on his right pectoral and another down lower, close to his hip. The rest looked relatively shallow and had even started scabbing in places.

Jared grabbed the disinfectant and poured a little into the first wound. His brother jerked away, landing on his back, and then bowed up off the floor, screaming in agony. "Stop."

"Hoyt, it's me, Jared. I'm trying to help you." A cold sweat broke across his brow, and his hands shook uncontrollably. He'd caused Hoyt pain, and he wasn't through yet.

Hoyt moaned and made a pitiful attempt to ward Jared away. "Please, no more." His voice was a moan, filled with desperation. Did Hoyt think Jared was his tormentor?

Grief such as Jared never imagined swept through him. All the long buried emotions rushed to the surface, bending him over under their weight. "I'll make the pain stop. It will all be over soon."

Jared opened the small box of morphine syringes and plucked one out. He leaned down, ready to plunge the needle into his brother's thigh. Just as Jared pulled his hand back, Hoyt opened his good eye, locking Jared in place. He didn't speak. He didn't move. And what Jared saw in his brother's gaze scared him more than any of the cuts on his body. Hoyt's gaze was empty.

Blank. Jared had seen that look before in shell-shocked soldiers on the battlefield. Some of them checked out and never checked back in, the experience of battle too much for their minds to bear.

"Hoyt?"

His brother gave no acknowledgment. Jared tried again. "Brother?"

Hoyt was an empty canvas. Jared reached for him, wanting to touch his shoulder, his arm, anything to make human contact and pull his brother back from the void. As soon as Jared's hand made contact with Hoyt's skin, he screamed and threw his hands out. The needle flew from Jared's grip. Hoyt rolled onto his stomach, then got up onto his knees. The violent action sent fresh waves of blood pouring down his back.

"Stop, you're going to hurt yourself." Jared was on his feet, crouched and ready to dive to catch Hoyt when he fell.

"Just kill me!" Hoyt's anguished roar boomed through the cave and ripped a hole in Jared's chest. Hoyt staggered to his feet, wavering like a willow in a hurricane.

He was out of control and would do more harm if he didn't settle. The needle was a few feet from Jared, and he lunged for it. Hoyt sensed his movements and dove, landing a weak blow to Jared's jaw before hitting the ground.

"Stop moving!" Jared shouted in desperation.

Hoyt rolled to his side, groaning in pain. "Please, I'm begging you. Just finish it. No more. No more."

Those anguished words ripped Jared's soul apart, sending wave after wave of sharp pain through his chest. Still, he gripped the needle and approached his brother, regret making his feet drag. "I'll make it stop, little brother." Jared dropped to a knee and plunged the syringe in Hoyt's flesh. Hoyt jerked and twitched, his movements like a fish out of water. "I'm sorry I wasn't there to protect you."

Regret tinged with acid boiled in Jared's blood. He would never forgive himself. Hoyt stopped jerking, the morphine working its magic. When Hoyt's head slumped to the floor, Jared picked him up and carried him back to the blanket, wondering all the while if Sparrow had been telling the truth. Had Hoyt's blame at the cabin been from delirium?

He picked up the disinfectant and gently dabbed at his brother's wounds, but his body felt like an empty shell, filled with nothing but despair. He watched himself work, cleaning and patching Hoyt's chest. He watched the fresh blood slowly seep from his brother's wounds.

Jared had never broken a vow in his entire life—he'd always prided himself on his word. But today he'd not only broken the promise he'd made to protect his brother, he'd shattered it to pieces.

Chapter Fourteen

Sparrow watched silently, holding in the urge to weep for the two brothers. She'd prayed Hoyt would stay unconscious through the cleaning, but he'd awoken and reopened his wounds. His pain was obvious.

But even worse was the agony on Jared's face. Silent tears trailed from his midnight eyes, and she didn't think he even realized he was crying. Her heart cried with him.

Jared tended to the smaller cuts first, then bandaged the two worst ones on his chest. After that, he carefully cleaned the slice on Hoyt's face. At least Jimbo had cut that one clean, using a good blade. It should heal without too bad a scar. But when Jared rolled Hoyt over to tend to his back, the sight was brutal enough to wrest a grunt from her.

Jared whipped his head around and she prayed he would ignore her. She didn't breathe again until he turned his attention back to Hoyt.

His brother's back was impossible to describe. It was as if someone had peeled small strips of it back like wallpaper off the wall. Only this was his flesh and blood. She gagged, unable to stop her bodily reaction to the gruesome sight.

Jared was in her face before he knew what he was doing. "How dare you fucking make a noise when you are responsible for this?"

Sparrow flinched back instinctively from the unfiltered rage and confusion on Jared's face. She should have looked away before he rolled Hoyt over. After all, the last time she'd seen what Jimbo could do with that knife, it had given her nightmares for years.

But this—this was altogether different. Because it was Jared's brother, and Jared thought it was her doing. That her hands had wrought this evil. Against her will, Sparrow's eyes watered. Hoyt's back was a massacre and Jared's face was a painting of anger and pain.

"I should do the same thing to you." Jared said, his voice a ragged whisper.

"Please, I swear to God I had no part in that. I could never…" Do something like that to anybody. How could he think she was capable of doing that to anybody? The thought sent a fresh wave of pain down her body.

"He said it was you. You were in the room. My brother does not lie. Your own adoptive brother said you took part in it. The only one denying it is you." Jared's hands slowly lifted and Sparrow swallowed convulsively.

He'd choked her earlier in his rage. It had been painful, but he'd let her live. Now his expression was turning borderline insane, and she didn't know if he realized what he was about to do. But she did.

And she didn't want to die.

"Jimbo set me up. Your brother was delirious. I could never do that to anybody. You've got to believe me. I was trying to help you find your brother and escape. I had you bound to my bed, helpless and at my mercy. If I wanted to trap you, I would have done it then!"

Jared's hands hovered directly in front of her now, his fingers curling into fist. She could see the indecision flickering in his gaze as bright and burning as a wildfire. "Because you're just as evil as they are."

Sparrow's gaze was transfixed on his hands as he clenched and unclenched his fists, his eyes black with the promise of retribution. And then he lowered them down and she breathed a small sigh of relief.

"I'm not going to kill you. That would be too easy. I don't need a knife to make you regret the day you were born."

Jared went back to his brother and Sparrow's shoulders drooped, she'd held her body so tense when he was near. Even still, small tremors shook her. Jared started to clean Hoyt's back and she quickly glanced away, unable to stomach the severity of his wounds.

She'd skinned all sorts of animals in her lifetime, but her hunting had been about survival. She and Squirrel ate the meat and sold the furs. But torture like that, it was pure evil, and deep down she realized that Jimbo couldn't possibly be sane.

The more she thought on it, the more convinced she became of Jimbo's guilt. The only possible answer could be that he thought Hoyt knew where to find the land deed and he had tortured him for the whereabouts of the document.

The only reason he would have hidden Hoyt and searched for the deed in secret was he wanted the mountain for himself. If he had that, he wouldn't need Miss Kay anymore.

The inkling of fear hovering over her laid anchor in her chest, weighing her down. Jimbo planned to kill Kay and take the land. There was no other explanation. And she was sure that once Jimbo started killing, he'd take out anyone who'd ever offended him. Including Squirrel.

By helping Jared, Sparrow had inadvertently screwed up Jimbo's plan, ensuring the big man would be out for revenge. He'd hunt them down and kill them…and then he'd kill Squirrel.

From the corner of her eye, Sparrow saw Hoyt's body convulse. She returned her attention to the brothers and watched as Jared poured alcohol on the open wounds, meticulously scrubbing and cleaning them. Then he applied some sort of salve over Hoyt's back before packing it and carefully winding a huge role of gauze around his torso.

When he finished, Hoyt lay on his stomach and Jared was drenched in sweat, his skin almost green.

Jared was hurting, and as far as he knew, she was the source of his pain. If Hoyt didn't wake up soon and tell Jared the truth, she was probably as good as dead.

But Sparrow wouldn't be with them that long. She would have to escape and return home. If Jimbo was as crazy as she suspected, no one was safe. It was her duty to warn them.

Jared scooted off to the side and pulled a canteen of water from his bag, and Sparrow's mouth immediately went dry. It had been too long since she'd had a drink of water or anything to eat. But she wasn't stupid enough to think he'd give her a drink. Not now.

His gaze cut to her and she immediately looked away, not wanting to see the disgust she was sure was on his face.

She wanted to remember the sweet gentle Jared from earlier. Before he'd suspected her of doing such a terrible thing.

"Drink."

She looked at him in surprise as he held the canteen up to her lips, but she drank greedily. The gag and the long journey had made her mouth as dry as over-tanned leather. "Thank you."

His smile was anything but kind. "Got to keep you healthy enough for my plans. Can't have you dying from dehydration, now can I?"

He was the first man she had ever kissed, and being around him, even for such a short while, had made her want. Made her hope. And now his every word and every action was intended to make her hurt.

Tears pricked her eyes and she quickly blinked and looked away, unwilling to give him more ammo. She had to toughen up, find that thick skin she'd spent her whole life growing.

And she'd have to find a way to forget the gentle and hurting man who had touched her heart. Because tomorrow, she'd escape and she'd never see him again.

***

Sparrow came awake slowly. She blinked, trying to take in her surroundings. A few seconds later she remembered they were in the cave. She lifted her head, her neck throbbing, and a million pin pricks of pain shot down her arms.

She couldn't remember falling asleep, but she'd remained tied to that rock. Every muscle in her body ached, and her hands were numb, her shoulders aching. The minuscule amount of clothing did nothing to protect her from the cold rock. She felt like a block of ice.

"Good, you're awake. Time to go." Jared's boots came into her line of vision first and Sparrow followed them up his legs, his lean hips, and his sinfully broad chest. He looked down at her, as refreshed as if he'd slept on a freaking featherbed.

She had never been a morning person, so the angry retort that came to her lips was probably best kept inside.

Jared squatted in front of her and held the canteen of water to her lips once more. Sparrow drank as much as she could, not knowing if it would be the last she was offered. The water splashed into her empty stomach and nausea rolled in her belly, followed by a grumble of hunger.

"I saved an MRE for you. I'm going to cut you loose so you can feed yourself." He seemed somehow more in control today. His movements were clinical and distant, and there were no longer those sparks of madness flickering at the edges of his eyes.

He disappeared behind her rock and the ropes loosened around her body. Sparrow held up her hands for him to cut the rope binding her wrists.

"Those stay. You can feed yourself that way."

"It would be a lot easier if you untie me." Sparrow grumbled.

"A lot easier for you to escape that way too. The rope stays." Jared thrust a tan plastic bag into her hands. The outside of it read Meal Ready to Eat. Sparrow pulled out a small pouch from inside it. *Chicken and gravy*. Hunger slammed into her so hard her fingers fumbled before opening the pouch. Inside was some strange looking goo, definitely not the chicken she'd envisioned. Was this some type of new torture he thought up?

She shot him a disgruntled look and he spoke up without her saying a word. "Military issue. Not the best thing in the world, but it's loaded with calories and carbs to give you energy. And it's the last thing you'll eat for a while, so I suggest you get busy. I want to get a move on before the sun rises."

"Thank you."

The benign expression on his face disappeared, and he frowned at her. "Don't thank me just yet. I'm just getting you back to my place."

Maybe. Or maybe he was starting to realize she couldn't have done this terrible thing? She could only hope. "How long until we meet up with your boat?"

He studied her intently before answering. "Couple of hours at the most."

Sparrow turned the pouch up to her lips, gulping half the package down. "How's your brother?"

Any hint of kindness in his eyes disappeared and she immediately regretted asking. "The same. You got a minute left. Quit talking and start eating."

He turned roughly from her and Sparrow cursed her stupid mouth. Before she'd asked about Hoyt, Jared had seemed to soften. Just a little. She ate quickly and watched as Jared repacked the bag and checked Hoyt. His brother seemed to have settled down some during the night. He wasn't shaking and moaning anymore, but he was almost deathly still. If she hadn't seen his chest rising and falling, she would've thought he was dead.

Then Jared stood in front of her again, holding out his hand, and she passed the empty package to him. He tossed it aside and held out his hand again. "Give me your hands."

She gingerly placed her hands in his and allowed him to help her to her feet. Her knees buckled and if he hadn't held her, she would've hit the floor again. Small needles of pain pricked all down her legs and feet as blood rushed back into her extremities. She didn't bother trying to hide her groan. She couldn't remember ever hurting this much, and in so many places all at once.

"Give it a minute. It's just the blood circulating."

Unable to speak, Sparrow nodded against his chest. He smelled of raw man and wild earth. Her senses went on alert. She became aware of his hands holding her up around the waist. The deep rise and fall of his chest as he took a breath. It was just plain wrong for fate to dangle such a fine specimen under her nose and then yank him away.

The last thing she wanted was for him to realize how quickly her body had betrayed her. Sparrow stepped back, surprised when he didn't resist and simply let go. But her legs held strong, and as the pain faded, she became aware of an urgent need. "I've got to pee."

"Follow me, already found you a place." Jared grabbed her arm and led her away from the cave, stopping before a small thicket of bushes growing between two trees.

The large pines acted as posts, and the bushes grew so thick they formed their own little fence. Not that she cared. She was used to having to go outdoors. There really wasn't much of a choice when she was out on a hunting trip. Sparrow walked around the bushes and shucked her jeans, thankful for the small thoughtful gesture of privacy anyway.

Chapter Fifteen

The girl had gone to the bathroom out in the open without protest. He'd been ready to tell her to suck it up, but there was no need. She had no shame.

And why did he like that about her?

"Let's move."

"Give me time to button my pants, okay?" she grumbled, grouchy in the early morning.

When she emerged, the first thing he noticed was the chill bumps covering her entire body, and for the first time, he took stock of the weather. He'd been so focused on his brother he hadn't thought about himself or her comfort. She made to walk past him, her movements stiff and uneven. Jared suppressed a cringe, knowing it was from the way he'd kept her tied up all night.

Dammit, he shouldn't care whether she was hurting or not. He should revel in her pain. But he couldn't, not with this doubt nibbling away his defenses. Maybe that's why his voice was so gruff when he spoke. "You're going to have to move faster today."

She wrinkled that curvy little nose, scrunching up her freckles and her full pouty lips. "If you want me to speed up, you're gonna have to lighten my load."

"And how do you expect me to do that? Carry my brother and the duffel for another mile?"

"Yes." Her one-word answer traced along the edge of annoyance and humor. He let annoyance win. "Since you're the one who helped put him in this condition, you'll have to suck it up. And if you slow me down, you won't like the consequences."

She flinched. Jared held her gaze, daring her to say anything, but she dropped her mysterious golden eyes. He grabbed her arm and pulled her back into the cave.

"Give me your hands."

He expected her to protest, but she meekly held up her bound hands. He quickly attached the lead rope to his belt. "You know what will happen if you slow me down?"

Still, she refused him her gaze, her stooped posture almost defeated. "Yes." Something about her stance sent guilt washing through him.

Jared retrieved the duffel and held it out for her. She took it, letting the back bang into her shins. He didn't miss the slight flinch. The bag hadn't felt that heavy to him, but he was over twice her size and weight. She really was a petite woman. A petite woman with beautiful, full breasts and achingly curvaceous hips. Even now he could see her nipples bead hard and tight against the material of her shirt. His hands itched to lift up her shirt and caress her.

Why shouldn't he? Jared groaned, lifted his hand and brushed the back of his knuckles over her breasts through the material of her shirt. She jerked at his touch. Her nipples budding even more. The bag pulled her arms straight down, forcing her breasts to mound over the top of her shirt. He rubbed her other nipple, soft and gentle, brushing his thumb back and forth over its tip until she trembled beneath his hands. Shit, his cock was aching and swollen. Eager to bury itself in her sweet depths. It would be so easy to take her right now. Right here. Already she leaned into his touch, seeking more.

Jared pulled on his control, forcing his mind away from thoughts of her parted thighs and soft lips.

Her head was tilted down to the floor as she meekly submitted to him. A growl of possession grumbled from his throat. He liked her like this. Liked knowing that she was trembling for his touch even though she feared him. She bit her lower lip and his control slipped. Grasping her chin in his hand, he lifted her face to his and took possession of her mouth, plunging his tongue inside deep and hard. Using her mouth to forget. To distance himself from the horror of his brother's torture.

Something almost animalistic took over and he deepened the kiss even more, winding his hand in her hair and holding tight. But instead of trying to struggle away from him, she dropped the bag and lifted her bound hands to his chest, grabbing onto his shirt and pulling him to her. His touch seemed to awaken something in her, and her open response stunned him. Drove him wild.

Before he knew it, he'd laid her on the ground and settled between her legs. He broke the kiss, both of them painting and hungry. He found the flesh between her neck and shoulder, and bit down, sucking her greedily into his mouth. He pulled hard, wanting her to remember she belonged to him now.

Sparrow moaned and arched up. Jared roughly pushed her crop top the few inches it took to expose her nipples. Those beautiful dark rose, tight buds begged for his lips. Greedy, he took the first nipple into his mouth, sucking hard and long until she cried out, and then he lapped at her gently until she settled down.

"Jared," she gasped, her hips undulating beneath him.

Jared pushed his hips forward, frustrated by the material separating them. He lifted enough so that he could yank at the button on her shorts.

"Jared. Stop."

He could just imagine her soft pink flesh glistening and wet. He yanked down her zipper. He needed to taste her there, to see if she was as sweet as he imagined she'd be.

"Jared, your brother." It was like she'd thrown a bucket of ice water in his face, Jared reared back onto his heels and yanked his hands from her body. Sparrow lay spread before him, her breasts bare, her legs wide open. He'd gotten so caught up in her that he'd temporarily forgotten about his brother.

Dammit. What the fuck was wrong with him?

His sat phone rang just then, and Jared jumped on the distraction, unsure what to say.

I hate you, but I want your body. The worst part was he was even more certain that she couldn't be solely to blame. She might have had some involvement; he couldn't completely rule that out. Not until Hoyt woke and told the truth.

Yeah, that would work out well.

He ripped open the phone. "Hello."

It was Merc's voice on the other end of the line. "We're an hour out. What's your status?"

"About an hour too. You got the medical supplies?"

"Yep. We'll be ready and waiting, brother. Just get here."

"Roger." Jared hung up, the phone call giving him a burst of renewed energy and purpose.

Hoyt's sleep had been much more peaceful last night than Jared's, who'd roused every half hour on the hour to check on his brother. Though he didn't want to admit it, he'd been unable to keep his gaze off his captive. He'd been miserable, through and through.

"Come on, they're almost there." His words startled Sparrow out of her thoughts and she quickly jumped to her feet, snatching the short top down in one movement. "Get the bag," he added. "Stay close."

He scooped Hoyt into his arms, avoiding the worst damage to his back, even though there was no way his brother could feel it. Jared had given him another dose of the morphine early this morning as soon as he started to twitch and moan in his sleep.

They headed out from the cave to the river where they could follow it south to the extraction point. The morning air was crisp and the sun just rising over the opposite mountain when they started on their journey.

When they were young, just boys, Miss Kay had taken them in after their parents' sudden death. Jared had been young and innocent and trusting, until the next day when she tossed them in the closet and shackled them both to the floor. He hadn't understood at first. He beat against the door, screaming and kicking, scratching at the wood until his fingers had bled.

But no one ever came.

And even then Hoyt, a few years younger, had tried to calm him down. He'd joked about the situation, saying it was a big adventure. Hoyt had always looked at the world like it was a bright and wonderful place.

But deep down Jared had known better.

They'd fed them a little at first, but after a while even that stopped. Jared and Hoyt had slowly starved to death in that closet. And even up to the end, when they'd been too weak to move, Hoyt had held out hope. But Jared had none. He'd realized they'd been fated to die just like their parents.

Until a golden eyed little girl stuck her head in the door and freed them …

Chapter Sixteen

Sparrow saw the boat through the trees, maybe twenty or thirty yards ahead. She couldn't make out the number of men on board, but the more there were, the harder it would be for her to escape. Dammit, she hadn't counted on them being so close. The sun had barely risen on the horizon. And as the sun rose higher, her chances for escape would grow even dimmer.

At least the heavy exercise of walking through the mountainous trail and lugging the huge bag had kept her warm enough. She still had her knife tucked into her boot, so as long as Jared didn't wise up and check her, all she had to do was wait for a distraction.

They marched out of the trees and down to the shore, every pair of eyes on the boat locked on them. Sparrow gulped as her gaze locked in on the tallest one. He was huge. His skin a deep tan, his midnight hair hanging to his shoulders. But it was his eyes that held her. They were…empty.

Another one, smaller than the giant, but still larger than most men she'd seen, jumped from the boat into the water and waded onto the shore. He had long brown hair that ran into a neatly trimmed brown beard. He focused on her for a split second before turning his attention to Jared. She knew when he saw Hoyt because his entire demeanor shifted from curiosity to aggression. "Mother of God."

Even though she'd had nothing to do with Hoyt's injuries, she shifted her gaze to the river, knowing what was coming next.

"Who did this?"

Silence followed, and unable to contain herself any longer, Sparrow glanced back at the men. All of them were all staring at her. She wanted to scream out the truth, that she was innocent, that she'd never do such a thing. But she dropped her gaze to the ground. She had a part to play, that of the meek, defeated little girl. As soon as they dropped their guard, she'd be gone.

"No way." The bearded man spoke again.

"She's coming with me until I know the truth." Jared's voice sent a shiver through her.

"Get them on the boat. I'm ready."

"Thanks, Aaron. I patched him up, but he needs real medical attention." Jared walked to the edge of the water, pulling her leash tight, and stopped at the edge of the boat. The giant lifted Hoyt from Jared and placed him in the boat. Jared turned to her, lifted her on board, and followed.

"Merc, put him here, on the blankets." Aaron knelt on the floorboards.

"Wait. Make sure you put him on his side." The boat shifted as Jared strode toward the others, leaving Sparrow with the choice to either follow or be thrown to the floor. The giant, Merc, gently placed Hoyt on the blankets.

The boat was unlike any she'd ever seen. It was camouflaged and big, like a cabin cruiser. The front of the boat boasted a metal platform where a large gun was mounted. Behind that was an open cabin with a steering wheel, and behind that a large open area with bench seating down the sides. They were arranging Hoyt to lay in the middle of the seats on the floor.

Aaron leaned over him, shined a light in his eyes and placed a hand on his head. "Jesus Christ, he's burning up. Did you give him anything?"

Jared shook his head. "All I had was morphine."

"Riser, give me that syringe of antibiotics. Merc, get us the fuck out of here as fast as you can." Riser pulled a syringe from the medical bag and Merc got behind the wheel. Jared pulled her over to the bench and pushed her down. He cut the rope holding them together and quickly tied it to a metal ring right on the edge of the boat. "Stay here."

Not waiting for her to respond, Jared went to kneel beside his brother.

Merc backed the boat into the water and gunned it down the river. The water was choppy and fast flowing from last week's storms, which had caused the river level to rise. The boat jumped and bumped through the rough water, but Merc didn't slow down.

"We've got to get his fever down. He might have a seizure if we don't. Maybe even permanent damage," Aaron yelled.

Sparrow closed her eyes, praying that wasn't true. Hoyt had to make a full recovery. He had to for Jared's sake, and for her own.

"Jared, hand me that IV bag, Riser, hand me the meds," Aaron spoke loudly enough to be heard over the sound of the boat's engine. He worked efficiently, first sticking a needle in Hoyt's arm and then feeding an IV into the back of his hand. He injected the syringe into that as well. "That should lower his temperature pretty fast. But it won't keep it down."

"I think his wounds might be infected. I cleaned him up the best I could last night, but I just…" Jared dropped his head into his hands, his voice trailing off on a ragged grunt.

Riser placed a hand on Jared's back. "Hey, man, you know Aaron is our best medic. He'll survive."

"Damn right he will, now help me get these bandages off of him. I need to see the damage."

The boat picked up speed. The river was wide and open for as far as Sparrow could see.

Aaron began cutting the bandages from Hoyt's body.

"The chopper's going to pick us up about five clicks from here. Hank loaned us a ranch house for you two to stay at and Dr. Jane is setting up for him there. You two can stay there as long as it takes for him to fully recover. That way we can keep this off the locals' radar," Riser said.

"Thank you." The ragged edge to Jared's voice tore at Sparrow's heart. Yes, he'd treated her harshly, but despite thinking that she'd mutilated and tortured his brother, he hadn't really laid a hand on her. That spoke to his true nature more than anything else.

Any other man would have killed Sparrow long before now. The worst thing Jared had done to her was to make her desire him.

"Hang tight, brother," Jared shouted. "We'll be at the chopper in less than fifteen minutes."

Their words registered. Fifteen minutes. If she got on that chopper, there would be no escape. And if Hoyt never woke up to profess her innocence…

A huge lump formed in her throat. It would destroy Jared for one thing, and he would never, ever believe her.

No, she needed to get as much distance from them as possible. Maybe one day, if Hoyt lived and found his way back to consciousness, Jared would realize the truth. But she'd realized how stupid her dream of finding a happily ever after with him had been. Sparrow was the white-trash daughter of a prostitute. Jared was not only the true heir to Crowe Mountain, but he was also a well-respected man in his own field.

Men like Jared Crowe didn't waste their time on scrawny little girls like Sparrow.

"Jared, these look great. I don't see any signs of infection." Aaron's voice pulled Sparrow from her thoughts once more, and she watched as he prodded and poked at the wounds on Hoyt's chest.

Jared cleared his throat. "Those aren't the ones I'm worried about.

Sparrow stiffened, her blood freezing in her veins. No way she wanted to be on this boat when they rolled Hoyt over. *Have to escape.*

"Five minutes," Merc said.

"I'll get a shoulder. Jared, you get his hip. Aaron, make sure we don't damage anything." Riser was already in action, reaching for Hoyt's shoulder. The men moved as one, efficient and precise—the perfect team.

They got Hoyt onto his chest and Aaron began to peel the bandages from his back. Sparrow tensed, steeling herself for the explosion. Jared's hand shot out and wrapped around Aaron's wrist. "Not from the top. Pull it up from the bottom."

Sparrow sucked in a breath and looked away. Jared left off the reason for his instructions. If Aaron peeled the bandages from the top down, he'd more than likely peel Hoyt's skin from his back. Again.

She felt the violence building in the air and tried to focus on the muddy water. The trees. Anything but the horror coming. But the dread was forming around her, inside her. Everywhere. And Sparrow could no longer deny the pull to watch Jared as his brother's back was revealed. Only Jared's steady gaze wasn't locked on his brother. It was locked on her. Sparrow's heart stopped. His gaze communicated one single word—revenge.

"Jesus Christ."

Jared looked away first and Sparrow was helpless to follow. Hoyt's back looked worse—oozing red blood and pus.

"Shit. It's infected, all right." Aaron rubbed a hand down his beard and Sparrow saw the worry in the small lines around his mouth.

"Chopper," Merc called out from the cabin. Sparrow heard the bird coming before she saw it. Then the helicopter swerved around a bend in the river, circled over their boat, and led the way down river. Sparrow couldn't make out a landing area, but the helicopter veered left and hovered a ways off the river before lowering down, seeming to disappear in the trees.

"We need to leave the dressings for now and let Dr. Jane handle it back home."

"Whatever you think." Jared ground out. The boat slowed and turned left.

This was it, she had to escape. Had to get the hell out of here.

"He's seizing! Hold him still!" Aaron yelled. Hoyt's body convulsed and the three men around him focused all their attention on him. Sparrow seized the opportunity, her hands shaking and her heart pounding faster than the blades on the helicopter. She pulled her knife out of her boot and cut the lead rope. Then turned the knife inwards, cutting as fast as she could through the bonds on her wrists.

She sliced her own skin in her haste, but the rope snapped free. No one looked her way. Hoyt flopped on the floor like a fish out of water and Sparrow felt a brief tinge of remorse for leaving at such a time.

But not enough to stick around and see if he made it.

Sparrow crouched on the bench and tucked her knife into her boot. The boat slowed even more. She climbed onto the ledge, surveyed the distance separating her from the opposite shore and dove in headfirst.

Dark water surrounded her, its freezing temperature stunning her into immobility. The cold air was nothing compared to the water. It stole her ability to think. To move.

Have to move. Have to survive.

Sparrow shook herself free of the haze and swam. She swam underwater as hard and as long as she could before surfacing.

She took the split-second to gulp in a deep breath of air, then dived beneath the surface once more, thankful for the dark waters of the muddy Mississippi.

Her arms and legs ached, but she didn't stop kicking. She didn't stop swimming. She just kept moving forward. Staying beneath the surface until her lungs felt liable to burst. When she couldn't take it anymore, she burst through to the surface, gulped in air, and turned to see if anyone had noticed she was missing.

The boat was docked at the edge of the river and men were scrambling to lift Hoyt and carry him onto dry land. She was safe.

For now.

Sparrow ducked beneath the water's surface once more. She'd made it over halfway, but there was still a long way to go. The Mississippi River was nearly a mile wide, even more so with the recent rain. Her energy flagged. She couldn't swim that long without having to surface for air. But she kept going until her vision started to blacken, only breaking through to the surface when she was on the verge of passing out.

"Sparrow!" Jared stood on the far shore, his muscles bunching to dive in after her. Merc hooked an arm around him, pulling him back at the last second.

Her cover gone, Sparrow continued to swim on the surface, moving with renewed energy. Adrenaline pumped through her veins. She didn't need to look back to know that Jared would pursue her. There is no way he'd let her go. Her only hope was to get to the other side and disappear into the woods.

She was so tired. Swimming against the current was sapping her strength, so she changed route and swam sideways and downriver at the same time, letting the current carry her away.

Why the hell she hadn't done that in the first place? *Stupid girl.* She could only blame it on her haste to escape. She hadn't been thinking about using the river to her advantage. She'd only been thinking about survival.

Finally, she reached the opposite shore, dragged herself onto dry land, and collapsed. She knew her life was in danger, but all she could manage was to lay there for a moment, gasping for breath and trying to summon the strength to move. Something that seemed impossible until she heard a boat engine crank.

Sparrow planted her hands on the ground and pushed up, her arms and legs numb. She shivered, chill bumps covering more of her body than her clothes, but she couldn't feel the cold.

Jared was speeding across the river, leaving her with only a few precious seconds to get a lead.

Sparrow took off running into the woods. She would keep this path, straight west, until she was deep enough and far enough to put a good distance between her and Jared. Then she would cut back north.

Already, the sun was gaining altitude over the mountains, highlighting her tracks. A blast of cold struck her bared skin, but she pushed on. At least the sun's warmth would keep her from freezing.

If only she had another secret cave to use as a hideout, she could stop for long enough to make a fire and dry her clothes. Her boots squished with every step and fresh rivulets of water streamed down her face.

"Sparrow!"

Jared's bellow startled her and she increased her speed. He was too close. There would be no stopping for fire. Sparrow pumped her arms, hoping to heat her body from the inside out, but each time she drew in a breath, her lips trembled and her lungs shook.

Her only hope was to rely on her knowledge of the woods. She'd grown up in them, knew them better than anybody. And while she hadn't ventured on this side of the river much, it couldn't be much different from home.

Home. What she wouldn't give for her trailer and a tall glass of whiskey. She'd have a campfire going in no time. Squirrel would be there too, leaned back on a log. If she closed her eyes, she could almost feel the fire kissing her skin.

The first shudder hit her hard, making her stumble and nearly fall. Sparrow grabbed a tree for support and wheeled around, disoriented. How far had she gone? The deeper into the woods she'd ran, the thicker the trees had grown. They seemed bigger, more threatening. Fresh moss scaled the sides of the trees like a disease. The tops of the oaks and pines melded together, trapping the light high above, withholding its life-giving warmth.

Sparrow drew in a deep breath and took off again, the effort taking more energy than it should have. She tried to jog, but it hurt too much to breathe. No matter how hard she pumped her arms, she couldn't get the blood to flow back into her fingers.

She wouldn't be able to keep up this pace much longer.

Think, Sparrow think. Squirrel had told her that her small size could work to her advantage. People automatically assumed she was a weakling. But she'd come from sturdy mountain stock. She had that same grit and determination forged in her blood. Forged by the very coal that grew deep in these mountains.

And thanks to old man Squirrel, she had more knowledge about tracking and survival than her entire family combined.

The last of her adrenaline slipped away and the stitch in her side grew too painful to ignore. Sparrow stopped and leaned against a tree. Another chill worked its way down her body, the cold wrapping around her like an ice blanket.

She had to find somewhere to hide and preserve energy. Sparrow flexed her fingers, the movement slow and stiff. Jared hadn't plunged into the freezing water. He would be moving at twice her pace. It was time to face facts. She had no hope of out-running him. Her only chance was to outsmart him.

Sparrow inhaled and stood tall. She lifted her hands over her head and flung them down as hard and fast as she could at her sides, attempting to sling some blood back into her numb fingers. After repeating the process for a few more seconds, she felt some measure of feeling return to her limbs.

She paused and listened to the chatter of the birds, mingled with an occasional bark and chirp. A rabbit scooted past her feet. These were all comforting sounds, familiar sounds. But she had to listen for the unfamiliar. Like limbs snapping and leaves crackling under heavy footsteps. But she heard none of that. Nothing that would give away Jared's presence or location.

Her chest tightened and realization stole across her. Jared and his team hadn't acted like normal people. They hadn't even acted like law enforcement. All their movements had been too precise, too measured. And they carried automatic rifles, not shotguns.

Sparrow attempted to swallow, but couldn't complete the process. Deep in her gut she knew that whatever those men were, they were deadly. And she couldn't assume Jared was anything less than an elite tracker.

She strained harder, listening for any disturbances.

Nothing. Not even a leaf crackling.

Slowly she opened her eyes and turned in a circle, studying her surroundings. She stopped in front of a giant old hardwood, its roots raised from the ground like gnarled fingers. He might be a good tracker, but she was better. He couldn't track her if she left no footprints in the dirt.

Sparrow tilted her head up, almost jumping for joy when she spied all the low hanging branches. The very trees that blocked the warm sun could also save her life.

Sparrow took off at a brisk jog, making sure to clearly mark where she stepped. A ways up she stopped, crouched, and jumped up to grab onto a branch that stretched right above her head. Once she'd climbed onto that, she made her way up the limb to the tree, circled the trunk, and climbed onto the next limb out. It took time and some fancy footwork, but she finally leapt onto the tree next to the old oak. After carefully descending the trunk, she stepped onto an uplifted root. Keeping her footsteps light, Sparrow walked across the series of roots, never touching the ground. When she was on the back side of the tree she leapt as far as she could and landed in a crouch.

That should trip him up nicely and buy her some extra time. Sparrow grabbed a fallen tree limb, still covered in fresh sprouts of leaves, and turned and began walking backwards, brushing the ground to cover her steps. After a few more minutes of slow methodical walking Sparrow stopped to listen once more.

She didn't hear anything this time. Not the birds, or the squirrels, or even a random deer. Her already racing pulse shot off at light speed. The animals sensed strangers better than humans did. Their lack of noise was a glaring alarm that the threat was near.

Sparrow gently laid the stick on the ground and eased behind the nearest tree, making herself as small as possible. Her heart pounded so loud in her ears she was surprised that the whole damn forest didn't hear it.

All these years she'd been the tracker. The hunter. She'd never thought she would become the pray.

She sensed his presence, even though she couldn't detect a sound of a single footfall. Pressing her back into the tree, Sparrow prayed that she'd covered her tracks well enough to fool him. The cold bark seeped through her already chilled skin. A violent shudder worked through her body and she bit her lip to keep from crying out.

The cold seeped into her like poison, taking over her fingers and toes, fogging her mind. She needed to move, needed to generate heat. But Jared's presence was an even stronger motivation to stay put. Sparrow dug her fingers into the tree bark behind her, the pain keeping her anchored in place.

Every primal instinct screamed at her to run, but she held herself there by willpower alone. She kept her breaths long, and slow, and light despite her wildly beating heart. She didn't know how much time passed, but eventually the sounds of nature returned to normal.

The deadly presence she'd sensed earlier was gone. She'd tricked him. Elations surged through her veins, and she jumped to her feet only to stumble back to the ground. A wave of dizziness assailed her. She got to her feet again, her legs lethargic and unresponsive. Now she was shivering uncontrollably.

She didn't need a thermometer to know her body temperature was dropping dangerously low. Sparrow realized with a start that the greatest threat to her life might not be Jared Crowe.

Chapter Seventeen

The river was nearly half a mile wide where Sparrow had swum across it. Jared had to admire her grit. He knew a lot of grown men who wouldn't have made it that far, but fear could do a lot of things for a person.

His admiration was cut short by her stupidity. The water temperatures were cold enough to cause hypothermia, especially when she had no chance to get warm. Jared had left his nearly dying brother to go after Sparrow, and now he'd probably have to save her from the deadliness of her own actions. Anger flowed through him as swift and dangerous as the currents in the Mississippi.

Jared still had his duffel. His unit had already taken Hoyt back to get treatment. *I should be on that helicopter, not chasing her.*

He'd struggled with his decision, but ultimately he couldn't let her go. He knew Hoyt was in the best possible care. Now, all he had to do was retrieve his prisoner and call for pick up. Easy enough.

He throttled the boat to the place where Sparrow had pulled herself out of the water. The steep dirt bank offered no spot for him to tie up, so he was left no choice but to head down river and tie off to a fallen tree. The last thing he wanted to do was lose this boat after the last one had been stolen.

Jared tied the boat to the tree, heaved the bag over his shoulder, and jumped onto land. He would have to backtrack some, but how hard could it be to find her?

He predicted a few hours at most, long enough for her to freeze and get sloppy. Jared had the best training in tracking the military had to offer. He and Hoyt were at the top of their class in reconnaissance. When he found Sparrow…he didn't know what he would do. He only prayed he'd manage to keep control of himself.

The image of Hoyt's mutilated back flashed through his mind. He'd nearly gagged from the smell after Aaron pulled the bandage off.

And it was all because of her. Didn't the fact that she'd run prove that?

***

Sparrow started moving again, denying herself the temptation to give up. Jared would see her escape as another betrayal and he was already pissed. Her last action might very well push him over the edge.

But no, she couldn't think like that. She wasn't going to die out here from the cold or by Jared's hand; she was pure mountain stock, by God, and she'd sure as hell make it back home. The dip in the river might have slowed her down a bit, but she wouldn't allow it to kill her.

She continued walking, keeping her footsteps as silent as possible. Careful and quiet.

As she went, she thought back to her happiest childhood memories, her mind slipping easily into a better time, eager to escape the aches and the pain and the cold of the present.

Each summer, she and her friend Susie had swum in Blue Hole pond and sunned on boulders in the hundred-degree heat. She concentrated on the memory of the warm sun bathing her body and the hot rock beneath her.

Susie's mom had been a whore just like Sparrow's. The girls had easily formed a bond over the fact they both had junkie mothers and no idea who their fathers were. The memory morphed into another one, only this time there was no sun shining down. There was only her trailer, cold and empty. Their window unit had quit putting out heat long ago. Sparrow had woken up late that morning, shivering. Her mother was still passed out in bed with a strange man.

Sparrow went outside to build a campfire before heading back in to wake her mother. She approached from Tootsie's side of the bed, having learned early on how dangerous it could be to wake the man.

As gingerly as she could, Sparrow poked Tootsie on the shoulder. "Mama?"

And, just like always, her mom didn't move.

Sparrow sucked in a frustrated sigh, her young eight-year-old mind not yet comprehending the real reason Tootsie didn't move. She wrapped her small fingers around her mother's arm, shocked at how cold her skin was. "Mama?"

Still nothing. Uncaring if she woke the man or not, Sparrow shook her hard. "Mama!"

Her mother never opened her eyes. She was cold, as cold as ice.

The memory wrapped around her, making her shiver even harder. She wasn't sure how far she'd traveled or in what direction. She didn't hear the river rushing nearby anymore, though, and when she glanced up to gauge the location of the sun, it had disappeared. Dark storm clouds gathered and made their presence known with a loud rumble.

At that instant the temperature seemed to plummet.

Sparrow had to make a decision. Try to find the river and follow it back home, praying all the while that Jimbo didn't get to her before she told Miss Kay about his plans, or start searching for shelter.

***

Jared realized his mistake after a good thirty minutes of walking straight out from the river. In the beginning, he'd easily followed Sparrow's tracks. She had made a mad dash

into the woods, disturbing every leaf, stick, and limb in her
path. Hell, even if he had never been trained in tracking, he
would've been able to follow her. But then her footsteps
dwindled and disappeared altogether. Foolish as he was,
Jared had continued straight ahead, assuming the girl would
be too scared and distracted to throw him off course.

Jared grasped that she'd once again fooled him, only
this time the only person he could blame was himself. How
many times would he underestimate her?

He stopped and checked his compass, careful to turn
and head back in the exact direction from which he'd come.
Somewhere along this path she'd diverged from her course,
and now he would have to find it.

A flash of lightning rent the air, followed by a boom
of thunder. The temperature steadily dropped, until Jared's
breath started fogging in front of his face. He slowed on his
track back, carefully watching for any signs. A branch broken
too high for an animal to make. A disturbance in the leaf
patterns on the ground. A footprint.

Each excruciating minute seemed to stretch out longer
and longer, putting more and more distance between them.
Worry shadowed his thoughts. It was cold out here. Really
cold, and she'd completely submerged herself in water just to
escape him. He spun around the moment he heard the river.
He'd missed it. Dammit, he'd underestimated her completely.

He'd seen proof of her handiwork on the walls of her
trailer. Seen her collection of knives and guns and bow and
arrows. And still…somewhere in the back of his mind he
thought of her as any other girl. Scared, cold, and alone in the
woods.

Jared laughed at himself. Idiot. *Hasn't she already
proved she isn't like any other girl?*

Jared changed tactics, and followed the trail back
from the river, stopping when it started to change pattern,
turning from a mad dash to controlled, measured steps, then a
fast run. Then nothing. Jared stopped and made a full circle,
carefully studying every nuance around him. A couple of

squirrels chattered overhead, a tree branch shifted, and a pine cone hit the ground, drawing his gaze up to the branches.

The oak was a huge beast of a tree that had to be at least a hundred years old. Its huge roots jutted up out of the ground, covered in moss.

That's when he saw it. The moss had been disturbed. Damn girl was a genius. He hadn't been able to track her because her feet hadn't actually been on the ground. Jared swept around the tree but saw nothing out of place. Even the most carefully placed footstep could leave a mark.

But she'd left absolutely no trail.

Jared closed his eyes and thought, where would she have gone? Where would anyone in her situation go?

Home.

Jared opened his eyes and headed straight north, his self-assurance growing with each step. He hadn't picked up her trail yet, but his instincts were firing hot. It wasn't long before he saw the tree branch and put the puzzle together. She'd covered her tracks. He started seeing footsteps and found the spot where she'd hunkered down behind a tree. No way she could've heard him coming through the woods. Hell, he'd barely been able to hear himself. What had given him away?

A raindrop splattered on his face. She wouldn't make it far dressed like that. After her dunk in the river, she had to be freezing. The rain and temperature drop would only make it worse. He cursed and pulled out his poncho. If he didn't find her soon she might actually die from hypothermia or exposure. He was in a race against time to save the one girl he'd vowed to destroy.

Chapter Eighteen

The sun had started its descent when he picked up her trail again hours later. His worry for her safety grew with every passing minute, as did his admiration. There were few people in the world he couldn't easily track, very few, but this slip of a mountain girl was testing him.

But even more alarming was her footstep pattern. She was dragging her feet, walking in an uneven path. Had she injured herself in her bid to out run him? He already doubted her involvement, but to have her really hurt because of him was too terrible to contemplate. She'd headed north and angled toward the river. The terrain had shifted, becoming steep and rocky. Jared ascended another rise and the land leveled out along a ridgeline. Up here the trees were nearly nonexistent, making her easier to track. Until he saw a sharp skid in the dirt where she'd obviously fallen. His fear skyrocketed. Had she tripped and leaned too far to the right?

No way. Sparrow had too much skill to fall off the side of a cliff. Still, he leaned over the edge and breathed a sigh of relief when he saw nothing but the rocks in the river.

He stood up, looking over the river valley, taking in the majestic mountain range. Tennessee held some awe-inspiring wonders. If only its people were as wonderful. Forcing back the memories, Jared turned to pick up where he'd left off.

He heard her before he saw her.

Moving away from the edge of the cliff, Jared eased back into the woods, walking carefully so as not to alert her to his presence. He spied her just beyond a dense cove of trees, sitting in a small clearing. She'd piled up some leaves and twigs and was trying to start a fire with two pieces of wood, but she was moving way too slow. Her hands shook so bad, she kept dropping the stick. Her chattering teeth sounded louder than a woodpecker tapping a tree.

He had just started creeping forward when she dropped the sticks. "I know you're there."

Jared stopped and hid his smile. "Told you I'd find you."

When she finally looked up, it was his turn to suck in a breath. Her blue lips stood out stark against her too pale skin and her pupils nearly swallowed her eyes. "Jesus, why didn't you stop?"

Her gaze narrowed. "Why? So you could torture me to death? No thanks. I've heard hypothermia is just like going to sleep, only you don't wake up. Besides, I have to get back and stop Jimbo. He wants the mountain and if he gets it, he'll kill Squirrel."

He'd pushed her to choosing death by exposure over him? Well, maybe he would make the same choice in her situation, but that sure as hell didn't mean he wasn't pissed off. Jared squatted next to her and made a grab for her arm.

Sparrow jerked away from him, falling on her butt. "Get away from me."

"Don't be stupid. I've got to warm you up."

She scrambled back on her hands and feet. "No thanks. Don't much care for your style of warming."

Jared pushed his remorse down and continued to stalk forward. "You think I want you like that now? Sorry honey, but even I have limits."

"You think I believe that? Stay away from me." Sparrow scrambled faster, but her elbow gave out and she fell to the ground. Only to push herself right back up. Jared forced himself to stop. Her expression had morphed from angry to frightened.

"What's it gonna take for you to believe me?"

Her harsh laugh turned into a deep cough, and it took all his strength not to yank her into his arms and cradle her against him. "Nothing. You've made your point very clear."

"Dammit, I just said that to scare you. If you don't stop and let me help you, you really are going to die."

She shook her head wildly, her teeth chattering even harder with the rough movement. His patience was at an end. It took him all of two leaps to grab her and lift her against his body.

"Let me go!"

"I'm not going to let you kill yourself." Jared locked his arms tight, careful not to hurt her.

She pushed against his chest and he barely felt it. But he did feel the freezing temperature of her body. Thunder boomed again. He had to find them shelter right now. Jared ripped off his poncho and wrapped her up in it to protect her from any more rain and hopefully trap in a little body heat. Then he picked her up, holding her in front of his chest. "I promise not to harm you in any way. It's fixing to start raining and the temperature will continue to fall. If we don't find shelter and heat, you will go into shock."

Her attempts to fight ceased and she sagged against him, out of breath and trembling. "I know. I was trying to find another cave, but I couldn't keep going."

"Smart." Jared started walking with Sparrow's sparse weight clasped in his arms. The threat of rain hung heavy in the air and grey clouds obscured any sunlight.

There were no more breaks in Sparrow's teeth chattering. Her entire body shook. Jared cursed and tried to squeeze her against as much of his body as possible, but there was only so much he could do while still moving.

"Sparrow, think. Any shelter you've ever heard of on this side of the river? Caves, hunting sheds, anything like that?"

"N-n-n-no—no—wait. The bear's den, where squirrel tracked his grizzly."

"Good girl, where is it?"

"Don't know for sure." She shuddered so hard he almost dropped her. "He said it's halfway up the tallest ridge you can see. And the top of the hill is as bare as an old man's bald head."

Great, a tall mountain in the Tennessee Mountains. Still, Jared looked around and nearly fell over in shock. The next hill over looked exactly as she'd described. "I'll be damned. Hold on."

Jared took off at a brisk jog, carefully shielding her face from stray branches. Her body temperature seemed to drop even more and adrenaline fueled his muscles. He had to find shelter *now*.

Jared began the ascent, his legs burning with pain. Didn't matter. He kept going, cursing when he had to slow down and wind around a smattering of huge boulders jutting out of the earth. At least the trees were thinner up here; the scraggly pines didn't have enough dirt in the rocky soil to spread their roots. He had to protect her. His woman.

Shit. Not his. No matter how much he wanted to possess her, he couldn't. Not until Hoyt woke and confirmed his suspicion.

He kept scanning his surroundings, watching for some small break in the earth signaling the cave. But he needn't have bothered. Suddenly, he was standing before a huge opening in the side of the mountain.

One that was more than large enough to hold an entire family of bears.

"Going to sit you right here for just a minute, make sure there aren't any animals hiding out in there okay?" Jared gently laid her down on the ground and propping her against a boulder.

Sparrow just leaned over on her side and tucked her knees against her chest. Without hesitation, Jared pulled his gun and went into the cave. He didn't have much longer before she went into shock.

The cave wasn't deep, so he cleared it in seconds, studiously ignoring the obvious signs that some animal had lived there in the past. He ran back out, grabbed Sparrow, and carried her into the cave. Once she was tucked against the wall, he said, "I'll be right back," then ran out to gather as much dry kindling and as many twigs as he could find. He returned with a small arm load, which he dumped next to Sparrow. "I'll have you dry and warm in just another minute."

Still no response, but her teeth were chattering as loud as gunfire in the cave. "Hold on." Jared made a fire faster than he'd ever made one in his entire life, and when he was sure the flame could hold its own, he turned to Sparrow.

Her pale skin was laced with blue veins and chill bumps. He didn't think she was even aware of his presence. He ripped the knife from his pocket and started to cut away her wet clothes. It was obvious she was in serious trouble when she didn't even protest him cutting off her shirt.

Next, he went to work on her boots. They were knee-high and laced up the front. Perfect to protect from snakebites but terrible when submerged in water. He quickly unlaced the left boot and yanked it off, then her damp sock. He repeated the process on her right one, and when he yanked it off, her knife clattered to the floor.

"Smart girl. I should've checked you for weapons." Next, he pulled at her shorts, but they were plastered to her body. He didn't want to, but he cut them off as well. She needed to get warm more than she needed to protect her modesty. He yanked his blanket from the bag, stripped off her panties, and rolled her into a cocoon next to the fire. Then he stripped and slid into the blanket with her, gasping when her skin made contact with his. She was like ice.

His concern kicked into overdrive and Jared started rubbing brisk circles on her back, attempting to warm up her core. Her entire body shook and shivered, and Jared's chest tightened with apprehension.

"Foolish girl, you could've gotten yourself killed."

"Safer than you," she stuttered. "You wouldn't believe me."

He felt a small measure of guilt. He'd done his best to frighten her, but he'd been so angry. It was awful to see her this way.

"C-c-clothes."

"They're gone."

She struggled feebly against him, but he swatted her hand away like he would a fly. "You don't have anything to worry about. I just want to get you warm."

"Why?"

"I just do." He couldn't tell her that seeing her like this tore at his insides. Or that he'd seen soldiers go into hypothermia under milder conditions, with half the amount of exposure. "I can't tell you, but I need you to get better, okay?"

What was wrong with him? Maybe he should be rejoicing at her pain. But that voice in his head—the voice insisting she couldn't do this thing, that she was innocent—was only growing louder.

"Jared," Sparrow gasped.

He loosened his arms instantly, realizing he'd been squeezing her tighter and tighter. She would flee him if she were able, and he couldn't blame her. He'd done his best to terrorize her. He wanted to hurt the person who was responsible for his brother's pain. But was that person really her?

He shook his head slightly. This wasn't the time for questions. His instincts told him to take care of her, and he never ignored his instincts. "Talk to me."

She didn't answer except for a fierce jerk. Jared rubbed her back harder, trying to create enough friction to produce heat. He'd isolated her between his body and the fire, but she still felt like ice. If she fell asleep, she might slip into a coma. And what the hell could he do about it out here?

"Sparrow?" Jared gentled his voice, trying to ease some of her fear. Still no answer. He leaned back and saw that her lids had slid shut, and alarm skittered through him faster than a scorpion across the hot desert sand.

"Open your eyes, dammit." Her lids fluttered but didn't fully open. Had he gotten so lost in his thoughts and anger and frustration that he let her slip away?

"Sparrow. Open. Your. Eyes." He punctuated each word, trying to somehow force his way into her consciousness. And he was rewarded by her pure gold gaze, making him feel as drunk as if they were the whiskey they resembled.

"What?" Her question was delivered in a groggy voice.

"I want you to talk to me."

"Why?"

So that you don't slip into a coma or shock. So that you don't die. "I'm bored. It's the least you can do since I saved you."

She grumbled a bit as he continued to try and heat her core temperature. "Just sleep." Her eyes slid shut again.

"No! Wake up. Talk to me."

She groaned, and *damn* it was sexy, punctuated even more when she opened those beautiful eyes again. "Let me sleep."

Over his dead body. "Tell me what it was like to grow up here."

Jared searched his own memories for any happiness he'd experienced here, but the most he could remember was the crisp air found only in the mountains. The hazy memory of his mother's smile. A pair of whiskey eyes piercing the darkness. But everything after that was simply darkness. He shook himself.

"Why do you care?" she grumbled.

"I just do. Now tell me. I won't leave you alone until you do."

They lay on their sides, faces only inches apart. Her body was gradually warming and he started to become aware of just how intimately they were pressed together.

"It was hard."

"Wow, really? That's all you've got?"

"You should remember what it was like. Hard work. Hard life. Hard people."

Yes, he remembered. He remembered every time he closed his eyes. Every time he woke up in a cold sweat and had to turn on the fucking lamp to ease the fear. "But I left, remember? Tell me something good."

Because he didn't want or need to hear what her life had been like after Miss Kay.

"I guess the only really good memories I got are of Squirrel. Everything got better after he took me under his wing."

"What do you mean?"

"He taught me how to hunt. How to fight and defend myself." Jared had another brief image of the scrappy little girl who had rescued him and his brother from that dark closet. For the life of him he couldn't picture her fighting anything bigger than a butterfly.

"Why did you have to defend yourself?"

"Jimbo. I had to fight against Jimbo and his brothers."

The image of Sparrow standing next to her hulking older brother filled him with fury. Jimbo could kill her with one punch.

"That bastard hurt you?" Jared was already intent on killing Kay, but Jimbo had just moved up to number one on that list. More so now, because if Sparrow was telling the truth about her involvement, Jimbo is the one responsible for what happened to his brother.

Sparrow gave a brittle laugh, which she punctuated when her teeth cracked together with another hard tremble. Jared tried to pull her more tightly against him, but they were already melded together so close they could be one person.

"Not after I nearly took his balls off with my knife."

Her knife. His brother. No—not going there. "So that's why you got the collection then? And why that Geraldine girl nearly pissed her pants when you slipped a knife around her throat?"

She nodded against him. He tucked her head into his neck, taking pleasure in the way her hot little breasts puffed against his skin. Her tremors gentled to the occasional shake.

"Tell me something else that you remember." Talking about her knives wasn't safe for either of them. The doubt growing in his mind about her involvement was close to taking over.

"I remember you. And how fierce you were that night I freed you."

Her whispered words shocked him. "Fierce? I don't remember that part of it." No, he remembered the pain. And Sparrow, of course.

"You were determined to protect your little brother. And when we escaped, you were determined to protect me too."

Her words tugged at his memory. Flashes of them running through the woods. Of Hoyt and Sparrow and him in the dark forest. "I wanted you to come with us."

She nodded against him and snuggled a little closer. Her feet wiggled between his calves, still cold, but not frozen.

"And you wouldn't leave with us."

Sparrow nodded her head again and let out a yawn. An occasional tremor still shook her; her temperature had warmed enough to safely rule out shock. But that wasn't the most pressing thought on his mind. "Why wouldn't you come?"

He remembered now, remembered screaming her name as she disappeared into the woods after refusing to leave with them. Remembered dreaming about rescuing her from this evil mountain. But those had been the dreams of a young boy.

Sparrow interrupted his thoughts, her voice no longer a weak whisper. "I couldn't leave my mom. She needed me to take care of her."

"Isn't that supposed to be the other way around?"

Sparrow shrugged. "Maybe in other parts. But if not for me, she would have gone hungry."

So after rescuing him and his brother that scared little girl had returned to this piece of shit mountain to take care of her mother?

"How old were you? What happened to your mother?"

She got very still against him, and Jared held his breath, waiting to see if she'd fallen asleep. Her words had been getting softer toward the end of their conversation, fatigue weighing her down as heavy as a damn boulder.

"I was eight when I found her dead," she said softly. "She'd overdosed on pain killers."

Holy shit that was fucked up. How awful it must have been for her to find her momma that way. Especially after staying on that mountain only for her. "And then Miss Kay took you in?"

"She let me live in her house. Made sure I was fed."

"What about protecting you from her sons?"

"She was busy. I needed to learn how to fend for myself anyway." In those words, Jared could hear the broken dreams of a young girl.

Sparrow spoke, "Miss Kay controls everyone. Everyone but her sons."

Chapter Nineteen

Sparrow woke up bundled in a cocoon of incredible warmth, with Jared's lips pressed to her neck. A chill shot down her spine, but it wasn't from the cold. She'd never felt so hot in her entire life. She tried to remember the night before, but the only thing that stood out was the memory of feeling cold, so cold she'd feared she would die from it. Apparently, Jared had had other plans.

Careful not to move, she studied him while he slept. Up close, his black hair appeared silky and she took the opportunity to run her fingers through it and learn its texture. They lay on their sides facing each other. She traced his arms, his thick neck and shoulders, fascinated by how soft his skin was over the hardness of his muscles.

He shifted and she came to the dawning awareness that she was naked. And he was damn near close to naked too. Bells went off, and she jerked against him, unable to hold still. Jared awoke immediately, his dark eyes holding her immobile.

"You made it." His sleepy smile was so sexy and sweet. Her heart flipped over hard in her chest.

"Apparently, I did." She buffeted her snarky comment by soothing a thumb over his cheek.

"Don't ever scare me like that again."

"It was because I was so scared of you," she choked out.

Instead of getting angry or even remorseful, Jared simply nodded. "I know."

And then he pulled her tighter against him and she became aware of every single inch of skin pressed to hers. She fought the urge to wiggle against him, but it was impossible to control her racing heart or the shallow breaths sawing in and out of her chest.

Sparrow swallowed, for some reason feeling like she owed him some sort of further explanation. But she kept her mouth shut, unwilling to give him more ammunition to use against her later. She wanted this calm version of Jared to stay around as long as possible.

"I know what you think I did... Why did you save me? Why didn't you just leave me there?"

"I honestly don't know." He pushed a stray strand of hair from her cheek, the feeling of his fingers sending delicious tingles along her jaw.

"What do you know?" Her heart raced faster.

"That I'm glad you're alive."

Her breath hitched under the intensity of his stare. There was no hatred in his gaze this time.

"I know I want to kiss you so bad it hurts." His roughly whispered words set her body on fire. She wanted his lips on hers too. She realized with the shock that didn't matter to her if he hated her, if he blamed her for the horrible thing she had not done, she wanted this. She wanted it right here. Right now. "What are you waiting for?"

Before she had time to suck in a breath, he pressed his mouth to hers. The touch was different this time, and her whole being was swayed by the way his lips felt so soft and yet firm against hers. And it was over much too fast.

"Is that it?"

He chuckled, "Not even close."

And then his lips sealed over hers once more, only this time there was no quick brush. He was forceful, commanding. He tugged on her lower lip and white-hot heat shot straight through her.

Sparrow gasped, and he took the opportunity to thrust his tongue inside her mouth, the sensation unlike anything she could have imagined. Jared's hands tangled in her hair, tilting her head and deepening the kiss. He explored her mouth and she mimicked his moves, learning the dance. Her hands found his shoulders and then his hair, yanking him to her, wanting to make this harder, bring it deeper. And he obliged. By the time they broke apart, they are both panting.

She didn't want him to stop. Never one to sit idly by and wait, she pressed her lips to his this time. Jared wound his arms around her, smashing her body to his. He broke the kiss, trailed his lips down her neck, and nibbled her throat, sending wave after wave of sensation through her body.

"I've been dreaming about those pretty breasts of yours. About how good they taste." Jared rolled her over onto her back and settled between her legs. His hardness made contact with her core through the material of his briefs. It seemed as if all her desire was centered right there between her legs.

Jared took her breasts in his hands and her body arched in response to his touch. "Your nipples are beautiful. Perfect for my mouth." He sucked one between his lips, and Sparrow cried out at the pleasure bordering on pain.

While he lavished attention with his lips, his fingers stroked her other nipple. The sensation was sweet torture. She tossed her head back and closed her eyes, her body overwhelmed with carnal need. "That's it, baby." Jared moved to her other nipple, this time drawing circles and flicking her tip before sucking it into his mouth. Her entire body arched off the floor as if he had some string tied around her, and with each tug, he lifted her higher.

His other hand trailed down her waist, skimming her hip, and then back up her thigh. She was needy and wanting.

And then she felt his fingers moving against her most private area.

"God, baby you're so wet." Jared took her lips in a possessive kiss. He began rubbing circles against her sex, and she was helpless to do anything but arch into his hand. Sparrow cried out in his mouth, but instead of releasing her, he rubbed faster. The tension inside her coiled and built, climbing to unexplored heights. Until suddenly her world exploded, and her body clenched and shattered in intense pleasure. Jared swallowed her cries, but she was lost to the sensation.

"That was it?" she said when she caught her breath a few minutes later. Jared lay atop her, kissing and licking and nibbling along her jaw and neck.

"That was just a taste honey."

Her eyes widened, "It gets better?"

"A thousand times better."

A thousand times better? She couldn't even imagine. Jared trailed kisses lower, moving between the valley of her breasts, circling her navel and kissing right below it. Alarm bells went off and she pushed at him. "What are you doing?"

"Kissing you." He grabbed her thighs and spread her legs wide. She gasped when she realized his intention and grabbed his hair, trying to pull him away. He ignored her protest. And then she felt his tongue on her, right there where his fingers had been only moments before. Her sensitive flesh screamed at the contact. "Jared!"

He didn't answer, simply continued the sweet torture, causing the tension in her belly to rise again. When she was on the verge of losing control, he stopped, and this time she tried to push him back down. "Please."

His chuckle was deep, dark. "Not yet."

She gave a frustrated sound, arching her hips up as he slid up her body. Jared took her lips in another fierce kiss and she was shocked to taste herself on him. The thought was so incredibly erotic. Before she knew it, her arms were around his neck and she was pulling him in for more.

***

Sparrow was a wildcat in his arms, just like he had known she'd be, and his cock was screaming to get inside her. But he knew he had to take his time, he had to prepare her. Because even though he couldn't sort all the lies he'd been told from the truth, he knew without a doubt that she had never been touched like this.

Her innocent, inexperienced kisses were making him so hurt for her, not turning him off as he might have imaged they would. Without breaking contact with her lips, he reached between them and teased her clit until he had her hips bucking to his rhythm. Then he slipped a finger inside. Sparrow dug her nails into his shoulder and cried out in his mouth and…fuck, he loved it. Loved her fierce, uninhibited response. Loved how tight and wet she was around his finger.

He eased his finger out and pushed it back inside, slow at first, letting her body get used to the intrusion. When she was ready, he slid in another finger, trying to stretch and prepare her. As he worked her with his fingers, he circled her clit with this thumb, wanting her to be wild with need.

He could feel her clenching around his fingers, so he knew she was close. He pulled out, yanked his briefs down, and settled between her legs before taking her mouth in another languid kiss.

Nudging her entrance with the tip of his cock was nearly intense enough to make him come right then and there. Careful to go slow, Jared called upon every single ounce of control he possessed and eased inside her as gently as he could. He worked like that, making shallow thrusts until his head was finally all the way in. Sweat poured from his head; his teeth clenched. Her mouth was open, her eyes wide, and she gasped and arched up to take him deeper.

"Hold still, I'm trying to make this easy." She felt so good. He was so close. The need to just bury himself deep inside her nearly overpowered him. Instead, he rose up on his elbows and clenched his jaw. Then he slowly eased out and pushed back in, a little bit deeper each time until he felt her resistance.

He had never taken a virgin before, but he knew he was big, and he'd heard it was painful the first time. Sparrow dug her heels into his butt, urging him onward. With a cry, Jared thrust forward, tearing through her resistance and burying himself to the hilt.

Sparrow cried out and wrapped her arms around his neck, pulling him to her. Every instinct inside Jared was screaming for him to move, but he forced himself to hold still. She was so tight she was strangling his cock.

Jared lifted up enough to see her face, scared she would be crying, but he saw no tears. Still, her eyes were closed, her lips pressed together in a tight line. She needed to relax or he would hurt her. He leaned down and nibbled her lips until she opened her mouth to let him explore her sensually. He reached between them and massaged her clit in small circles. When her hips arched against his, he knew she was ready again. As gentle as he could, he eased out and thrust back in with one long slow stroke, never breaking contact with her mouth.

Again and again he repeated this movement, controlling himself until he couldn't breathe, he couldn't think. He tore his mouth from hers, nearly coming undone at the sight of her heavy-lidded eyes filled with pleasure. She was the sexiest sight he'd ever seen.

Unable to take it slow any longer, Jared thrust hard and fast. She was so tight, so fucking tight, he didn't know how much longer he could hold back. He circled her clit again and again, until her eyes went wide and she screamed his name. She spasmed around his cock. Her response pulled his own orgasm free and he yanked out, spilling his seed on her belly.

All his strength gone, he collapsed and rolled to the side. There was no way in hell he could separate from her now. He'd known it would be good with her, but that had been mind-numbingly incredible. Possessive need overtook him and he knew he could never harm her. Knew she had to be innocent.

Chapter Twenty

"That was incredible." Sparrow stretched and rolled over, throwing an arm and a leg across his chest and thighs.

Jared lay on his back, his hands propping up his head, his eyes closed and a small smile twitching on his lips. "Absolutely."

"Is it always like that?" She wasn't dumb enough to think she was his only one. Frankly, she didn't care. But she was curious to know, because she couldn't honestly conceive of feeling this way with someone else.

"No, it's not." His words were soft and gentle. His big calloused hand covered her much smaller hand and pulled it to his lips for a kiss. Even that simple touch was enough to send a little spark of electricity all the way to her toes.

A contentment that she'd never before experienced filled her body, making her muscles as loose as a weeping willow blowing in the breeze. He'd opened her eyes to a whole different side of life, and she looked forward to more.

Dreamed of more with him.

"Let's do it again."

He cracked his eyes open and turned to face her. "Now? You're not too sore?"

She moved and felt a twinge between her thighs. The ache from him filling her, stretching her, was still fresh. "Not so bad. I can do it." She leaned down and nibbled on his bottom lip, finding that to be one of her favorite parts of his body. Along with his chest, his stomach, his shoulders, and his arms… Okay all of him. All of him was perfect.

Her words drew out a chuckle and he flashed his teeth at her in a big grin. "You might not be too sore, but I'm worn out." He made a dramatic sigh and lay back on the ground.

Sparrow slapped his chest and immediately kissed the red handprint she'd left. When his arm wrapped around her and pulled her hard against him, she felt full of emotion. He was holding her like he cherished her. And he'd loved her like he wanted to possess her.

Last night and this morning had changed everything. He'd showed her so much and she'd given so much to him in return. And that small flicker of hope had reignited inside her soul. A part of him had to know she was innocent—otherwise he could never touch her that way.

Maybe they really could have a life together, set up a place for Squirrel. And she could leave Crowe Mountain for this man. She knew it with every fiber of her body. "You must be old then. Do you need a nap?"

Jared cracked open one eye and glared at her. "You think I can't keep up with you?"

Sparrow made her eyes wide and innocent looking. "I'd never say that. You just reminded me of how Squirrel has to stop and catch his breath after he walks too long. I assumed it was like that for all older people."

Jared let out a growl, flipped her back onto her back, and nudged her legs apart. When she felt his hardness nudging her entrance, her eyes went wide.

"Does this feel like an old man?" Jared grabbed her hands and stretched them above her head. His other hand explored her body.

"I can't tell," Sparrow gasped. She knew she was poking the bear, but he was being so cuddly and lovable and easy to rile.

Jared traced down her collarbone, passed her breast, and rested his fingers at her ribs. Then they dug into her flesh, tickling her until she cried out for him to stop.

"Take it back," he demanded, continuing the torture.

She was laughing so hard tears ran from her eyes. "I take it back. I take it back. Stop."

He stopped and then his mouth crashed down over hers, making her dizzy with desire. Without warning, he thrust inside her with one long stroke, filling her so much she couldn't breathe. Couldn't do anything but exist in this moment.

Jared leaned back and this time his gaze was intense. Something inside her heart cracked and reached out to him. She cupped his cheek, wanting to ease whatever burden was hidden behind those dark eyes.

And then he pulled out slammed home again, driving all conscious thoughts from her mind. Jared let go of her hands, grabbed her legs, and wrapped them around his waist. "You better hold on little girl, I'm about to show you what this old man can do."

■ ■

"Here, I'm afraid these are the only things that survived last night. I had to cut most of your clothes off." Jared held out the white and black panties.

Sparrow took them from him, a slight blush staining her cheeks. "Still can't believe you undressed me."

"Believe me, I would rather have undressed you under different circumstances. Something I plan on doing in the near future, actually."

Sparrow ducked her head and yanked on the panties, but not before Jared saw her blush deepen to bright red.

Damn that made him happy. Something he hadn't really felt since…since he didn't remember. He was so confused. Twenty-four hours ago, he had been almost one hundred percent certain Sparrow had been the one to torture his brother. But her reactions, her words, and his gut instinct all screamed that she was innocent.

He had no doubt that Jimbo was a liar through and through. But how could he refute his own brother's accusations?

Sparrow slid on the panties and damn him if he didn't want to rip them off and make love to her all over again.

Especially considering the small arrow pointing straight down to her pussy with the words "Insert Slot B."

Obviously, whomever she'd borrowed the outfit from either had a sense of humor or thought their lover was dense enough to need the instructions.

Sparrow stood, her arms crossed in front of her, vulnerable and unsure" Why don't you go dig in my bag, there's a shirt of mine you could wear?"

"Thanks." She crossed to his duffel and bent over. Instant lust slapped him in the face. The back of her panties read "Insert Slot C." All sorts of new images flooded his mind. Images of him bending her over, possessing every single part of her. Shit, he had to do something or he would take her again.

"Toss me that phone, will you? I want to check on my brother." Thank God for sat phones. Sparrow came up with his shirt clutched in one hand and the phone in the other.

"I really hope he's okay."

Not knowing how to respond to that, Jared took the phone and walked out of the cave.

Merc was the one who picked up. "You're late checking in."

Jared blew out a deep breath, noticing the morning chill, and swept a hand over his head. Mist surrounded them, sunlight creating an otherworldly glow in the heavy haze. "Hit a few complications."

"Did you secure the package?"

The package? Jared turned to see Sparrow struggling into her boots. He had placed her panties and boots next to the fire last night to dry. "Roger."

"Good, I'll notify the boys to get the chopper ready. What's your ETA for extraction?"

"Two hours."

"Roger that."

Fear gripped him suddenly, and he steeled himself to ask the question he'd been avoiding. The real reason he'd called. "Did he make it?"

He heard the rough pain in his voice, but he couldn't do a damn thing about it.

"Yes. I think he's going to be okay. Doc got him stabilized, dumped a shitload of antibiotics into him, and cleaned up his back as best she could." Merc paused and Jared knew he wasn't through.

"And?"

"She did the best she could with his back and chest. But there's going to be scarring."

Jared's gut tightened instantly. Pretty boy Hoyt Crowe was going to wake up a fucked up mess.

"You there man?" Merc asked.

A huge knot had formed in his throat and Jared had to fight to get words past it. "Yeah. Just bring the chopper, I need to see him."

"Already done."

He turned to see her packing up camp in his long T-shirt, those provocative panties, visible only when she bent over, and her knee-high snake boots. So small and innocent looking. "Thanks."

"Chopper's on its way. I'll call if there's a change." Merc disconnected the call. Jared slid the phone into his pants pocket, unable to take his gaze off the girl in the cave.

His instincts screamed that she couldn't have harmed Hoyt. But how could he trust his instincts when she made him hard as a rock and he was fucking panting after her like a dog in heat? He couldn't trust himself.

He had to get her home. Hoyt would wake up and tell him that Sparrow had not been involved. He had to. And then they could all proceed with their lives.

Sparrow approached, bag in hand, looking for all the world like a lost little girl in that huge army green T-shirt. He took the duffle, set it on the ground beside him, and gave into the urge to pull her into his arms. She curved into his body, like she'd been crafted just for him.

"Everything okay?"

Unbidden, he felt tears prick his eyes. He squeezed her tighter to him so she couldn't see and pulled in a shuddering breath. No, nothing was okay. His brother had almost died and he didn't fucking know if she'd taken part in torturing him. "Yes, he's stable."

"That's great news, isn't it?" She tried to pull away, but he wouldn't let her. He squeezed her to him, unwilling and unable to let her go just yet.

How fucked up was he that he was drawing comfort from a woman who could be responsible for his brother pain?

Jared cleared his throat. This wasn't him; he wasn't indecisive. He didn't question himself. He made a plan and he stuck to it. And now he needed to get to his brother and find out the truth.

"Yes, it is." Jared let go and bent down over the bag, pulling out the small blanket she'd folded neatly inside. "Wrap this around your shoulders. If we move fast, it'll help keep you warm."

Only Sparrow didn't accept the blanket from him. From the way she stood there staring at him, biting her lower lip, he knew he wasn't going to like her next words. "I can't go with you."

Chapter Twenty-one

Please understand. Please understand. Please understand.

Jared's expression had been so agonized when he hung up the phone. He was scared to death for his brother, and she thanked God that Hoyt was okay.

But he wanted to get back as soon as possible, and Sparrow couldn't do that. She couldn't abandon Squirrel to Jimbo. She had to make Jared understand that as soon as she did, she would return to him.

Jared let out a sigh, but he didn't budge. "You and I both know you're going to come with me, so take the blanket."

"I want to come with you, but I have to go home first. I have to stop Jimbo. I think…I think he's fixing to kill Kay and take over the mountain. Then he'll kill Squirrel." Saying the words out loud unleashed the shiver she'd been holding back. Squirrel was the only father she'd ever known.

Jared's expression of resignation disappeared and he all but snarled at her. "Don't fucking say her name. You know what she did to me."

Fighting the instinct to take a step backwards, Sparrow closed the gap between them, tilting her head back to stare at the man who was stealing her heart. She caught her breath at the stray thought. Was it possible to fall in love so fast?

But you met him all those years ago. He was the boy you rescued.

"Jared, I know. And it disgusts me too. It's not her I'm worried about. It's Squirrel."

Jared flinched and she laid her hand on his chest.

"He's a grown man who can look out for himself. If he's really in trouble, he can go to the police." His expression was fierce and she knew it was out of concern for her this time.

"You've been gone a long time, but there ain't no law on Crowe Mountain. The only law is made by Miss Kay."

"Enough," he roared flinging her hand from his chest. "I can't stand to hear her name again. And I don't care why you want to go back, I'm not letting you leave. You're coming with me whether you want to come or not."

Pain exploded inside her chest. How could he talk to her like that after what they'd shared? "Please try to understand. I swear to you I will come back to you. All I need is enough time to warn her. I owe that much to her."

"I don't care what you think you owe that monster. You're coming with me." He made a grab for her, but Sparrow jumped back and cried out.

"You think I trust you to come back? Do I look like an idiot?"

Sparrow stumbled back, a huge ache burning in her chest. "What do you mean? Last night..."

"Last night was just sex. Don't think that you can use your body to try and control me. I'm not that stupid."

Every word was a bullet to her heart. Agony coursed through her veins, curling her fingers and toes. She felt a wild hysteria bubble up inside her. She'd given herself to him completely, wholeheartedly, but he had only been using her.

No, not him, she assured herself. *He's just saying those things to be mean and hurtful.* Her heart refused to believe what her mind was telling her. "I may not be as experienced as you are, but I know last night was more than just sex. You felt it too."

"Wake up, little girl. You should have listened to the old man's advice. I had you seduced from the first moment I saw you."

It took every ounce of her power not to crumple to the ground. He was telling the truth. What had been the most amazing, life-changing moment of her life had been nothing more than a planned attack on his part.

"Why?" Her voice was whispered and broken but she didn't care.

"Why else?"

And suddenly his words from the previous day came crashing back into her mind, destroying her. He'd told her hadn't he? He'd told her he would use her body, just like a whore, and that she would succumb to him.

"Oh, God." Sparrow shoved her hand into her mouth to hold the sob back. He'd taken her virginity and turned her into her worst nightmare. A whore. A slut who'd begged for his touch.

Her thoughts whirled as out of control as an explosion in the coal mines, and she felt her heart collapse within her chest. Although she remained upright, there was a gaping hole inside her. The tears threatened to fall form her eyes and she hated that he saw that weakness in her.

He took a small step toward her "Sparrow?"

She had no defense against him. No defense but her knife. If he thought she was a monster, then she'd show him what a true monster really was. Sparrow ripped her knife out of her boot and held it in front of her, ready to attack. "No!"

Jared's gaze hardened. "Drop it, now."

"Stay back."

"All you're doing is convincing me that my brother was telling the truth."

"I'll make you regret this, Jared Crowe. "

He lunged and she dove sideways, tucking into a roll before lunging back up on her feet. The move repositioned them so that she was on the side of the woods and Jared stood at the entrance to the cave.

"You and I both know you won't make it. Hell, if it weren't for me, you'd be dead right now."

"Oh, I'll make it all right." Sparrow pulled the knife back and took aim. "And you know if it weren't for me, you'd be dead too."

Jared tensed. The moment he sprung, she threw her knife straight at him and took off running.

***

Jared ducked. Still, the blade grazed his cheek and he felt warm blood trickle down his neck. He took off after her with a roar, crashing through the woods like a man possessed. She'd gotten a small head start on him, but not nearly as much as she would've if the knife had sunk into his flesh as she'd intended.

The hill sloped sharply down and he watched as she flew through the woods, pumping her arms faster and faster. She was going to kill herself if she didn't watch out. "Sparrow!"

She didn't break pace, so he zigzagged behind her, dodging tree limbs and rocks. She jumped over a fallen log like she had wings on her feet. And he followed.

She wouldn't get away from him. He wouldn't let her. He had to have her, had to keep her with him until he knew the truth. Jared forced his breathing to slow, calming his heart. He'd pursued plenty of criminals before, and this should be no different.

He pushed himself harder, breathing in through his nose and out through his mouth, efficient like a machine. Closed the gap between them until he could practically reach out and grab her hair.

Sparrow glanced over her shoulder and cried out. She banked left, trying to throw him, but he was ready for her feint. Jared pounced and tackled her to the ground, making sure to roll beneath her so that he took the brunt of the fall.

Sparrow struggled in his grip, scratching and kicking. Jared locked his arms around her and simply squeezed until she stopped struggling.

"Let me go," she screamed, making one last half-hearted attempt to escape his grip.

"Never." His words must have fueled her. Sparrow managed to rip one arm free and throw a punch. Jared cocked his head to the right, so her knuckles only grazed the ridge of his jaw. He shackled her wrist and flipped her over, pinning her beneath him. He shoved her arms to the ground above her head. "Stop it, dammit. I don't want to hurt you."

"Too late for that," she spat. She glared up at him with venom, but he could also see the pain lurking beneath the anger.

A drop of his blood dripped from his face onto hers. "You threw a knife at me."

"I don't usually miss what I aim at." Sparrow struggled again and he leaned the full weight of his body into hers, effectively cutting off all movement.

"So you were trying to kill me then?"

"No, I don't kill people. Just wound." Their faces were inches apart. Her hot breaths fanning his face from exertion.

Against his will, Jared felt his cock rise to the occasion. "Obviously. Otherwise I wouldn't be here in the first place."

She'd shown him just how effective she was with a knife. The doubts he'd had about her abilities to hurt his brother grew thinner. And then there was the fact that she was struggling so wildly to get back to her family, the same family who had nearly destroyed him and Hoyt. "You used me."

Guilt slammed into him, but he ignored it. She needed to understand that she was coming with him whether she liked it or not. And the last thing she needed from him right now was sympathy. "You mean you used me, don't you? You took me prisoner first. You tried to seduce me for information first."

"But I let you go."

Jared placed his face directly in front of hers. "Don't expect the same from me."

"I hate you." Maybe if she'd screamed the words it would've been better, but her whisper was full of loathing and pain. Her aim struck true and he jerked back, giving her precious space to wiggle free of his grasp. He had seduced her, but not to use her. The need he'd felt for her had been too strong to ignore. It was like she'd taken control and he'd been helpless to stop it.

Sparrow rose to her feet and he followed. He needed her almost more than he needed to breathe, and yet he couldn't trust her. Not yet. Maybe never. He had to get to his brother. Had to find out the truth. And so help him, if she really had been the one to torture Hoyt...

"I'm sorry you feel that way." Jared reached down and pulled the rope from his bag. "It's going to make for a long journey together."

Sparrow stared at the rope and shuddered. Then she shocked him to his core by walking back to him, her gaze wary. "No rope, Jared. I can't take it anymore."

He studied her, watching for the slightest indication that she was lying. "I can't trust you not to run."

Sparrow held out her wrists and he saw the raw wounds from before, wounds he'd given to her. She squared her shoulders and looked him dead in the eye. "They hurt."

If she'd acted defeated, or submissive in the least, he would have thought she was lying. But Sparrow was a fighter. She was only showing him that his actions had consequences. Shit. "Okay. No rope. But you walk in front of me, no more than a foot at all times."

She graced him with a nod and dropped her hands. "Fine."

His gaze wandered back to her wrists again. Fuck. He couldn't leave her like that. "Hold on, I've got some ointment and bandages."

Jared dropped the rope and squatted to dig through his bag. "I'll need to wash the scrapes first." Where was his disinfectant? He finally located it and stood. Sparrow had made her way to the edge of the small clearing. "Don't," he said, the word simple but full of warning.

"You used me." Sparrow eased a foot back. The hill sloped down sharply behind her. If she weren't careful, she would tumble down the side of the mountain. She'd been nearly unconscious last night, so she hadn't seen the steep incline.

"Sparrow, stop now. You're going to fall and kill yourself." Jared tensed, ready to launch after her.

"I'd rather be dead than be with you." Her words cut him like the knife she'd thrown earlier. Only this time, it hurt much worse.

"Don't be stupid. You almost died last night. You and I both know you won't survive out here. Not now. Not like this." Dressed in his T-shirt and those panties.

"You know nothing about me and what I can and can't do." Sparrow lifted her chin. "And now you never will." She took off down the steep slope without warning, her blonde head disappearing.

Jared dropped everything and ran after her. The slope was littered with rocks and small tree sprouts. Sparrow dodged them all, zigzagging down the hill, picking up speed as she went. Jared accelerated after her, doing his best to dodge the obstacles in his path, vowing with every step that he'd tie her up and never free her after this. She was totally unreliable. She continued to take his weaknesses and use them against him.

They were about halfway down when Jared leapt forward and made a grab for her. Sparrow looked over her shoulder and squealed. She ducked left, barely missing a tree limb to the throat. Jared's heart plunged into his stomach at the thought of what might have happened.

"Sparrow!"

She glanced back again and that was all it took. Her foot caught and she tripped, her momentum throwing her downhill. He watched in horror as she threw her hands over her head and was flung across the harsh terrain. Jared ran faster, harder. He had to stop her. Had to save her.

The bottom of the hill approached at high speed. Down there, the trees grew thick and large. If she slammed into a trunk going this fast, her bones would break. Adrenaline fueled his legs and Jared gained on her. She looked like a rag doll being thrown down the mountain. *Almost there.* He could practically reach her.

Bam! Sparrow hit a small tree and rolled sideways. Her arms went around her stomach, but her body kept going. Jared's heart pounded hard in his ears, drowning out everything else. *Faster. Get to her.*

Sparrow slammed into a boulder next, and the huge rock stopped her completely. Jared raced to her side. She didn't move.

The seconds it took to reach her seemed to stretch into hours. Jared ground to a stop and dropped to his knees. Sparrow lay on her side, her eyes closed and blood running down her face from a wound on her temple. Jared leaned back on his heels and roared with fury. Too much. The last few days had been too much.

His brother. Sparrow. The mountain. Miss Kay. His mind seemed ready to explode.

His hands shook as he checked her for broken bones. Fuck, he was losing it. She was his punishment for failing to protect Hoyt. This dangerous, confusing woman he could not trust but could not stop thinking about. Jared gently rolled her to her back and lifted her shirt, wincing at the bruise forming on her hip. At least the fall hadn't crushed her ribs.

He had to pull on all of his training to keep focus. He'd been in situations a million times worse without losing his shit, but this slip of a girl was fast stealing his discipline. Jared swept her whole body, checked her pulse. Everything looked fine except for her head wound. A goose egg had already popped up on the spot where her head had been struck. Jared took the edge of her shirt and gently dabbed at the wound, cleaning as much of the blood and dirt away as he could. When he finished and closely inspected the wound, he relaxed. She would have one hell of headache when she woke up, but she would wake up.

And then he would tan her ass for scaring him to death.

Chapter Twenty-two

A while later Sparrow awoke, her head throbbing. An ache that was made worse by the fact that Jared had slung her over his shoulder and was currently traipsing down a steep hill.

The day's events rushed back to her, and a surge of helpless anger hit her. He'd used her. And, gullible fool that she was, she had fallen for his charms.

Just like that time the Crowe boys had dared her to jump off that tree limb and swing from a high rope, she'd fallen hard. Only this time she hadn't broken her arm; she'd broken her heart.

Now her hands were bound behind her back and she was helpless. Helpless and alone with the most powerful man she'd ever encountered. A man who wanted her to suffer because he blamed her for doing something she hadn't done.

If her situation weren't so perilous, she would laugh. Her whole life she'd spent perfecting this tough-girl persona. She was legendary in these parts for her skill with the knife. Could throw farther and more accurately than anyone within a hundred miles, and now the very person she had fought so hard to create—to become—would be her downfall.

Fate was cruel.

Jared stopped and she realized they had reached the river's edge. There was his boat, tied to a fallen tree.

"I know you're awake. I've got to set you on your feet." Why was his voice so gentle? And why was he bothering to warn her? He could just dump her on the ground. Then he bent forward and eased her feet to the ground before slowly standing beside her, holding onto her arms so that when the wave of dizziness crashed over her she didn't crumple.

As soon as the world stopped spinning, and her head stopped pounding so hard that she couldn't see straight, Sparrow glanced up at her captor. He lifted a hand to her face and she instinctively flinched away. Some emotion flickered across his eyes then disappeared. He finished the action, gently brushing the hair back from her temple. "You got a nice goose egg there, but I think you'll be okay. How do you feel?"

"Like my head met the wrong end of a rock."

The corner of his mouth lifted in a smile, causing a small flutter in her chest. Damn the man. He wanted to punish her for a crime she hadn't committed, and here she was thinking about how nice his lips looked. *Idiot.* She had inherited more of her mother's DNA than she'd originally thought.

"I'm going to lift you into the boat, and it would be in your best interest not to struggle."

His boat floated a little ways out from the shore, and she could just see herself sinking to the bottom of the river, hands bound behind her back, drowning in three feet of water. No thank you. She would escape, that was a foregone conclusion. It was just a matter of when and a matter of how. "I'm all yours, sir."

Jared smile disappeared. Good, let him stay mad, she wasn't about to stroke his ego.

"You should remember your life is in my hands now. You should play nice."

Sparrow fluttered her lashes and gave him a smile. "Of course, anything you want, sir."

Jared growled and scooped her up. "Wildcat."

Sparrow didn't bother to answer, because he had no idea just how wild she could be. He stepped off the bank into the river and she tilted precariously to the side, but her only choice was to rely on his strength to keep her out of the water. Not that she couldn't swim if her hands were free. "Be careful!"

"You think I'm going to let a little water take you from me?"

Jared plopped her down on a hard bench in the boat before quickly giving her his back to untie them from the log. As soon as he bent forward, she planted her booted foot on his butt and gave a hard shove. Jared went flying into the water and came up with a roar.

"You looked like you needed a bath." Sparrow smirked. Squirrel always said she was really good at poking the bear.

But when his big hands bore down on the side of the boat and he leapt inside with an agility that amazed her, she started to rethink her decision. He was on her in the next second, his hand wrapping around her shoulders, forcing her backwards until she was nearly bent over the side. It seemed as if the gentle Jared had snapped and a primal beast had taken his place.

"You'll regret that." His voice was rough and harsh, his black eyes obsidian. Rivulets of water ran down his body and dripped onto her.

"Careful, you'll get my new shirt wet."

One second she was leaning backwards, the next he had tossed her over his lap and flipped the T-shirt up to expose her panty-clad bottom. "What are you doing?" she shrieked.

His answer was to deliver a smack right on her ass. "I told you not to test me." Smack!

The blow was loud but not that painful.

"You think I'm scared of a little spanking?" she asked.

Smack! She sucked in a breath and bit her lip. The sting wasn't so bad.

Smack! "You will listen to me." Smack! "You will not fight me." Smack!

The burn spread out across her skin, morphing into a sensation she could not name. The blows were landing a little harder and Sparrow could no longer keep her silence. She cried out, struggling from his grasp, but Jared's answer was another spank. This one landed directly below her butt cheeks, smacking her most private area. It sent shockwaves of awareness through her body and something else. She was getting aroused.

Shame filled her, hurting her worse than any small amount of pain she'd experienced from his spanking. How could she be aroused by this? How could she be aroused by a man who'd taken her captive? A man who didn't trust her?

Tears ran unchecked down her cheeks as he ripped her up from his lap, forcing her to sit across his legs. His features were still twisted with rage, but when he saw her tears, the hard line of his mouth softened. Before she could react, his lips covered hers and she responded with a wild abandon, craving his touch with an overwhelming yearning.

As Jared possessed her mouth, his hand fell between her legs and she spread them for him, eager for his touch. When he found her wet, he ripped back from her, his breathing harsh. "You're wet for me."

His fingers delved inside her panties, circling her most sensitive spot until she bucked into his hand and cried out for more. He drove his fingers into her without mercy, bringing forth moan after moan of pleasure. She felt his lips close over her bare nipple and realized he'd ripped her shirt up to suckle her there. The pleasure converged in the center of her body, building and building. Roaring filled her ears. Her body tensed. So close, so needing…

He stopped and withdrew his fingers, pulling her shirt down and sat her up. "What?"

It was then that the roaring grew louder and she realized the sound hadn't been coming from inside her own head—it was the helicopter appearing over the mountain.

Jared grabbed her hair, gently tilting her head back until she was forced to look into his eyes. "The next time I won't stop."

Chapter Twenty-three

Jared toed the thin red line of insanity. The girl who'd captured him and tried time and again to escape him, who'd maybe hurt Hoyt, had kicked him in the water. She deserved his anger. And he fucking wanted to bury his cock inside her so deep he never came out.

The only thing that gave him comfort was the way she was squirming on that bench, as eager for him as he was for her. But for once, she kept her mouth shut. Jared slammed the boat into reverse, pulling into the river, and sped straight toward the helicopter.

Thoughts, images, ideas of what he would do to her when he got her home consumed him. There was no use denying the primal instinct to take her. He longed to possess her.

Her sweet body responded to his so intensely, her little moans and reactions more erotic than anything he'd ever experienced. Her pussy had clenched around his finger tight and wet... fuck, his cock throbbed. He needed relief, but relief would be a long time coming.

He ran the boat up onto the opposite sandbar, killed the motor, and hopped down, then turned back to lift Sparrow out. The last time he'd left her unattended, she'd nearly escaped.

"You caught her." Merc's question was more of a statement as he stood in front of the helo, arms crossed, muscles bulging. Hunter and Cord followed him out.

Jared set Sparrow down on the sand and pushed her in front of him, reaching past her shoulder to grasp Merc's hand in greeting. "I always catch what I hunt."

Something clicked in Jared's head, and he realized Sparrow was only wearing his T-shirt and her panties. At least his shirt came down almost to her knees, essentially covering her. But a surge of jealousy took him unaware and he found himself stepping in front of her, blocking her from the gaze of his teammates. His most trusted friends. He didn't miss the look that Merc gave him after that telling action.

Jared prepared to defend his actions, but there was no need, Merc changed the subject. "Good thing you're here. Hoyt took a turn for the worse after we got off the phone. He's been calling out for you."

Fear and guilt shot through Jared. He'd been so consumed with Sparrow, he'd let thoughts of Hoyt fall to the wayside. "Tell me."

Sparrow leaned in close, and Jared glanced over his shoulder to see her pressing into his back. Her gaze was locked on Hunter, who now stood to their right and was looking at Sparrow like he wanted to kill her. It was probably the same way Jared had looked at her. Only for some reason, it wasn't okay this time. "She's mine. No one else touches her."

Hunter held silent for a long moment before moving away. Hunter was Task Force Scorpion's team leader. He took each soldier's life personally responsible. He'd saved Jared's life on more than one occasion, just as Jared had saved his. The members of the unit were as close as blood brothers. Each willing to give up his life for the others.

But Jared wasn't willing to give up Sparrow.

"Why don't we discuss this on the helicopter. Cord will take the boat home. But we need to get you to your brother pronto." Merc gestured to the open door of the small black helicopter.

"Roger." Jared picked Sparrow up and snapped her into the small padded seat of the helo. Her hands were bound behind her back, and he knew it was uncomfortable, and a small part of him enjoyed her discomfort. He made a mental note to check her wrists when they got safely in the air to make sure the binding wasn't too tight. He climbed in next to her, staking his territory. Merc followed and sat across from them as Hunter climbed into the pilot seat and cranked up the helicopter.

Cord pulled out in the boat and turned downriver just as the helicopter lifted off the ground. Tension stretched tight in Jared's insides. "Tell me now. Will he live?" The words cut him up like razor blades.

"I think so. But the doctor is there and she can fill you in when we land. It wasn't really his physical health I was talking about." Merc scrubbed a hand over his jaw, glanced first at Sparrow and then back at Jared. Sparrow held his teammate's gaze with her chin lifted, as defiant as ever.

Jared didn't miss her small flinch, but she didn't cower. His own mind was on the verge of breaking, He kept seesawing back and forth with the struggle of whether or not to believe her.

"It's his mind. He keeps rambling and calling out your name. No one can figure out what he's talking about, but he's just…he's not really lucid right now."

Jared's chest tightening until it felt like it would implode. "Does the doctor…" He couldn't finish the sentence. Couldn't even bear the thought of his brother losing it, locked up in some mental institution.

Jared was responsible; he should've been there sooner. He shouldn't have forced Hoyt to come with him in the first place.

"The doctor hopes hearing your voice will at least soothe him, get him through the worst of it."

The hour-long helicopter ride flew by. Hunter touched down in the field directly next to their headquarters on Hank James' property. Hank, a war veteran himself, was Hunter and Ranger's father. He'd allowed Task Force Scorpion to set up a temporary operating base on his property last year. The setup had proved incredibly useful for their covert ops, as Hank had plenty of land with access to the river and the biggest roads.

Jared didn't know how many acres Hank owned on Broken River Ranch. He had multiple dwellings and structures stretched out across the property. A large tan metal building had been converted into the team's headquarters. On the complete opposite end of the property, Hunter and his new wife, Evie, had just finished building a house. And now Jared and Hoyt Crowe had been set up in one of Hank's other ranch houses.

"Tell your old man how grateful I am to him for putting us up like this," Jared said to Hunter.

"No problem, man. He'd do it for any of us. I've got a Jeep waiting for you. Follow this road until it forks, then hang a right and you'll be at the house." Hunter handed Jared the keys.

Jared swallowed, unable to speak. He was so close to seeing his brother again. But what if Hoyt never really came back?

Merc clapped a hand on his shoulder. "Hey man, we're all here for you. I'll come with you, make sure you've got everything you need."

"Thanks." Jared didn't bother trying to hide the rough edge of emotion in his voice. Instead, he focused on moving forward. Without a word, he pulled Sparrow out of her seat and carried her to the waiting Jeep. Once she was secured in the backseat, Merc climbed into the passenger seat and Jared drove.

The fall air wasn't quite as chilly down here, but it still had a bite to it. Jared gunned it down the dirt road, dust flying behind him. The trees rushed by in a haze of green and orange. He took the turn Hunter had described and pulled to a stop in front of a white ranch-style house with a long rambling porch across the front.

"Get her for me, okay?" Jared waited on Merc to nod before exiting the Jeep and walking on shaking legs into the house. He couldn't let Sparrow distract him now, not when he was so close to seeing his brother. He was already so confused by her.

He slammed the front door open and rushed through it, only to come to a grinding halt. It was so silent. Was he too late? His heart sped up as fear licked down his spine. An agonized moan came from the hallway to his right. Jared ran in that direction, stopping abruptly when he came to the first doorway.

Dr. Jane Hartsfield stood with her back to the door. Hoyt lay on his stomach on the bed with his eyes closed, the sheets kicked off, his skin pale and sweaty. An IV and various other electronic devices were hooked up to him.

Fresh white bandages covered most of his body, including the left side of his face. Jared watched as Hoyt twitched in his sleep, his eye darting beneath a closed lid.

Hoyt jerked and screamed out loud, twisting as if in agony. "Jared! Don't leave me."

"Hoyt, this is Dr. Hartsfield, and you're safe here." The doctor tried to place a hand on Hoyt's head, but he just bowed up off the mattress. "Hoyt, listen to me. You are safe. I won't let anyone hurt you."

"Not her. Not her, please. Make him stop." Hoyt's cries tore something dark loose inside Jared and he had to grab onto the doorframe to keep from falling to his knees. Hoyt jerked and the IV pulled from his arm, spilling Hoyt's blood.

Jared pulled himself from his stupor and dove for his brother's arm. Dr. Hartsfield grabbed a bandage. "Hold him still, I'll have to tape that one shut." Jared couldn't manage to speak. His brother was as pale as death, tossing his head back and forth on the pillow.

She bandaged his hand. "You need to talk to him. Let him hear your voice."

Jared was lost and locked in his own world of regret. "What can I say?"

"I don't care. Just talk and hold him still." The doc went about checking all the electronics as Jared stared at his brother, his mouth suddenly dry.

"Hoyt, it's me, Jared. I'm here." Hoyt stilled, but as soon as Jared stopped speaking, he started to thrash again. "I've got you brother. You're safe, with me. Don't worry about anything. I'm going to take care of you, but you've got to calm down before you hurt yourself."

Hoyt seemed to settle, and even though Jared didn't have a clue what he was saying, he kept on talking.

"That's good," the doctor said calmly. "Can you grab his other hand? I need to replace the IV, and it's the second time I've tapped that arm." Dr. Hartsfield walked around the bed and started touching Hoyt's arm, searching for a vein. Jared leaned over and took his brother's other arm, holding him to the bed.

Hoyt's breathing was shallow and rapid, and sweat drenched his hair and pillow. "Can't you give him something for the pain?"

"I have. He shakes it off faster than most. I've avoided tying him to the bed, but if he keeps thrashing around like that, I'll have no choice." Doc met Jared's gaze, communicating silently with them. The last thing a soldier rescued from captivity needed was to be bound.

"Okay, I'll hold him. Can you give him something to calm him?" Jared felt so helpless as she inserted the needle into Hoyt's other arm.

"Yes, I will as soon as I get the IV in." She taped the needle to his skin then plugged the tube into the free end. When the clear liquid from the IV bag started to flow, Dr. Hartsfield pulled a syringe out of her pocket. "This is a sedative. I can give him a dose every four hours. We are just going on three right now. I'll give him this one dose early, but he can't take much more. If he doesn't start to calm, I'll have to admit him to the hospital."

Jared swallowed and nodded. A hospital meant involving the police. Which would entail handing Sparrow over to them. "I'll stay with him. Get him to calm down."

When she looked at him, there was pity in her gaze, and Jared hated it. "I hope so. He's been through a lot of trauma, both physical and mental. I've done what I can for his injuries, now it's up to him on the rest."

"Will he wake up?"

"There is nothing stopping him from waking once the sedative wears off. But Jared, there's no guarantee your brother will be the same man he was before."

Raw acid burned Jared's throat and made his eyes water. All Jared had ever wanted was to protect his younger brother. That's why Hoyt smiled more than Jared. That's why he laughed more. That's why he was able to sleep at night when Jared's rest was wracked by nightmares. Hoyt had been so young when they escaped Crowe Mountain; Jared had thought the memories of their captivity long erased from his mind. And he'd done his best to keep it that way.

Now that decision had been taken out of his hands.

***

Sparrow stood just inside the door, watching Hoyt struggle, with Merc holding her arm. From the doctor's haggard expression, she could tell Hoyt had been doing that for a while now. Anguish ate at her. Jimbo's handiwork had left deep wounds, wounds from which Hoyt might never recover.

Sparrow swore right then and there that she would kill Jimbo. He'd tormented enough people to deserve death. When she heard the warning the doctor delivered to Jared, a knot of dread unfurled in her belly. Jared already blamed her for this. There would be no escaping the blame if Hoyt was never in the right mind to explain.

Jared led the doctor from the room, brushing past Sparrow with a look of rage. She backed up a step and bumped into the solid wall that was Merc. Placing his hands on her shoulders, he anchored her where she stood. "You go nowhere without him."

Jared returned a second later without the doctor and grabbed Sparrow's arm in a bruising grip. "Where did you set up the room?"

Merc gestured to the second door past Hoyt's. It had large heavy-looking locks. Merc inserted a key and opened the door. "We thought you'd want to keep her close. Your bedroom is connected through a shared door."

The room was much larger than her own, and besides the sturdy four-poster wooden bed, there was a dresser and two nightstands. Another shut door stood on the right side of the room. Merc followed her gaze and said, "That door goes to Jared's bedroom."

Jared's grip tightened painfully on her shoulders as he propelled her forward. "Thanks for setting this up."

"Anything I can do to help. I'll stick around for a while and make sure everything is okay."

"No need. I've got this." Only Jared wasn't looking at Merc when he spoke. His ice-cold gaze had locked on to her.

"You sure it's a good idea to be alone with her right now? I'm more than happy to stay."

Jared finally broke his stare and looked at Merc, who was leaning casually in the doorway. Oh, how she hoped he would stay.

"I've got this. I'll check in later."

Sighing, Merc pushed away from the door and handed Jared the key. "Roger."

After he left, Sparrow became aware of just how alone they were. And just how dependent her life was on the man standing before her. A man who once again looked like he wanted to strangle her.

Dammit, she wasn't some simpering female. She didn't do this thing, and she'd be damned if she cowered under his misdirected anger. "I didn't do anything to your brother. You know it. Deep inside you know it."

"My brother says you did. Who do you think I believe?" Jared's voice cracked with emotion.

"Your brother was out of his mind with fever. He didn't know who I was."

"Shut up! My brother is half dead, but he's still asking me to keep him away from her. *Her.* Who is that if not you?" Jared advanced on Sparrow and she retreated until her knees bumped into the footboard.

She was trapped. "I swear, he—"

Jared roared his fury and Sparrow wished in that instant she could run away. But she was imprisoned between the animal he had become and the bed.

"One more word out of your mouth and I'll tie you to the bed. Do you understand?"

She trembled and cursed herself for the fear. Her whole life she'd been fighting bullies who tried to keep her down. And now she had to fight the man to whom she'd willingly given her body and soul. "You wouldn't."

Jared collected himself, but that crazed fire in his eyes was still there when he yanked her up by the arms and tossed her onto the bed. He grabbed her wrists and bound them to the center of the headboard. Then, without another word, he turned and left room.

"Jared! Don't do this!" She was so angry with him, and yet what remained of her heart was breaking.

He returned a few minutes later with more bindings. "I'll do to you what you did to me. Let's see how well you like it.

He grabbed the closest ankle and she kicked out, but her efforts were futile against his strength. He bound each foot to a separate bedpost, leaving her spread eagled and half naked. "You're going to regret this. I swear to God you'll regret it."

He knelt on the bed, his grin humorless, and wrapped a gag around her mouth, effectively silencing her comeback.

Sparrow was completely vulnerable to him. Humiliation swamped her. She'd trusted this man so much, and he still didn't trust her. He still didn't believe that what they felt for each other was real. And she had no idea how she could change his mind.

But she would die before she let him see how much he was hurting her.

"You can look at me like you want to kill me all you want. But you'll stay like this until I'm ready to deal with you."

Jared strode from the room and slammed the door behind him, the ominous click of a lock snapping into place sealing her fate.

Chapter Twenty-four

Jared shoved his hands through his hair and stormed down the hall. His mind was twisting in so many directions he felt ready to explode

Part of him already regretted his actions against Sparrow, but part of him was still imagining her slicing her blade into his brother's flesh. If he stopped and asked himself, really asked himself, he didn't believe her capable of it. Not unless she was the best actress who had ever lived. Maybe those were simply his brother's feverish ramblings...

Jared turned the corner back into his brother's bedroom to see Hayden James, Hunter and Ranger's little sister, sitting on the edge of the mattress, holding Hoyt's hand and stroking his arm and face.

"What are you doing in here?"

She looked up at his voice, tears streaming down her face. "Who could do this to him?"

Jared wished he had a straight answer for her, because with every minute he doubted it was Sparrow.

"Don't worry. I think we've got her."

Hoyt drew in a shuddering breath, twitching even as the sedative flowed through his veins.

Helpless agony surged through Jared, completely taking over his logic. He wanted to hurt something or someone so bad his entire body shook.

"Her? You think a woman did this to him? Women love your brother. I can't believe one would actually be capable of hurting him."

"Before my brother passed out, he all but pointed his finger at her." The words delivered in a voice that was shaking more than he'd like, and the memory of finding Hoyt chained up in that rotten shack sent another shiver through him.

Hayden wiped away her tears with a shaking hand, her pale blue eyes haunted. "I want to see her. I want to see the person that did this to him."

"No, you stay away from her."

"You're not the only one that loves him, you know?"

Her statement caught him off guard. Jared pulled his head out of his ass and studied her. She was caressing his brother with such gentleness.

Hayden was in love with Hoyt. How had he not realized that sooner? Hoyt had been the one to stand by Hayden after her betrayal this summer. She'd been taken advantage of by one of their Team members, who'd been married at the time. And who'd also been Hayden's brother's best friend. Still, while Jared had known they were close, he'd assumed it was more of a big brother kind of relationship.

Apparently, Jared wasn't as good at reading women as he'd thought.

"Hayden, I don't want you near her. Do you understand?"

Her gaze hardened. "If she really did it, I want you to hurt her. Hurt her like she hurt him."

He ran a hand through his hair and sighed. There wasn't a chance in hell he could hurt Sparrow. Not even if Hoyt woke proclaiming her guilt. He was in too deep. "I'm not sure how long you've been here, but I think it's time for you to go home."

"I'm not leaving him."

What the hell was up with all of these stubborn women in his life? "Do I need to call your brothers? You know they'll listen to me."

"You can call the entire police force of the state of Mississippi, cause that's what it will take to drag me from your brother's side." Dammit, tears were building in her eyes again and that vulnerable little tremble started on her chin. A chin she poked out stubbornly.

"Your dad then. You shouldn't be here." But he hadn't chosen the right words. He knew that instantly from the triumphant gleam in her eyes.

"Daddy's the one who told me to stay as long as I needed."

Motherfucker, the girl was good. "You could give your brothers a run for their money, you know?"

She nodded and sniffled. "They say the same thing." And then her gaze softened. "Why don't you go take a shower and clean up? Not to be indelicate, but you look like hell."

For the first time in the last forty-eight hours, Jared took notice of his appearance. He'd been traipsing through the woods for days without a shower or bath. He didn't need to take a big whiff to guess how he smelled. But he didn't want to leave his brother.

Hayden must have sensed his thoughts. "I'm not leaving his side. If anything changes, I'll come get you, but I think you're pretty safe to take a quick shower. Besides, do you want him to see you like that when he wakes up?"

She was right, but still…

"I don't care if I'm in the shower, come and get me if anything changes in the least. I'll leave the door unlocked."

"I promise."

Jared stepped out of the room and turned down the hall. Merc had said his bedroom joined up to Sparrow's. He strode past her door without stopping, resisting the urge to lean in and check on her. She was fine. He'd done no worse to her than she had done to him.

He entered the next door on the left to find another sturdy wooden bed, just like the one to which he'd bound Sparrow, half naked and helpless. His gut tightened with lust.

He needed a cold shower to take his mind off his captive. His mood was skating the line between lust and blind fury, and every little thing that happened threatened to tip him in a different direction.

His bag lay on the bed and Jared quickly dug into it, pulling out toiletries and a change of clothes. Once he had what he needed, he headed for the shower.

The bathroom boasted a claw bathtub beneath a sunny window, a long granite vanity with two sinks, and a large tiled shower. He stripped and turned on the water, stepping beneath the spray. Jared leaned forward and placed his forearms on the cold tile wall, letting his head fall between his hands.

His chest tightened like a vice. He'd failed to protect Hoyt. He'd failed his brother. The violent swirl of emotions struck hard and warred within him, needing an outlet.

He took a deep breath and tried to get under control. The last time he'd acted on his emotions, he'd nearly killed them all.

***

Sparrow wasn't sure how long she lay alone in the dark room, but it was long enough for her bladder to shrink to the size of a tiny balloon. She hadn't thought of bodily functions on the trip here. She'd been too concerned with simply functioning. Period.

She yelled, but the sound was muffled by the gag. Part of her hated Jared Crowe. Hated him for what he'd done to her, for the fact that he still refused to fully believe her, for the way he'd treated her like a whore. But another part of her, for which she felt nothing but disgust, felt mercy for him. On some level, she even understood.

God what a weakling you are.

She'd allowed what she felt for him, what they'd done together, to steal her reasoning and turn her mind into a puddle of mush. And now she was actually making excuses for his behavior. She was sick.

She'd caught a glimpse of his brother laid out on the bed, as white as the sheet covering his body. It was obvious that despite the scar running down the side of his face, Hoyt was a very handsome man. Or he used to be. Sparrow cringed, knowing just how much Jimbo had enjoyed destroying that pretty face.

But what hurt her even worse than seeing Hoyt in such pain was the agony etched into Jared's features as he stared down at his brother. He truly loved Hoyt—with a depth that Sparrow envied. She'd wanted a relationship like that her whole life, longed for someone to share such a deep connection.

The minutes stretched into hours. The need to pee grew until it was strong enough to make her squirm. Sparrow had no way of knowing what time it was or how long she had been there. They'd boarded up the window so tight that not even a hint of sunlight filtered through. Even the table lamp was turned off, enclosing her in complete darkness. But she didn't mind the darkness, not really. What bothered her was the not knowing. Would Hoyt be okay? Would he ever wake up? Or would Jared hate her forever? God, why did that thought hurt her so much?

What she wouldn't give to be back in her own trailer hanging out with Squirrel. Maybe even helping him check traps. No matter how awful her life was in the mountains, it was still her home. The only home she'd ever known.

In the space of one day, she'd been forcefully torn from everything she'd ever known and thrust into a hopeless future.

Fatigue pulled at her eyes. She'd been through so much. Her head hurt and her hip ached. Maybe if she got some sleep, she'd see a way out of this mess. And tomorrow, she could face the day with perspective. The kind that didn't involve panting over Jared.

Chapter Twenty-five

Sparrow jerked awake, her heart beating fast enough to crack her sternum, sensing a presence in the room. She couldn't see anything in the darkness, but she knew someone was there. She tried to talk, but the gag muffled her voice.

Without any ability to move or speak, she was forced to listen to the person's footsteps as they walked around the bed. She craned her head in the direction of the sound, fear choking off her air. If it were Jared, he would have already spoken.

No, this was someone else.

The lamp clicked on and Sparrow blinked, temporarily blinded. When her vision cleared, she stared up at a young woman, about her own size, with long blonde hair and beautiful blue eyes. Eyes that were filled with loathing.

"You are the one? You hurt Hoyt?" Her voice had a strong southern accent, but it was soft and melodious.

Sparrow tried to respond, but the gag silenced her.

The girl reached for it and pulled it out of Sparrow's mouth. "Thank you." Her mouth and throat were parchment dry, her lips cracked from being stretched, but at least she could talk.

"I didn't do it for you. Answer my question." The girl crossed her arms.

"Could you get me some water? My mouth is really dry."

"Not until you tell me. Did you hurt him?"

Sparrow watched the tears forming in the girl's eyes, knew from how red rimmed they were that she'd been crying. Sympathy tugged at her conscience. "No. I didn't touch him."

"Then why did he say you did?"

"I don't know. He was out of it. I was standing there in front of him…maybe I'm just the first thing he saw after he came to." Maybe Sparrow could talk her into freeing her. "What's your name?"

"Hayden. Hoyt doesn't lie." Hayden's cheeks stained pink and she briskly wiped at her tears.

She would have to play her cards just right. Hayden was young, and most definitely vulnerable. If Sparrow could just get her hands free she could use her to escape. "I didn't say he did. I think he was disoriented. Do I look like I could do that?"

Hayden studied her for a long time. "You don't look like you could, but I know enough to realize that doesn't mean anything."

"Please, can I have a sip of water?" Sparrow pleaded, hoping she sounded pathetic enough to get her way.

Hayden sighed, "Okay. I'll be right back." She left and returned a moment later with a bottle, which she uncapped and held to Sparrow's lips. Sparrow drank greedily, savoring each drop. When she'd gotten enough, she nodded and Hayden set the bottle aside.

"What happened to your head?" Hayden indicated Sparrow's temple.

I was rash and stupid and almost got away. "I fell and met the wrong end of a rock."

Hayden winced and Sparrow felt an inkling of hope. The girl seemed sympathetic enough. "Hayden, I haven't gotten to pee since yesterday. Any way you could take me to the bathroom?" Maybe this could be her way out.

She backed up immediately, and Sparrow knew she'd pushed too fast. "No. I can't. I'll get Jared."

"No! Wait. Don't get him."

"Why not? I'm sure he'd let you go to the restroom."
Hayden hovered near the bed, leaning toward the door.

Come on, Sparrow think. Why would she not want
him to take her there? "I-I can't go in front of him." Sparrow
did her best to look frightened and embarrassed.

And it worked. Hayden approached the bed again and
Sparrow's heart leapt into her throat.

"I'm sure he'd give you privacy. He's really not a
bad guy."

Sparrow shook her head, "No, he wouldn't. He made
me go in the woods with him standing there." She held back
her snort—as if she'd cared. When Mother Nature called, you
answered. Plain and simple.

Sparrow chanced a peek to see Hayden put her hand
around her throat, her stance shifting from foot to foot. Time
to drive it home.

"Please, I was so mortified. I've never done that
before, ever. I-I-I don't think I can take it." Sparrow
squeezed her eyes shut and turned her head, as if fighting
back tears.

"Oh, no. I don't know. He'd kill me if I untied you. I
mean..."

"No, I wouldn't kill you. But I'd be fucking pissed."
Jared's deep voice startled them both. Sparrow jerked around
to look at the door and Hayden jumped a clear foot.

"Hayden, didn't I warn you to stay out of here?"
Jared walked into the room and took Hayden's hand. A wave
of jealousy overtook Sparrow. What was she to him anyway?

"I'm sorry. I just had to see for myself." Hayden
glanced at her then back to Jared. "I'm not so sure she could
have done it, Jared. She's so petite."

Jared cupped Hayden's cheek and it was all Sparrow
could do not to scream. He obviously felt something for the
girl. His touch was too familiar. Too gentle. Dammit, why
did she care if he was in love with another woman? He
certainly didn't seem to care too much for her.

"She may be, but she's deadly."

"No, Hayden, you're right. There is no way I could have done that to a grown man," Sparrow said.

"Shut up," Jared snapped and then turned to look at the beautiful blonde. Sparrow saw red.

"Go on back to my brother's room. I'll be there in just a minute," Jared said, gentling his voice.

Hayden bit her lip and looked at Sparrow again.

"Don't leave me alone with him, please!" Sparrow asked.

"Enough! Hayden, get out of here. I'll deal with her."

Tears appeared in the girl's eyes and she ran from the room. Sparrow watched in sorrow as her one chance at possible escape slipped away.

"You took advantage of her," Jared shut the door and then came to tower over her. He'd showered and changed clothes, his clean scent filling her nostrils.

"Can you blame me? She was an easy mark, plus, you haven't really left me a choice have you? I'm not going to just lay here and let you hurt me."

Jared put his knee on the bed next to her and the mattress dipped under his weight. "Who said I was going to hurt you?" He placed a hand on her exposed knee and traced it lightly up her thigh. Chills raced after his touch and Sparrow clenched her jaw, fighting the sensation.

"You did. Many times."

Jared switched to her other leg, tracing just high enough for her to feel the heat from his hand near her core, but stopping before he actually touched her there. He repeated the motion, softly caressing her thighs and barely avoiding her core. "I was angry."

He lifted the hem of her shirt, exposing her belly. Sparrow started to shake. "What are you doing?"

"I'm touching you." He continued with the light circles around her navel. She sucked in, hollowing out her stomach in an attempt to escape his touch.

"Stop. I don't want this," Sparrow said.

"Then why are there goose bumps across your skin?" Jared continued.

"I'm cold." That was a lie. His fingers were setting her on fire.

"Maybe you would like a hot bath to warm you up?" Jared held her gaze.

A bath would be heaven on earth. She was coated in dirt and sticks and dried blood. She could almost imagine how terrible she looked and smelled. But why would he offer her such a luxury? "What do you want?"

"I want your cooperation. I will untie you and let you take a bath if you promise not to try and run." Jared continued to caress her belly, sending little waves of pleasure rippling over her flesh.

Sparrow licked her dry lips. "That's it? Just promise not to run? Done. Now untie me."

Jared's smile was too secretive, too knowing as he stood and untied her feet and then her hands. Tingles of blood flow licked her fingers when she finally lowered them. Jared helped her up, but he left her hands tied together. When her feet were on the floor, Sparrow said, "My hands."

"Of course." Jared produced a knife from his pocket and Sparrow gasped when she saw it was hers. He cut through her bindings and tucked it back in his pants.

"That's mine." Sparrow gingerly rubbed her wrists.

"Spoils of war. Come on." Jared led her through the connecting door. Sparrow did a quick scan of his room—the exit door was shut and shutters were drawn over the single window. "They are all locked, and I have the key." He propelled her past a large bed with a beautiful but worn quilt and led her into a bathroom as big as her living room.

Sparrow let out a low whistle. "Fancy."

"I've already run your bath. I didn't have any women's clothes so I laid out another one of my shirts."

A black shirt lay folded in a square on top of a long gleaming vanity. There was a towel and cloth beside it. Sparrow walked over to the vanity and ran her hands over the shiny surface. She nearly squealed when she saw the bath tub.

"The toilet is through the door there." Jared indicated a smaller door in the corner and Sparrow rushed to it, slamming it closed behind her. Once she had emptied her over full bladder, she emerged into an empty bathroom.

Holy crap, he had really meant it. She could have a bath in this real live movie star tub. Sparrow shucked her shirt and panties in record time. She dipped a finger in the water and almost cried. It was steaming hot and perfect. She stepped in, careful to hold on to the high sides, and sat, submerging herself up to her chest.

Nothing in her life had ever felt this good.

Sparrow closed her eyes and leaned back. Thoughts of Jared intruded on her peace. Why was he softening? Had Hoyt woke? She ruthlessly pushed the thoughts away, greedily wanting to relish every second. When the water started to turn tepid, Sparrow dunked her head beneath the water and grabbed a bottle of shampoo off the shelf behind the tub. She quickly washed her hair, savoring the sweet smelling shampoo. Then she grabbed the cloth and washed her body, frowning when she got to her dirty feet. No wonder Jared had wanted her to have a bath; she was filthy.

The tub was so deep, she had to stand to wash the rest of her body. Sparrow grimaced when she skimmed her hands over her bruised hip. She was lucky that it was the worst of her injuries, of course. She could have easily broken her bones in that fall.

"Now, that is a beautiful sight." Jared's voice filled the bathroom and Sparrow fought the urge to dive under the cover of water.

"So much for a peaceful bath."

He scanned her from top to bottom and lingered on her hips. He strode forward and reached for her. Sparrow plopped down in the water, not ready to give up her safe haven yet.

"Your hip looks worse."

She shrugged. "I don't feel a thing."

Jared sighed and a look of resignation crossed his features. In the bright light of the bathroom, she could see the lines of fatigue and worry etched around his eyes and mouth. He'd trimmed his beard, leaving only a dark sexy shadow covering his jaw. "How's your head?"

She'd almost forgotten about that. The pounding and the headache had eased earlier today. "Terrible."

"That was a stupid move on your part." He backed up, leaned against the counter and crossed his ankles.

"More like desperate." It had broken her to think he'd taken her virginity without feeling anything for her, that she'd let this man use her.

Jared made a sound close to a growl. "You will not ever do that again, do you understand?"

Sparrow dropped the cloth into the tub, knowing her time was over. "Can you just go, please, so I can dry off?"

He shook his head slowly from side to side. "I think I'd rather stay."

The thought of performing such an intimate act in front of him filled her with embarrassment and longing. But when he arched an eyebrow, daring her to protest, her back stiffened. If he thought she'd cower from showing a little skin, he had another thing coming. Sparrow placed her hand on the rim of the tub and stood, making sure to take her sweet time stepping over the edge and onto the fur rug on the floor.

Sparrow sauntered over to the towel he'd left out, making sure to bend a little more than necessary to grab it. Sparrow Pickney cowered from no man.

Chapter Twenty-six

Sparrow bent over to grab the towel, and all the oxygen seeped from the room. Any thoughts Jared might have possessed about embarrassing her evaporated. The girl was shameless, and fuck all, he loved it.

When she turned and began drying off, her movements sensual, he rubbed a hand over his mouth, fighting to keep the groan inside. All the blood rushed from his head straight into his cock. She was an enigma. He'd taken her virginity, proof she'd never experienced another man's intimate touch, and yet she moved like a seductress. Punishing him by turning his plans on him. Before he knew it, Jared was crossing the room, his feet taking him to her of their own accord.

When he finally stood before her, she clutched the towel between them, and it was then he saw her hands shake. Not so bold after all.

Her hair hung long down her back, and her freshly scrubbed skin soft and silky to the touch. "You're driving me crazy."

She stiffened. "I'm not trying to. All you have to do is release me. You'll never have to see me again."

"Never." The thought of losing her now sent a wave of fear through him. She belonged with him. "You're mine."

He drew her to him, slamming his mouth down over hers. She gave a weak protest and then wrapped her hands around his neck, pulling him down to her. The towel fell to the floor between them, and then her naked chest was pressed into his, driving him past reason.

Jared cupped her ass, lifting her and wrapping her legs around his waist. He turned and set her on the bathroom counter, closing his lips over her nipple, his eyes sliding shut in pleasure. "We shouldn't do this, but God I want you so bad."

She arched into him, panting. "Don't stop."

He stood and ripped off his shirt, needing to feel her flesh against his own. "Never."

He slipped a hand between them, and when he found her wet and hot for him he nearly came in his pants. Jared knelt before her, pushing her knees wide as he lowered his head between her legs and licked her clit with long, slow movements. Sparrow gasped, her fingers digging into his hair. Fueled by her response, he sucked her clit between his lips, lapping at her until she arched into him uncontrollably. He took her like that until she cried out and he tasted her juices as she came.

Feeling as if he would die if he didn't bury himself inside her, Jared stood and ripped off his pants. Then he yanked her off the counter, turned her around and drove into her from behind in one deep thrust. "Jared!" She screamed and slapped a hand on the mirror in front of her, the other grabbing onto the counter for support.

All he could manage was a growl as he gripped her hips and slammed into her over and over. He watched her in the mirror, watched her eyes grow heavy lidded and her mouth open with a whimper each time he thrust. He was so close, and he could see she was too. He reached around her and flicked her sensitive clit until she convulsed around him, milking his own orgasm free.

Jared fell forward, catching himself on his arms to keep from crushing her. Sparrow laid her cheek against the counter and closed her eyes, breathing hard. Seeing her so replete from pleasure filled him with a sense of contentment and intensified his feeling of possession.

"You're so responsive. So beautiful."

She smiled and hummed when he skimmed a finger down her back. Although he wanted to stay there all night, Jared forced himself to pull out. He handed her back her towel, wanting to cry when she wrapped it around her body. Then he heard her stomach growl and realized he hadn't fed her. "Put on your shirt. I'll get you some food."

"Okay." Sparrow pulled on his T-shirt, and seeing her in his clothes did something strange to his insides. He buttoned up his pants and pulled her into his bedroom, through the connecting doors into hers.

Her eyebrows swooped down in confusion. "I thought we were getting food?"

"I'll get you food. I'll be back in just a minute." At least he hoped he had food, he hadn't explored the kitchen yet to see if it was stocked.

"Can't I go with you?" She was looking up at him, her eyes luminous.

"I'm sorry, but no." He watched her hopeful expression fall and the relaxed curve of her smile drop. His anger surfaced. What did she expect him to do? Just forget everything? Forget Hoyt's accusations? He had to know for sure, it was the only way…

"Jared, how long are you going to keep me here?"

The question caught him off guard and he answered without thought, "Until Hoyt wakes up."

She wrapped her arms around her middle. "And what's going to happen when he tells you I wasn't involved?"

The question brought him back a step. This question of her innocence had kept niggling at him lately. At some moments, he felt so certain. At others, less so. But if it were true, if she really hadn't done it, he'd kidnapped her for no good reason. "We'll know what happened when he wakes up."

Her eyes deepened from gold to amber. "And what will you do if he doesn't wake up?" She was looking at him like a wounded bird.

When he didn't respond for a good long while, she looked at him—through him—and said, "You're scared he'll wake up and tell you it was a big mistake. You can't face the fact that you screwed up."

"My brother doesn't lie!" he shouted, frustrated, and pulled her to him again.

She rose on her toes, meeting his challenge. "He might not have lied, but he was delirious. And deep down inside you know I'm telling the truth!"

She planted her palms on his chest and pushed, but he didn't budge. A fact that only seemed to make her angrier. "You can't keep me here forever!"

Jared's shoulders and neck tensed to near snapping. "I can…and I will!"

Jared stomped from the room and slammed the lock home. Their pleasant interlude had turned into a disaster. And all because he couldn't stop thinking about her. All because he desired her so much that he was willing to overlook his continued confusion about what she had—or hadn't—done.

Jared roared and punched the wall, smashing a fist sized hole in the hallway.

"Jared?" Hayden stood in the door of his brother's room, her eyes wide. "Is everything okay?"

His shoulders heaved as he attempted to regain control. But his stomach was so tight he thought it might snap his spinal cord. Jared extracted his hands on the wall, unable to gentle his voice. "Fine."

"Oh, okay," she stammered.

Hayden looked afraid of him, and yet he hadn't even yelled at her. Sparrow had screamed right in his face and punched him in the chest. The differences between the two women were striking. The gentle breeze of Hayden didn't hold a candle to Sparrow's roaring flame.

"I need to get some air. I'll be outside if anything changes." Jared stormed out of the house and slammed the back door behind him, sucking in huge gulps of fresh air.

He stared up at the night sky, trying to reign in his feelings and failing miserably. Sparrow's questions haunted him. If she really were innocent, he would have to live with the fact that he'd mistreated a girl who had done nothing but try to save him. .

Chapter Twenty-seven

A full three days passed without Jared coming to her room. At first she was furious. He'd used her again, and just like before, she'd fallen for his touch.

Merc was her only contact with the outside world. He'd brought her brand new clothes to change into and some books and magazines to help pass the time. He even brought her a radio, so she could listen to music. Three times a day, he would bring her trays of food and escort her to the bathroom, and that was it. She flinched at the cold contact whenever he touched her. And unlike Jared, he looked at her with lifeless eyes completely detached and unfeeling.

She couldn't really complain about her circumstances. They'd fed her more in the space of three days than she usually ate in a week. The clothes she wore now were brand new – she'd pulled the tags off them herself. Sparrow smoothed her hands down the soft cotton dress. She'd never worn clothes that hadn't already belonged to someone else.

Her bed was soft, the sheets even softer and the bedroom was the size of her whole trailer. But no matter how luxurious her room, it was still a cage.

Sparrow had to face facts; she had feelings for Jared Crowe. Deep feelings. Feelings that he was intent on destroying.

Sparrow had survived for years on her wits and on the land. She hadn't had many friends outside of Squirrel. So conversation wasn't a necessity for her, but day after day of being locked in that little room with only the low glow of a small lamp was wearing her down.

And as much as she hated to admit it, she missed Jared.

At least he hadn't ordered her to be chained the bed again. As the week went by, her nerves grew more and more taut as she kept thinking about Jimbo's betrayal.

She knew she was missing something. She thought hard about the week before. Everything about it had seemed so normal. Miss Kay had ordered Sparrow to make her rounds, collecting money from their distributors and girls. Checking stock at the bars, making sure none of the bartenders were stealing liquor.

Jimbo and Bob were in charge of collecting money for the dope. They pretty much stayed out of each other's way altogether unless Miss Kay called them in. Nothing had been reported stolen or missing. Jimbo's movements had been as predictable as the sun rising. When he was done with his chores, he would grab Geraldine and disappear into his house.

Think, Sparrow, think. There had to be something else. But the only theory she'd come up with was that he'd hidden Hoyt in that shack without Miss Kay's knowledge because he hoped to steal the deed. And that worried Sparrow more each day.

The only thing that broke up the monotony was hearing Hoyt's intermittent screams. Not exactly a peaceful break. Each time it would catch her unprepared and she would leap to her feet, her heart racing, and rush to the door to press her ear against the smooth wood, trying to pick up on what was going on.

By the last day of the week, Sparrow thought she was losing her mind. She could only sleep so much and most of the time ended up pacing the confines of her room. If something didn't change, she would lose it. She needed the outdoors, the sun and the wind on her face. She needed to do something, to be useful.

When Merc brought her breakfast that morning, Sparrow snapped. "You can take that food and shove it up your ass."

Merc just grunted and kicked the door shut behind him. He went to the bed, taking the same path he always did, and placed her food tray in the same spot as before.

Sparrow stopped him, and crowded his personal space. She didn't even flinch when he stood to his full height and towered over her. "You have to let me out of here. I'm losing it. Just take me outside for five minutes, that's all I need, I swear."

Merc stared down at her and Sparrow held her breath, hoping that he might speak to her, say anything. Instead, he just turned and walked to the door.

In a rage, she grabbed her tray of food and slung it as hard as she could. Merc ducked sideways at the last minute and glared at her.

"Talk to me, dammit!"

He glanced from the scattered food to her. Then he opened the door and simply walked out, ignoring her completely. When she heard the lock slide into place this time, she collapsed to the floor a sobbing mess. This was what Jared wanted, probably, to break her spirit. She would do anything to get out of this room.

Sparrow jumped to her feet and ran to the door, pounding on it with all her might and screaming at the top of her lungs. When no one came, she ran to the dresser and started ripping out drawers. They were empty, she'd discovered that on the first day, but she needed to destroy something.

When she finished with that she'd started on the bed stands, she moved on to the bed, tearing the single fitted sheet off in a rage. She was in the process of stomping over to the drawer on the floor, intending to throw it, when the door slammed open and Jared stood in the doorway.

"What the hell are you doing?" He looked terrible. He'd lost weight, his eyes were bloodshot, and his hair was tangled like he hadn't slept or eaten all week. She ruthlessly

crushed the concern she felt for him beneath her heel. He'd
abandoned her.

"I need out of this room! Now!"

"You've lost your mind. Did you destroy the
dresser?" Jared stared around incredulously.

She ripped the drawer off the floor and chucked it at
him with all her pent-up fury. "Not yet!"

Jared ducked sideways, the drawer barely missing is
shoulder, and slamming into the wall behind him. "Don't do
that again."

Sparrow picked up another drawer, pulled it back
over her head, and hurled it with all her might, smiling in
satisfaction when it bounced off his solid chest.

Jared grunted from the blow. "Stop it! Don't you dare
pick up another one."

"How could you leave me alone this whole time?" she
asked, her voice cracking. "How could you not come back?"
Sparrow's chest heaved with the pressure of her feelings.
He'd made her feel things for him and then left her high and
dry. Again.

"That's what this is about? Because I've been gone
this week?"

"I could care less if you were dead in the street." *Not
true*. She'd stayed awake at night craving his touch. He'd
driven her mad with his absence in every way possible.
Sparrow picked up another drawer and held it at the ready.

"Sparrow, put that down right now." He pointed a
finger at her, his eyes starting to glow with anger.

"Gladly!" She chucked it again. Only this time Jared
ducked and dove for her, his shoulder slammed into her
stomach as he tackled her to the bed. Sparrow struggled,
slapping and scratching and punching anything she could.
She landed one good solid smack against his cheek and
savored a surge of satisfaction. But not for long.

Jared trapped her wrists in his hand and shoved them
over her head, pressing them into the mattress. "You really
have lost your mind."

"Because of you!" She arched up, trying to buck him from her body, but his weight pinned her down.

"Me? You want to see what I've been doing all week?" That wild look returned and he yanked her from the room. "Want to see what I've been so busy doing?"

He led her into Hoyt's room, the bright light streaming from the window blinded her. Sparrow threw her arms over her head, trying to block out the excruciating brightness.

Jared didn't give her time to acclimate. He ripped her around, forced her back to his chest and pinned her arms to her sides. When he spoke again, his breath was hot and heavy in her ear. "That's what I've been doing. Taking care of my brother."

The bandage on Hoyt's face and chest were gone. Black stitches curved up the side of his cheek, holding together the long cut running the length of his face and pulling his lips up to the side. The hundreds of small cuts on his chest had crusted over; the two deep ones that were held together with stitches were swollen and angry looking.

Hoyt gasped, his eyes still closed, and arched off the mattress, rolling onto his side as his body convulsed.

Jared released her and ran for his brother, quickly holding his arms down, and Sparrow could see why. There were multiple bandages up his arm where he'd ripped the IVs out. And from what she could see, there weren't many places left to put one. No wonder Jared looked so haggard. "Is this what he's been like all week?"

"No, this has been a good day."

Sparrow approached the bed slowly. "Why don't you strap him to the bed so he won't hurt himself?"

Hoyt jerked sharply and Jared grunted, trying to keep him under control. "Tried that. He just fought harder and ripped open all his stitches."

"Can't you give him something that'll knock him out?" Hoyt continued to shake in Jared's grip.

"Not for another hour. Doc's regulating his meds pretty heavy because he's had so much."

Sparrow glanced around the room, searching for anything to help. That's when she realized the door was wide open and Jared was on the other side of the bed, fighting his brother. This would be the perfect opportunity to escape.

But she couldn't do it. She couldn't leave Jared like this, no matter how much he'd hurt her. No matter how the last week had driven her crazy. And seeing the torment on his face was tearing her part.

Sparrow approached the bed with caution, silently waiting on Jared to yell at her. She'd never cared for anyone this sick, so she didn't really know what to do. There was a washcloth on the bed stand, so she picked it up and laid it across Hoyt's forehead. He didn't throw her off, so she counted that as an accomplishment.

He shuddered hard and she watched the veins pop in Jared's arms as he held his brother down.

A long lock of curly blond hair fell in Hoyt's face and Sparrow reached out to brush it out of his face.

"He's not getting any better. The infection's gone…all he has to do is wake up. But he won't. He refuses." She felt Jared's bone-deep grief as if it was her own.

"May I try something? I used to have nightmares when I was a little girl. I remember my mother singing to me to calm me down. She was good at that."

She half expected Jared to deny her. "I'm willing to try anything."

Sparrow scooted up to the top of the bed, near Hoyt's head, and threaded her fingers into his hair. The thick strands were matted together with sweat. Sparrow closed eyes and thought back to her childhood, trying to remember the words. They came to her, as if her mother were there whispering in her ear. Sparrow sang the sweet lullaby, her voice soft and soothing as she gently caressed his scalp, praying that her voice would help ease this tortured soul.

Chapter Twenty-eight

Jared was transfixed by Sparrow's voice as she softly sang the sweet haunting lullaby. He felt himself relaxing, lulled by the tune.

But also by the girl singing it.

Realization struck him like a bolt of lightning. Someone who cared as deeply as Sparrow could never inflict unimaginable pain and torture. Regret crawled the walls of his stomach and he closed his eyes under the weight of his guilt.

He had been desperately wrong and he didn't need his brother to wake up and tell him that. The facts were all there, staring him in the face.

When Sparrow finished the song, she opened her eyes and gazed deeply into his. The rest of the world seemed to melt away, and it was just the two of them and this incredible passionate bridge connecting them together. A bridge he intended to cross.

"Sparrow." His voice was thick with emotion.

Seeming to understand his silent plea, she reached for his hand. His fingers closed around hers and he felt something warm expand in his chest.

Then he heard a sniffle from the doorway, and when he looked up, the spell had been broken. Hayden stood there dabbing at her eyes with a tissue. "That was beautiful. And look how you calmed him."

A blush rose on Sparrow's cheeks and Jared realized she was probably not used to getting praise. Something he planned to rectify soon.

He cleared his throat and let go of her hand, gently releasing Hoyt so that he lay fully on the mattress. "Hayden, would you mind sitting with him for a moment?"

Hayden met his eyes with a look of understanding. "No, I just woke up from my nap, so I'll be good for a while."

Jared rose from the bed and walked around it, taking Sparrow's hand in his own and leading her from the room. He bypassed her room and went straight to his, shutting the door behind him.

Sparrow faced him, her gaze open. Her trust nearly destroyed him. He'd hurt her so many times, and yet she hadn't given up on him. She was willing to try again. Jared took her into his arms and lowered his lips to hers. He intended to put every ounce of his feelings into that kiss.

***

Sparrow broke the kiss and stepped back, reveling in the sight of him. He was wearing low-slung jeans and a black muscle shirt, revealing biceps carved out of molten lava and honed into rock-hard steel. His wide chest narrowed like he had been cut with a knife. Black shirt. Black hair. All darkness. Like dark chocolate. Good for her in small quantities. But it could give her a heart attack if she ate the whole package at once.

She swallowed as she became achingly aware of her vulnerable position. If he lifted the hem of her new dress, he'd reveal everything God had given her. Jared stood staring at her like she was going to be his appetizer, dinner, and dessert all in one.

A strange sort of heat came over her body, like a fever. Delirious. She couldn't move. Her body felt like it was floating, drifting in and out of itself. Touching that heat and pulling away, like a moth to a flame, then returning once more.

Jared growled, the sound vibrating his chest. Sparrow snapped her heels together, hoping to hide the flood of heat building between her thighs. The raw edge of lust that they'd been skating along was about to cut them in two.

She arched toward him as his massive arms closed around her waist, lifted her up, and laid her out on the bed like a morsel he couldn't wait to devour. Jared pushed her flat and she spread her legs willingly, savoring the feel of him as he settled on top of her. He was huge, his corded muscles and wide chest could easily suffocate her, but he held himself up on his elbows, supporting his own weight. His hands caged around her head, holding her hostage for his mouth. She wanted to tell him he didn't have to do that, she wasn't going anywhere, but she couldn't move.

Sparrow wiggled, seeking his hands on her body, but he held back. He stayed right there, driving her wild with his mouth on hers. He didn't stop until she was moaning and struggling for more. Finally, he broke the kiss and she sucked in a breath. His lips trailed down her neck, pausing to deliver feather light kisses.

"Jared." She pulled him down, silently begging for him to take her.

But he pulled up. "No. I want to do this right. You deserve better." He lowered his head to press kisses across her skin again, never taking too much. The barely there caresses drove her wild, but left her wanting more.

"You don't have to."

Jared stopped all together and took her face between his hands. "Yes, I do. I need to show you that I believe you." He kissed her gently. "That I cherish you." He kissed her again. "That I need you." This time he took her mouth deeply and Sparrow felt every nerve in her body respond.

"I'm so sorry I didn't believe you. I was a fool. Please forgive me. Stay with me, let me spend the rest of my life making it up to you."

"I've already forgotten." She grabbed his hair and tried to pull him down to her, but he resisted.

"I've taken you before, and loved every damn minute of it. But today isn't about me. It's about you." Jared threaded his fingers through hers and pushed her hands over her head. Then he lifted her dress from her, leaving her completely naked.

"You're so fucking sexy. So perfect." He reached a hand out and gently caressed her tummy. Sparrow sucked in a breath.

"Jared, please!"

He fell forward, taking her lips and then trailing down her neck, stopping at the hollow of her shoulder to suckle. After a few seconds of that torture, he moved lower, lavishing attention to her sensitive breasts. He licked. Teased. Tormented. Never sucking too hard. Never drawing her into his mouth. It was as if he were scared to hurt her.

She was losing her mind.

Chill bumps raced across her skin, trailing behind his hand as it drifted down, circling her navel and then moving back up to gently squeeze her breasts. She arched into his touch as his lips trailed to the other side of her neck and both his hands moved to cover her chest, massaging her aching breasts until she was ready to scream.

"Jared." Sparrow gasped and grabbed his shoulders, sinking her nails into his skin. "I need you. Please." She needed him to take her like before. But he refused, intent on proving some point.

Finally, when she was ready to groan in frustration, he took her nipple between his lips, drawing on her softly. "Harder. Suck harder." Sparrow tugged his hair, silently communicating her needs.

"No. Not tonight. All I've done is take from you. I intend to give to you tonight." Sparrow wanted to sob at his words.

"But I need you to do it harder. I want it." Sparrow took his face between her hands and forced him to look at her. Really look at her.

"I want this to be perfect for you." Jared said, but she could see the flicker of indecision in his gaze.

"Well then stop pussy footing around." Sparrow threw down the challenge and held her breath. Praying he would accept.

Jared growled and ripped her hands over her head. Liquid flooded her thighs. His mouth closed over her nipple, and this time he sucked hard, drawing her fully inside the hot depths of his mouth. Then he bit down and she cried out, but not in pain. The burning intensity roared out of control. When he finished with that one, he licked and sucked her other nipple, driving her past the point of awareness. Logic. Control. He lavished attention to her breasts until she thought she would snap.

Sparrow sobbed from the pleasure. She'd thought it was great before, but tonight, tonight something huge had happened between them. There was a deeper, more special connection. One that touched her soul.

Jared trailed kisses down her belly and settled between her thighs. "Do you want me to touch you here?" His voice was rough, more of a command than a question, and she nodded eagerly.

"Say it. Tell me you want me to touch you there."

Sparrow licked her lips, burning with need for him to pleasure her. "Please, please touch me there."

Her body arched into his touch in accordance with her words. His mouth closed over her clit with a growl and held there, licking and tasting. Sparrow rode his tongue unashamed. Screamed out her pleasure when he slipped a finger inside her. She needed oxygen, but not as much as she needed his body on hers. In hers.

He tore his mouth from her and he sat up, leaving her cold and alone. She jerked forward, trying to drag him back down, but he shackled her wrists and dragged them overhead. Then he smiled at her—an animalistic, possessive smile, and she melted.

He reached down and flicked her clit, causing her to arch into his touch. He repeated that process, rubbing feather soft then pressing hard until she panted. She felt his fingertip slip inside her and pull out, then massage up and around her clit before dipping in again. When she was close, he stopped the slow languid strokes and rubbed in hard small circles. The pressure building inside her broke. She spasmed arcing off the bed and finally drifted back down in a hazy cloud of lust.

"That's a good girl." Sparrow tried to regain her composure, but all she could do was close her eyes. The bed shifted, and then she felt something warm and hot on her clit. Her eyes flew open to see Jared's head nestled once more between her thighs, his hands pushing her legs wide. His tongue licking her clit in one long slow stroke, reigniting the fire. Another long stroke. The small flame burst back into a raging wildfire.

"God you taste like honey. Sweet. I can't get enough." She couldn't take her gaze off the erotic sight. Never in her life had she imagined anything like this. One of his hands trailed from her thigh to her center and she felt his finger probing her entrance once more. Only this time he pushed in further until he filled her. He worked the finger in and out, his knuckles grazing against her skin. He felt so good. So right.

The pleasure built inside her again, and she knew if he continued she would burst. Then he put two fingers inside her, stretching her, and she lost all thought.

"God you're so tight."

She sobbed, needing more. "Please."

He came up on his knees, tore off his shirt, and jerked his pants down. Then he nestled between her legs, touching her entrance with his rigid cock. "Are you sure?"

Sparrow wrapped her legs around his waist and dug her heels in. "Yes!"

Jared thrust forward, filling her in one long stroke, leaving her gasping for air. She'd never felt so full. So right.

Jared dropped his head to hers and closed his eyes as if pain. "Fuck you're tight. Squeezing me like a goddamn glove." Sweat beaded on his forehead and dropped onto hers.

He pulled almost all the way out this time and thrust forward again, driving even deeper, stretching her more.

"Please, Jared." He lifted his head and kissed her gently, cradling her face between his palms. He lifted his hips, pulled out and then drove forward, not stopping until he bottomed out.

And then he repeated the move, the slow friction hot. Building. Again and again, his slow strokes drove her wild with pleasure.

"Jared, please." She knew she was begging, but didn't care. She needed him to take her harder. Lay claim to her.

He growled and slammed in hard and fast, and her entire body jerked in response. He drove into her like that until Sparrow was mindless, moaning and begging. She couldn't take it any longer and burst into a thousand pieces. No longer one body but countless floating particles around the room. Sparrow felt him jerk on top of her, followed by his own groan of pleasure.

Jared collapsed against her, his heavy weight welcome as she drifted back into her body. He stayed inside her, stretching her, and she never wanted him to leave.

Jared placed soft, tender kisses on her cheeks, her nose, and then her mouth.

A while later, when they'd settled and simply lay together in bed, caressing each other, Sparrow broached the subject that had been bothering her all week. "Jared, I know you don't want to talk about this. But I have to at least warn Kay about Jimbo. If he takes over the mountain, I'll never make it in time to save Squirrel." Sparrow sucked in a breath, anxiety tripping up her heart. What if he refused?

"How about you call her in the morning?" Jared's open response pulled tears from her eyes.

Sparrow nodded, unable to speak past the emotion clogging her throat.

They'd not only faced the bridge between them, they'd crossed it.

Chapter Twenty-nine

The next morning Sparrow rolled over in an empty bed. Savoring the languid ache, she stretched. Even the sheets felt different, somehow softer, and yet her skin felt more sensitive. Just thinking about the way Jared had held her sent a rush of chills across her body.

The shuttered window blocked out all light, leaving her without any idea of the time of day, but her stomach grumbled, indicating she'd slept past breakfast.

Sparrow rolled from the bed and dug in the sheets for her dress, slipped it on and ran to the restroom to relieve herself. She flipped on the lights and leaned in close to the mirror, studying her reflection. The glow of happiness couldn't be denied any more than she could stop a huge grin from spreading across her lips. Lips swollen from earth-shattering kisses.

It meant so much to her that Jared had agreed to let her call Miss Kay and warn her about Jimbo. After all he'd suffered at Kay's hands, somehow Jared had found a way to overcome the hate in his heart, and he had done it for Sparrow. No one had ever scaled such a hurdle for her before. They'd crossed some invisible barrier, reaching an altogether different level. One that involved trust and respect and love.

Even though Hoyt hadn't awoken to confirm her story, Jared *believed* her. The thought filled her with happiness and a newfound energy. Already missing him, Sparrow quickly combed her fingers through her hair and ran to the door of the bedroom, turning the knob to yank it open. Only the knob wouldn't turn.

She gripped it harder, putting all her strength behind it, but still it wouldn't give. Her heart beating uncontrollably in her chest, she ran to her own adjoining bedroom and tried the door. The knob didn't budge. Dread slammed into her, nearly knocking her to the floor.

No. No way, not after last night. He'd been so tender, so sincere. She refused to believe the solid evidence of the locked doors. Sparrow drew back her fist and pounded, screaming Jared's name.

The lock clicked and relief hit her so hard her knees almost buckled. But when the door opened, Merc was the one standing there. A wave of dizziness assailed her senses and she grabbed the dresser. "Where's Jared?"

For once, Merc answered her without hesitation, "He left."

She clutched the dresser tighter, her fingers turning white under the strain. "Where? Why is the door locked?"

"Why wouldn't it be?" Merc's answer sucked the life out of her.

"Last night, he-he said I was free to—"

Merc held up a hand, cutting her off mid-sentence. "Jared didn't say a word to me about letting you out. So, until I hear otherwise, the door stays locked and you stay inside."

"Wait." *He couldn't have. Not again. Please, not again.*

Sparrow stared, dumbfounded, as Merc shut the door in her face, the ominous click of the lock falling into place stealing her ability to breathe. Pain exploded across her chest and radiated down her arms and legs, curling her fingers in response.

She formed a tight fist and punched the door. Jared had betrayed her. Again. And in the worst possible way. Last night had meant nothing to him, absolutely nothing. How many times would she fall for his tricks? How many times would she let him trample her heart before she broke past fixing?

The answer came swiftly—never again. Never again would she let him touch her. Sparrow pulled on every ounce of strength she possessed, trying to shut down her emotions and distance herself from the situation. But she hurt so bad…

Think, Sparrow. She angrily wiped at the tears on her face. There has to be a way out of this place. She dashed into Jared's bedroom and tried the window, but it was locked tight.

The bathroom—there was a window over the bathtub. Sparrow ran to it and tried to slide it open, but that, too, was locked. Only she could see sunlight through the outside shutters in Jared's bedroom, and she realized it wasn't actually boarded it up. He'd probably never planned on giving her free reign of his bedroom.

She dashed back into his room, and dove for his open bag on the floor. How he must have laughed at her ignorance. Her stupidity. *Dumb hillbilly.*

Well, this hillbilly had survival skills, and she wasn't about to let some asshole break her. She'd picked more locks then half of the residents of the Boone County jail. She tossed his clothes over her shoulder, about to give up hope, but when she lifted a pair of pants a heavy black knife fell out of the pocket. Sparrow picked it up, its heavy weight a familiar comfort, and smiled. Not only could she pry the window open, she could leave him a nice little message for the trouble.

Sparrow flipped the blade and ran her thumb down the edge, her grin growing when she got a small sliver of blood. Jared Crowe would regret the day he'd laid eyes on her.

Sparrow made quick work of her gift to her captor and popped the window lock with ease. She peeked out first and then jumped down onto the soft green grass in the side yard. Nothing but trees, trees, and more trees surrounded the house. Her own personal playing ground. But if she stayed close, he would catch her. Even if he had to get his whole team involved.

And if she couldn't make that call he'd promised her to make, Sparrow's new knife had a date with Jimbo's throat.

She snuck to the corner of the bright white house and peered around into the front yard. A large four-wheel drive truck was parked next to an older red car. She gazed with longing at the truck, but the chrome pipes sticking out the back would ensure that half the county heard her crank it up. The little red car would have to do.

Sparrow ran across the lawn in a crouch then came to a stop beside the truck. It was almost a sin to slash the new mud tires, but hey—it was her or the rubber.

As the air hissed from the tires, Sparrow got into the car. She was in the process of yanking the starter wires from underneath the steering wheel when sunlight glinted off a pink glitter diamond on a keychain hanging from the ignition. Like stealing whiskey from a passed out drunk.

Sparrow cranked the car up and eased from the drive, increasing speed the farther she got from the house. She didn't bother taking a last look in the rear view. She'd left her heart behind, but she didn't regret it. If Jared was so intent on destroying it, he could have it. The only requirement where she was headed was to be cold-blooded and cutthroat. A broken heart would just get in the way.

Chapter Thirty

Jared arrived back at the house after getting his ass reamed by his commander for going off grid, especially since the last time one of their teammates disappeared, he'd ended up dead. Colonel Grey not only had a reputation for being the most lethal interrogator in the Special Forces, he was deadly in his own right. At least the rest of the team hadn't been present to witness him barely avoiding a rank demotion.

Not only had Jared broken the rules with he and Hoyt's clandestine mountain getaway, he'd put his team in danger for his own personal vendetta.

But all of that mean almost nothing after last night. Sparrow had given him the gift of her heart, and he intended to cherish it, nurture it, and do whatever it took to protect her. Opening himself to her had been far easier than agreeing to help contact Kay, but it had been impossible to deny her.

Jared floored the gas pedal in anticipation of seeing her again. He'd hated to leave her this morning, looking so damn beautiful it made him struggle for breath, but they'd stayed up all night making love, and he hadn't wanted to wake her.

Somewhere in all this action and misery and mind-numbing sex, he'd fallen in love.

Jared pulled into the drive of the little white house, frowning when he saw Hayden's car was gone. She'd promised to stay with Hoyt until Jared returned from his meeting. A sense of foreboding sent him running up the stairs and in through the front door. He didn't slow until he was at his brother's door. But Hayden was sitting next to the bed, just like he'd expected, reading a book. She frowned when she saw him. "What's wrong?"

Jared gave a shaky laugh, "I just got a feeling. Thought something had happened while I was gone."

"No change, except he slept much better. Doc reduced his meds, so it's only a matter of time now before he wakes up." Hayden folded her book closed and offered him a smile. Struck by her calming beauty, he found himself hoping Hoyt realized what a gem he had.

"Great. Just let me know when you need to head home and I'll give you a ride."

Hayden cocked her head to the side and dropped her brows. "Why? I can drive myself."

"Your car isn't out there. Thought your dad must have dropped you off."

She got up, crossed to the window, and pulled the blinds up. "Where the heck is my car?"

That sense of foreboding returned and Jared joined her on the other side of the room. "You mean you did drive it over here this morning? I thought I remembered seeing it when I left, but I figured my mind was playing tricks on me."

"Hell, no." Hayden pulled out her cell and dialed. "Dad, did you come get my car?" Jared watched as her lips pressed into a tight line. "Okay. No, its fine. Maybe Hunter needed it."

She disconnected the call and immediately dialed again. "Hunter, did you or Ranger borrow my car this morning?" When Jared saw the look on her face, he didn't have to stick around to know the answer.

His heart racing with alarm, Jared ran from the room, only stopping when he reached Sparrow's door. It was shut. He tried to open it. Nothing, the door was locked. His was locked too. Stomach tight, he banged on the door. "Sparrow!"

No answer.

Jared shoved a hand into his pocket for the keys, only then remembering he'd left them on the kitchen table. He hadn't thought he'd need them anymore since he'd left the doors unlocked this morning.

Was she pissed he'd left without saying goodbye? Dammit. Jared ran to the kitchen to find Merc leaning back at the kitchen table, sipping a cup of coffee.

"Why are the doors locked?"

Merc looked at him in surprise. "Since when did you want them unlocked?"

Jared's eyes slid shut with dread. If she believed he'd locked her in after last night, after all the promises he'd made...

"Did you talk to Sparrow this morning?"

"Yeah, the girl tried to talk me into letting her go." Merc snorted and then took a sip of his coffee, calm as he could be as Jared's world came crashing down around him.

"And did you?"

"Of course not, do I look stupid? She's still in there. Locked her up tight myself." Jared could barely hear Merc's answer over the roaring in his ears. He hadn't thought to tell Merc. Hadn't thought about anything but returning to her as quick as he could.

"Give me the keys!" Jared held out his hand, barely able to restrain himself from launching across the table and strangling his teammate. Merc gave him a strange look, tossed him the keys, and he took off at a sprint down the hall.

She'll never forgive me.

Jared fumbled with the keys, nearly dropping them in his haste to unlock the door. He slammed it open, but it was just as his heart had feared. It was deserted.

"Sparrow!" Jared bellowed and raced into his connected bedroom. The emptiness was a living, breathing thing contracting the walls. She'd destroyed his bed. His comforter and sheets were ripped in shreds. Feathers littered the floor. Even worse was the large heart she'd carved into the wall with a huge 'x' over it. The room shrunk, cutting off his oxygen.

She was gone.

Jared dropped to his knees and roared in agony.

"What the hell is going on?" Merc raced into the room, gun drawn. He glanced down at Jared and swept past him to clear the bathroom. "Shit, she got out the window."

Jared barely registered his words. "I told her that I believed her. That she was free."

"You're not making any sense, man. When did you decide to free her? Didn't you think she was the one who tortured your brother?" Merc holstered his nine millimeter and came to a stop in front of him.

All Jared could manage was a weak shake of his head. After everything he'd done to her, she'd still trusted him. She'd given him everything. Her body. Her heart. "I was wrong. She didn't do it."

Merc winced. "Looks like she was pretty pissed."

"What on earth?" Hayden entered the room, stopping just inside the door. "What happened? Where's Sparrow?"

"Gone. She's gone." Jared couldn't find the strength to get off the floor.

"I knew it. My car...she took my car." Hayden slapped a fist into her hand.

If she had a car, there was no telling how much of a lead she'd gotten. He'd never be able to catch up with her.

Merc tossed a set of keys on the floor in front of Jared. "Take my truck. She can't be that far. You know where she's headed."

Home. Last night she'd begged him to help her to get in touch with Kay. Now Sparrow would be headed home to that monster. If Kay knew she'd helped him and Hoyt, it might mean the end of her.

"You're right." He picked up the keys and got to his feet. "Thanks." Jared brushed past Hayden on the way out. "Watch out for Hoyt."

His brother would be fine; his life was out of immediate danger. But Sparrow was headed straight into the hornet's nest. This time, it was Jared's turn to save her. Jared exited the front door, stopping a few feet from Merc's four by four.

The rims sat on the ground, leaving the truck immobilized. She'd cut the tires.

"Those tires cost a fortune!" Merc had walked up behind Jared, and now he stood staring at his truck in shock.

"Jared! Come quick!" Hayden yelled from the house.

Jared and Merc exchanged a look and then bounded into the house, following Hayden into Hoyt's bedroom.

Jared nearly stumbled when Hoyt met his gaze with clear blue eyes.

"Jared?" Hoyt croaked out, his voice hoarse.

Relief swept over him in a tidal wave, and Jared grabbed Hoyt's hand and sunk down onto the mattress. "I'm here."

Hoyt offered a weak smile, "Duh, you're sitting right next to me."

Jared broke into a burst of laughter. "Yes I am. You scared the crap out of us."

Hoyt gazed around the room, stopping on Hayden, who stood at his other side. "How long have I been out?"

Tears fell down Hayden's cheeks. "Over a week. We've all been so worried about you."

Hoyt made to lift his hand and wipe her tears, but then yanked it back, his body stiffening, and spat out a curse. Jared watched helplessly, devastated that his brother would suffer from such a small movement. "Why am I on my side? And why the fuck does it feel like someone poured acid on my back?"

"You don't remember?" Maybe it was better that way. He wouldn't have the nightmares. The haunted days.

"No. I remember going into the woods to take a piss and that's it. What happened?" Before Jared could stop him, Hoyt rolled onto his back and let out an immediate bellow of agony.

"No! Don't move. Let me call the doctor." Hayden ran past Merc, who was standing guard at the door.

Jared helped Hoyt roll back onto his side, and Merc rearranged the pillows to help prop him up. "When you went missing, it took me a couple of days to track you down. By the time I found you, you were almost gone."

"The shack." Hoyt's voice dropped and his eyes widened.

Jared nodded, "It was Kay and her son."

Hoyt finished his sentence for him, "Jimbo." A severe shudder racked him, shaking the entire bed. Sweat beaded along his lips and his pupils contracted to pinpoints.

Shit. Jared would take a bullet for his brother. But he was powerless to stop the memories. "I got you out of there and we helicoptered you back home. Dr. Hartsfield has been treating you here, away from the hospital."

Hoyt paled and continued to shake, his gaze going distant. Fear skittered up Jared's spine and he squeezed Hoyt's hand. "Stay with me. You're safe now."

"It was so dark. So small. He kept coming—coming with the blade." Hoyt moaned and arched his back, fighting some invisible memory.

"You're not there anymore. I have you. I'll keep you safe." Claws of helpless fury and apprehension took hold of Jared. Dr. Hartsfield's concern was forefront in his mind. *It's not his physical injuries I'm worried about.*

"The girl. She helped." Hoyt struggled and Merc had to help Jared keep him on the bed. "No! Stop!"

"What girl?" Chains wrapped around Jared's chest, tightening with each word. He knew it wasn't her, but he had to hear the words.

"Don't know." Hoyt grunted, jerked.

"What did she look like?"

"The crow on her wrist. She had the knife. Please! Stay away!" Hoyt screamed and fought their hold, fueled by demons from hell. His insane rage gave him enough strength to throw Merc, who had at least fifty pounds and a foot height on him, off the bed.

Panic took hold of Jared. He'd seen a crow on one woman's wrist. The whore Geraldine. And Sparrow was headed right back into the hornets' nest.

"I won't let you take me back!" Hoyt's eyes rolled back in his head and he convulsed.

"Hoyt! Hoyt, stay with me brother. They can't hurt you anymore." Jared watched in horror as Hoyt seized, unable to stop him. Unable to draw him from his hell.

"Move!" Dr. Hartsfield appeared at Hoyt's side with a syringe. She shoved it into his arm without hesitation. "He's got to calm down. Hold him."

They each grabbed an arm and forced Hoyt over onto his stomach, unable to keep him on his side. "No!"

"Why isn't it working?" Jared nearly yelled at the doc.

"Give it a second. Just don't let him go," Dr. Hartsfield said.

Jared watched as Hoyt's jerks turned to twitches and finally stopped all together as he slumped into the mattress. Merc wiped a hand across his head and dropped to the floor beside the bed.

The sound of Hayden's weeping filled the room. A hand settled on Jared's shoulder and he jerked, startled, and looked up into Dr. Hartsfield's sympathetic eyes. "He will be all right. This is normal in the beginning."

Jared wanted to ask what she meant by *the beginning*, but he couldn't say the words. The doctor squeezed his shoulder and then went to check Hoyt's vitals. "Everything sounds good. He's reopened a few wounds, and I'll have to change his bandages and check his stitches, but that's it for now. The sedative I gave him should keep him out for a while. I will go ahead and call you in a prescription for oral sedatives. But I suggest that as soon as he's healthy enough, you bring him to see a counselor. No matter how strong Hoyt is, he's going to need help getting through this."

"Anything. I'll do whatever it takes." Jared pulled himself off the floor and shoved his hands in his pockets to hide the shaking.

"I'll stay. You go and finish what you started," Hayden said.

Jared floundered, full of guilt and questions. Should he leave Hoyt after his break down? Could he?

How could he not? He loved Sparrow with all his heart and the thought of her in danger made his blood freeze in his veins.

"I can have the helicopter ready to go in an hour." Merc crossed his arms and waited.

Jared looked at his brother, unconscious on the bed. Fresh blood steadily seeping through his bandages. Broken.

"Let's go. I'm going to make them pay for this, and then I'm going to burn that mountain to the fucking ground."

Chapter Thirty-one

Sparrow pulled off the road about a quarter mile from the Crowe compound and put the little car in park. Luckily, she discovered Hayden's purse tossed carelessly in the backseat, along with a shiny new credit card in her wallet. Sparrow had made a couple of pit stops along the way. Now thanks to Hayden, she had on blue jeans and a shirt that actually fit, new boots, and a brand-new knife sharpened on a diamond cut grinder.

It was only midafternoon, and under better circumstances, she would have waited for darkness to fall, but too much time had passed. Miss Kay might already be dead, Squirrel in danger. The thought fueled her with adrenaline and she took off through the woods.

Sparrow wound through the trees with ease, the trek familiar. Her trip up here seemed to take forever, made even worse by the fact that she couldn't get Jared's betrayal out of her mind. Last night replayed in her mind over and over again, taunting her with her own stupidity. His sweet whispered words and promises. Lies. All lies.

She hoped he showed up on her mountain again, cause this time she'd be ready. And her heart would be surrounded by a wall made of bricks and mortar.

This was her home, her lifeblood. And she would protect it to her last breath.

A little while later Sparrow was nearing the camp, close enough that she could just make out the back of Miss Kay's house. She crouched down, watched and waited. Most of the camp's residents were still up, getting ready for the night. She'd have to be real careful to not be seen. Especially since Jimbo's house was right next to Kay's.

Sparrow crept out from the safety of the tree line and made her way to Kay's back door. There wasn't a porch, just a small set of concrete blocks leading to the entrance. Sparrow briefly contemplated knocking, but decided against it. There was too much of a risk that Jimbo would be inside.

She slowly turned the knob and eased the door open inch by inch. The back room with its polished floorboards came into view. Just beyond that was the kitchen, and then Miss Kay's bedroom on the end. Sparrow stepped inside and shut the door, stopping to listen as someone moved around inside the house.

She took out her knife, held it at the ready, and entered the kitchen. Miss Kay had her back to the room, and was leaning over the stove, stirring up a pot of something delicious. Sparrow inhaled, her eyes closing at the familiar smell of home. "Beef stew is my favorite."

Kay spun around, a pistol in her hand and aimed directly at Sparrow's chest. "I wondered when you'd come slinking back."

Sparrow steeled herself, knowing it wouldn't be easy to convince Kay of the truth. "I've been trying to get back here for a week."

"You should've stayed gone with your lover. I know you helped that boy escape." Kay tensed, her broad shoulders squared at Sparrow.

"I didn't run away with him. He kidnapped me." Sparrow gripped the knife handle tight, praying she didn't have to use it.

"Not what Jimbo said. He said he seen you taking him away. Said he tried to stop you too."

Sparrow snorted and put her free hand on her hip. "Oh yeah, did Jimbo tell you he had Hoyt Crowe tied up in that old shack?" Sparrow watched Miss Kay's expression for any flicker of recognition, but saw none.

"Hoyt Crowe's been dead for over a decade. Both them boys are."

"No, he's very much alive."

Kay's mud brown eyes narrowed. "How do you even know about that boy?"

"Cause I caught Jimbo torturing him for information on the location of the deed to Crowe Mountain." Sparrow dropped the bomb and sat back to see how it would land. Kay would either believe her or kill her. Either way, Sparrow was ready.

"Nobody owns this mountain but me." Kay's voice came out as soft but deadly as a rattle snake.

"I know, I would have warned you sooner, but Jimbo tried to have me killed. And then—" Sparrow toed the floor, forcing the lie to her lips, "—then that man I'd taken captive escaped and kidnapped me. Been trying to get away this entire week."

Sparrow prayed she looked properly embarrassed. Such a thing would have made her look like a fool in front of everyone on Crowe Mountain. And Kay would have punished her, severely.

"You're telling me my own flesh and blood son is planning to betray me?"

"Yes. Why else would I risk my neck to come back here and warn you?"

Miss Kay shook her head. "No. Not my Jimbo."

"You know as well as I he's greedy and he likes to hurt people." He preferred to torture and maim and peel the flesh from people.

Miss Kay seemed to shake herself and Sparrow prayed she would lower the gun. Prayed she'd believe her. Her entire world was riding on it. "I've got to hear it from him with my own ears." Miss Kay gestured toward the front door with her gun. "Outside, now."

Sparrow walked out the front door with her head held high and her knife tucked in her waistband. Everyone stopped and stared as Kay led her down the front porch at the point of her pistol. Kay Crowe didn't hold her gun on someone unless she planned to pull the trigger. The late afternoon sun cast a low glow over the open dirt courtyard. Small groups of men huddled around tables, gambling, while their evening entertainment perched on their laps. The whores were giving it their best to earn some money for the night.

Kay marched Sparrow to the front of Jimbo's house next door and hollered, "Jimbo Crowe! Get your ass out here right this minute!"

Floorboards creaked as his footsteps filled the clearing. The front door swung open and Jimbo marched out, buttoning up his pants. Sparrow watched as his aggravated gaze turned fearful. Then infuriated. "I see the little traitor came crawling back begging for scraps."

Before Sparrow could defend herself, Miss Kay said, "She's got a pretty interesting story. One that I couldn't believe, thought you might like to hear it."

Jimbo dropped his arms to his sides and leaned casually against the door frame, though Sparrow could see every muscle in his body tense. "Now Ma, you know I don't care about no stories."

"Oh, but I think you'll like this one."

Sparrow felt the barrel of the gun dig into her back and fought back her anxiety. Jimbo was too dumb to think fast on his feet. He'd trip up, and then he'd reveal his true nature. He tried to appear casual, but the worry was clear on his face.

"You want to know how I ran this place for so long? Because I'm always thinking ahead. I got people everywhere. I know everything."

Jimbo straightened from the door, his meaty hands clenched into fists. "Whatever that little bitch told you is a lie."

"Seems she knows things she shouldn't. That she couldn't possibly know. Things she claimed to see with her own eyes. Girl says you're planning to betray me."

Miss Kay's voice rang loud and clear. Jimbo seethed with hatred and Sparrow squared her shoulders. She wasn't scared of him, not anymore. "Why don't you tell her what you had planned, Jimbo? Tell her about the land deed." It was a gamble, but it paid off when Jimbo's skin went pale. Still, he was a stupid man and he didn't know when to quit. "You mean you want me to tell her how I caught you trying to steal it?"

"Me? I wasn't the one hiding a prisoner in the old shack."

Jimbo smirked and leaned back against the door frame. Alarm bells went off in Sparrow's mind. He appeared too confident.

"Ma already knows about what you did, girl. About how you helped your prisoner escape. I told her I tried to stop you, but that fella knocked me out and I got the scar to prove it." Jimbo pulled a clump of dirty red hair back from his temple, revealing a jagged red wound.

Sweat beaded across her hairline and she scrambled for a better explanation. "Did you tell her about stringing Hoyt Crowe up in that shed?"

Gasps filled the clearing, but Sparrow didn't dare take her gaze from Miss Kay's boy.

"Everyone knows the Crowe brothers died a long time ago. If you're going to lie, you at least need to speak sense."

"I saw you with my own eyes." Sparrow felt control slipping from her grasp.

"I would never betray my ma. But I will kill for her." That familiar hard glint lit Jimbo's mud brown eyes. Sparrow felt the hard press of steel dig into her back and grief settled heavy on her shoulders.

Miss Kay's whispered words practically scalded her ear. "I told you, you shoulda stayed away."

At that moment Geraldine, drunker than Cotter Brown, stumbled out the front door. It took her a minute to realize what was going on. Once she did, she slapped her hand over her chest and nearly fell over sideways. "Oh Lord! Miss Kay, I swear to you I was gonna tell you. I tried to stop him. I swear to God. Please don't kill me."

Jimbo turned on her in a flash and knocked her to the ground. "Shut up you filthy whore!"

Geraldine was either too drunk, too stupid, or a shade too much of both. She wailed, crawling on her hands and knees off the porch, and reached out to grab the bottom of Kay's long dress. "I swear I tried to stop him, but he threatened to kill me. I never wanted to betray you."

Sparrow felt a wave of darkness behind her as Kay pulled the gun from her spine. Sparrow side-stepped out of the line of fire.

"Dammit Ma, you gonna believe that filthy whore? She's crazy."

Geraldine's practiced tears stopped in an instant and she turned on her lover. "You didn't say that when I was riding you like a lazy horse a minute ago."

"Shut up." Kay booted Geraldine, and the rail thin girl went rolling. Jimbo pushed away from the door frame, his hand sliding up to his waist band. Sparrow tensed and reached behind her back to ease the knife from her pants. She held it by the very tip, carrying it low and out of sight.

Kay aimed the pistol at her son. And for the first time in her life, Sparrow saw the woman's hand shake. "You betrayed your own kin?"

Any semblance of love disappeared from Jimbo's face and he sneered, "This place needs a man to run it. You don't let me run the heroin, and you're costing us a fortune."

Kay's eyes bulged and she locked out her elbow, lowering her finger from the side of the gun to hug the trigger. "This is all about drugs and money. You're too stupid to run this place."

Sparrow took a small step closer to Kay, trying not to draw Jimbo's attention and failing miserably. "This is all her fault. Ever since you adopted her, you favored her over your own sons."

"That's a lie." Sparrow gasped. She'd fought tooth and nail for every ounce of respect she'd earned from Miss Kay.

"I always knew you'd turn out to be a coward like

your daddy. He was always looking out for himself, rather be fucking some whore than taking care of business," Kay said. "Only way you're getting control of this mountain is over my dead body."

Sparrow flinched as Kay pulled the trigger. The entire courtyard echoed with the sound of a hollow click. Kay pulled the trigger again and again and still nothing happened.

"Now see that's where you're wrong, Ma. I've been planning this for a long time. You can pull that trigger all you want, but that gun ain't gonna fire."

Jimbo lifted his own pistol, aiming at his mother. Sparrow froze, her heart stopping.

"If you'd just listen to me, I'd let you live. But there ain't room but for one leader. It's time for you to step aside."

Jimbo's finger dropped to the trigger in slow motion. Sparrow lifted her knife and let it fly, diving sideways at the same time. An explosion boomed through the air. Sparrow heard a thud and felt her body jerk backwards and then fall to the ground. Kay stood, her face pale with shock. Stunned, Sparrow followed her gaze to see Jimbo drop to his knees, Sparrow's knife embedded in his throat.

"Sparrow, hold on. I'll send Bob for the doctor." Kay dropped to her knees beside Sparrow and yelled out for Bob Crowe. She ripped a kerchief out of her dress pocket and shoved it against Sparrow's shoulder. Pain erupted down her arm, making her gasp. But it was nothing next to the satisfaction of seeing her knife protrude from Jimbo's neck. Her arms and legs felt like they were going numb and black edged around her vision. Sparrow embraced it, silently praying she'd pass out, her mind unable to process the horror.

"Where's that boy? Bob!" Kay shouted and pushed against Sparrow's shoulder. She tried to listen for his footsteps, but all she could hear was the blood pounding in her ears.

Then she heard the ominous click of a gun being cocked and saw the nozzle of a pistol press against Kay's temple. Sparrow met Miss Kay's eyes and saw the banked fury burning there.

"You're right, mother. Jimbo was too stupid to run this mountain. I tried to bide my time, but I couldn't stand back and watch you two run this place into the ground."

So both my boys have betrayed me," Miss Kay whispered.

Suddenly Geraldine appeared out of nowhere and landed a vicious kick to Kay's side. Sparrow watched helplessly as she fell over, gasping for breath. Geraldine spat next to her head and said, "You and Jimbo were so easy to play. Now it's my turn to be queen of the mountain." And then Geraldine wrapped her arms around Bob and planted a deep kiss on his lips. So they'd been planning this together all along.

Bob broke free and turned back to face Sparrow. "Have to thank you for taking him out for me. I really wasn't looking forward to it."

"Screw you." Sparrow said and coughed harshly as the burning fire spread across her chest and her vision went blurry.

Geraldine clapped her hands and jumped up and down like a little girl cackling. "Can I kill her? Please?"

Patting her on the back, Bob gave her a benign smile. "Anything for my girl."

Geraldine bounded up the porch and yanked the knife out of Jimbo's throat. The realization of what she was about to do made Sparrow's chest go tight. Geraldine returned to kneel next to her in the dirt. She placed the bloody blade at Sparrow's jugular. "'Member when you held that knife to my throat? Payback's a bitch, ain't it?"

Sparrow closed her eyes and tensed, waiting to feel the sharp slice across her flesh. Then she heard a dull thud and she looked up to see that Geraldine had tumbled to the ground—a small bleeding hole in her forehead.

Bob screamed, "Geraldine! Baby!" He swung his gun around wildly as his gaze darted around the clearing. Finding no one, he settled back on the two women at his feet and took aim. "You'll pay for that."

Another red dot appeared in his forehead and Sparrow

watched the life leave his eyes as he dropped to the ground next to her.

She should have been frightened, but she couldn't seem to get a firm grasp on reality. She was floating, her vision losing its crispness at the corners.

"Sparrow!" She turned to see Jared running full out from the woods, a rifle raised and ready. "Dammit, Sparrow, answer me."

Sparrow opened her mouth but couldn't quite figure out how to say the words. She concentrated, focusing on getting her lips to move, "Jared…"

Chapter Thirty-two

Jared dove to his knees just in time to see her eyes slide shut. Terror gripped him, piercing his heart like a knife as he doubled over her. "Wake up baby, don't do this to me."

"She ain't dead, just passed out."

Jared ripped his gun from the ground and pointed it straight at Kay Crowe, all of his pent up rage concentrated in his trigger finger. "This is all your fault."

Jared shook with the effort to regain control. But all he could see was Sparrow's lifeless body next to him. Although Kay hadn't pulled the trigger herself, he felt certain she was responsible.

He leaned in, pressing the end of his rifle to Kay's head, ready to put a bullet into her brain. His need to avenge and protect ripped a guttural cry from his lips. "You tried to kill us! We were just little boys! Why?"

Kay looked at him, her gaze afraid but resigned. He wanted to scream at her for being calm when the things she had done to him had tormented him his entire life. When she didn't answer his question right away, he pressed harder, bowing her backwards under his fury.

"Jared, stop. I can't let you do this." Merc approached, his weapon raised, scanning the crowd that had gathered around them.

"You have no idea what she's done to me and my family."

"I know, but you'll regret it if you kill her. Besides, think of what that would do to Sparrow." Merc's no nonsense words penetrated the fog of rage. "Put it down, brother."

Jared tried to lower his weapon, he tried really hard, but he couldn't unlock his arms. "Tell me."

Kay sighed, her gaze skittering to Sparrow before returning to him. "I guess you're gonna kill me no matter what. There ain't no big deal about it. I wanted the land, plain and simple. When your ma and pa died, I saw the opportunity and took it."

Red colored his vision, his muscles bulging with exertion. "You locked us in a closet. Left us to starve to death!"

"Yeah and you escaped. So, you had it tough growing up. Welcome to the fucking family." Kay held his gaze even as Jared fought with every ounce of control he possessed not to kill her. Not to finish it.

"Jared, you need to make a choice," Merc said. "Save your girl or have your revenge. I'm not so sure you can have both." He backed up to him, constantly shifting and keeping the crowd in sight. "But you gotta make a choice now cause these hillbillies are getting antsy."

Jared shook his head, trying to physically get his emotions under control. Blood seeped from Sparrow's wound, spreading over her shirt in a growing circle of red. Her life was slipping away. He knew then he'd choose her every day for the rest of his life. Jared lowered his gun, slung it over his shoulder, and stood. "Your entire family betrayed you. Now they're dead. And everyone here knows that the true heirs to Crowe Mountain are alive. Good luck with that."

Jared gently scooped Sparrow into his arms and walked away. The people in front of him parted to allow him through, everyone but Squirrel, who stood at the very back, a bag thrown over his shoulder and his knife at his hip. "You got room for one more young fella?"

"You're coming if I have to drag you." Jared kept walking, heading straight to his waiting truck. He laid her in the back seat and then ran around to the other side to climb in and put her head in his lap. Her skin was only one shade darker than a piece of paper. Blood splatter covered her face and shirt and arms.

"Dammit, Merc. Hurry up!"

Merc climbed into the driver's seat and Squirrel hopped into the other. When Merc sped out of the compound, Squirrel turned around. "Don't worry, boy. That girl's got grit in her veins."

"Sparrow?" He gentled his voice like a caress. No response. He raised a hand, unable to control its shaking, to touch her face. Still nothing.

Jared had trouble meeting Merc's gaze in the rearview mirror, but he forced himself to do it. Regret flooded him when he saw the pitying look in his friend's eyes. He clenched his jaw. "She's a strong woman. She's going to make it."

Even if she never spoke to him again, he'd make sure she lived. He could live with regret. He'd done it his entire life.

But he couldn't live without Sparrow.

***

"You're going to have to set me up a permanent room if you keep bringing me new patients." Dr. Hartsfield rose from inspecting Sparrow's newly stitched gunshot wound. "She looks great. The bullet came out without any permanent damage to tissue. She should recover fully with lots of rest and care.

"What about when she wakes up? She saw a lot of death. Do you think she'll be like Hoyt?" The words tasted like acid on his tongue, but he forced himself to ask. Sparrow needed him to be strong.

"I've seen men check out for less." Doc shrugged, "Some come back, some don't."

"She's scrappy. She'll wake up just fine." Squirrel sat in an old folding chair next to her bed, his gaze fixed on Sparrow.

Jared didn't know if the old man was trying to convince them or himself.

"I'll be back by to check on her and your brother again tomorrow. Notify me if there's any change. But Jared, she's been through a big trauma. It may take some time for her to recover."

He'd put Sparrow in his own bed, unable to stand the thought of her being any farther away from him. Now he had her, a bit damaged on the outside, but still alive. He could only pray she wasn't destroyed on the inside. Like his brother.

If only he'd kept a better eye on Hoyt. If only he'd believed Sparrow sooner. If only he could turn back time and rescue them. He'd never let either of them go.

"It ain't your fault. That girl was destined for something big. You can't stop fate." Squirrel pulled a small flask from his pocket, took a swig and then offered some to Jared.

"No, thanks." He didn't deserve the least respite from his suffering.

Suddenly, Jared heard a crash and ran to Hoyt's room, hot on Dr. Hartsfield's heels. They both skidded to a stop in the doorway to his brother's room, Jared nearly plowing her over. Hoyt was on the floor on his hands and knees, a broken glass of water splattered out before him. He was pale and gasping for breath, but he was awake.

After he and Doc helped Hoyt back onto the bed, Jared grabbed his brother's hand. "You scared the shit out of me, bro. Don't ever do that again."

Hoyt offered up a weak smile "Swear. Won't ever do it again." He coughed and immediately groaned.

"I'm glad to see you're awake, the doctor said. "I need you to answer a couple of quick questions. Where are you hurting?"

"My side hurts like a mother."

"Anywhere else?" she asked.

"No, it's all good."

Jared smiled. The doctor smiled too. "Well, I think other than a few bruised ribs, you'll survive."

Jared met the doctor's eyes. And the look he saw there soothed his soul. The IV bag was still attached to Hoyt's arm, so Jared righted the knocked over stand. All the other lines going into him had been ripped out, but the doc said they weren't needed anymore. Jared leaned over and touched his head to Hoyt's. "I'm glad you're back."

Hoyt squeezed his hand. "Me, too, bro."

Hoyt closed his eyes and fell asleep. Dr. Hartsfield touched Jared's arm and indicated for him to follow her out into the hall. "He's okay. He's just resting. It's going to take him a long time to get his strength back up, and he may have to do some physical therapy, but I don't see any reason why he can't get back to a hundred percent physically."

Jared's heart skidded and jumped at her words. His entire focus for the past few weeks had been on life and death. Now he could finally focus on making sure his brother found his way out of the quagmire of nightmares—and on making sure Sparrow made a full recovery.

That night, he slept in bed with Sparrow with the door open, listening for any sounds from Hoyt's room. Dr. Hartsfield had injected her with painkillers before leaving. Jared fell asleep praying she'd forgive him when she awoke.

Chapter Thirty-three

Jared was ripped from his slumber by a loud scream. Sparrow thrashed and kicked and screamed louder. He barely restrained himself from throwing his body over hers. Instead, he grabbed her arms to hold her down, but she didn't stop thrashing her head from side to side, mumbling and sobbing.

"Sparrow. Wake up, it's me, Jared. You were having a bad dream, honey." Her breathing hitched, but she stopped screaming. Her eyes fluttered open; for a split second her gaze was blank, but then awareness took over.

Her breathing hitched, and then she sucked in a broken breath and emitted a low keening wail that broke on a sob. The sobs wracked her body, ripping him in two. His need to protect and soothe her was his only conscious thought as he wrapped his arms around her and pulled her against him, careful not to put pressure on her injury, and rubbed soothing circles on her back.

"I...I killed him." She managed between crying.

"You were trying to protect your home." Jared wanted to wrap her in a cocoon and take away every last drop of her pain. His first kill had given him nightmares, and *he* was a soldier.

"Oh God, I can't believe he…"

"Hush now. It's over. You're safe."

"I should have known. Should have—should have done something sooner."

Jared felt nothing but anguish. "No. There was no way for you to know. You're not evil like them. I know that."

Tears gathered in Jared's eyes and he let them fall, unashamed. "It's my fault. If only I'd listened to you sooner, you would never have gone back. I'm so sorry."

She continued crying and Jared didn't know what else to say. So he simply held her until her crying softened to hiccups and then the hiccups faded into the soft even breathing of sleep. Jared watched the sun rise through the window before sleep claimed him.

***

The next few days faded together for Sparrow. She spent most of her time in bed. She just wanted to lock the rest of the world out. Her emotions were raw and ripped wide open. Part of her was still very angry with Jared. Another part longed for his comfort.

They compromised. He slept with her every night, holding her tight, but it didn't go further than that. And during the day, he came to check on her, but he also gave her plenty of time by herself.

Squirrel would often come sit with her. They would sit together and play checkers or just talk. It was during one of these visits that she was finally forced to talk about it.

"You know he's hurting too." Squirrel leaned across the table and took a sip of the water. Sparrow jumped his red marker. They were playing checkers again, and it was a close game. "I've never seen a man so tortured over a girl before," Squirrel added. "You must've done a real number on him."

Sparrow leaned back in her chair and lifted an eyebrow. "Or maybe he's the one who did a real number on me. He didn't believe in me. He doesn't trust me. What kind of relationship can be built on that foundation?"

Squirrel double jumped her two. "I talked to his brother. Jared has never been in a real relationship before. And never with a firecracker like you. The only thing he's ever known is war. Combat. Fighting. Not exactly the kinda thing that makes a man trustin'."

The words reached inside and touched a part of her. It made sense to her. "But I'm not his enemy."

"No. You're worse. You're a girl." Squirrel smiled and jumped another of her checkers.

"And what's so wrong with being a girl?" She leaned forward, letting him know she was not okay with that statement.

Squirrel held up his hands in surrender. "Nothing 'cept that boy ain't got no idea how to handle a girl."

Heat rose to her cheeks and suffused her entire body. Jared knew exactly how to handle a girl. He had handled her with expertise. And she'd lapped up every bit of it.

"All I'm saying is you should at least talk to the boy. He screwed up. He knows it. And I'm tired of watchin' him mope around here like he's out of whiskey."

As if on cue, Jared called from the kitchen, "Supper's about ready."

Squirrel looked her up and down, sniffed, and said, "You need a bath."

Sparrow tried to look affronted, but couldn't quite pull it off. She hadn't change clothes in two days. She knew she looked a mess and smelled like one too.

"Think on what I said." Squirrel got to his feet, walked to the doorway, and shouted, "Better have me some potatoes. Don't like all them green vegetables you keep cookin'."

Sparrow got to her feet and turned to the dresser to grab a change of clothes. Hayden had brought over a whole bag of them for her to wear until she recovered enough to buy some of her own. She didn't avoid her reflection in the mirror this time. The girl staring back at her looked older, harder, and about ten pounds underweight. Her hair was messy, her clothes ill fitting. Was this the girl she wanted to be for the rest of her life? A shadow of herself?

Maybe Squirrel was right. Maybe it was time to try trusting her heart again. Hopefully this time it wouldn't almost kill her.

Sparrow went to bathroom and took a bath. She'd just finished towel drying her hair when she heard a soft knock at the bedroom door. "Come in."

The door snaked open and Jared poked his head inside. "Listen, I know you don't want to see me or be around me and I can't blame you for that, but you have to eat."

His words carried a firm command, yet there was still hesitance in his tone. Sparrow turned to face him, a slight smile on her face. He really was the most handsome man she'd ever laid eyes on.

As he eased his way into the bedroom, his gaze raked over her like hot coals, setting her skin on fire. "Sparrow, I…" He rubbed a hand through his hair and blew out a frustrated breath.

"Yes?" she asked.

"I think you need to eat more. You're losing too much weight. And if it takes me leaving to make you feel comfortable, I'll do it."

"Why would I want you to leave?

His dark gaze snapped to hers. "Because you hate me for what I did to you. I shouldn't have left that morning without talking to you first. Without letting Merc know what was going on. I ignored my instincts until it was too late. It's all my fault and I can never make it up to you. *Never.*"

She decided to have a little bit of mercy and took a stroll across the room. Sitting down on the bed, Sparrow curled a leg beneath her. She had on a low-cut top and fitted cotton pants. Hayden had called them yoga pants. Whatever that was. She knew she didn't exactly look sexy with the black sling around her arm, but his eyes locked on her with banked heat.

Sparrow leaned over and picked at the bedspread, "So let me get this straight. You screwed up, and now you're just fixin' to give up?"

She watched as his jaw ticked and he slowly closed and reopened his glittering eyes. "Listen, I deserve that. I know you don't want to be near me. I promise, as soon as I can, I'll find somewhere else for you to live."

"What if I'm comfortable right here?"

The dark circles beneath his eyes looked like small bruises. His cheeks had hollowed out too. She'd been so focused on her own misery she'd failed to notice his.

"Here?" His face was a mask of confusion. As if it didn't even occur to him that she might be giving him a second chance. Hell, maybe he was afraid to let himself believe it.

Sparrow realized that she was going to have to take the bull by the horns, so to speak. She got to her feet, unfolding her body from the bed, and walked to him. Reaching up, she cupped his cheek. "Yes, Jared. Here with you."

He trembled as his hands wrapped around her waist. "With me? After what happened?"

"You made a mistake. I'm sure I'll make mistakes too. And I think if you love someone you should fight for them. Not give up on them."

Jared ducked his head and sucked in a shuddering breath, resting his head on hers, his lips inches away. A tremor passed down her body and chills raced across her flesh. Her heart rate accelerated from the slow, steady rhythm of a woman full of confidence to out of control.

"Sparrow, I love you. I don't want you to leave. Will you please stay with me?"

She nodded, tears forming in her eyes. Part of that hollow burning in her chest eased just a little bit. "I love you too. And I'm not going anywhere."

His lips close over hers, taking possession of her mouth, and she opened willingly to him. Heat coursed through her body. He slid to the bed, pulling her down with him, careful of her arm. But any pain she'd felt was forgotten as he slid between her thighs and worshipped her body. Sparrow slipped into a cloud of bliss from which she never wanted to return.

Epilogue

Hoyt leaned his head against the bedroom wall, the sounds of Jared and Sparrow making up was a soothing balm to the soul. They would be able to heal together. They would be able to move past what had happened. They would move on.

And he would be stuck here, trapped as a prisoner in his own body. A body that didn't belong to him anymore. He turned away from the wall then, took a sip of his orange juice, and got up to shut his bedroom door. He sat down on the bed, fingers clenching the covers. Images of being trapped in that small room slashed at his mind and a cold sweat broke out across his body. His scars from all the cuts seemed to reopen and bleed. His throat closed off, and he hunched forward to suck in air that didn't seem to exist. He put his hands on his knees, gasping at the sharp pain in his chest as his rib cage constricted around his lungs.

A part of him knew that he was having a panic attack. Hell, he probably had some form of PTSD after all that shit he'd survived. But that was the logical part. And right now the logical part of his brain only made up about zero point five percent.

Terror sent him to his knees and he crawled to the bedroom door, pulled it open, and collapsed half between the rooms, clutching at his chest and sucking in air. *Slow. Count to ten.* He repeated the mantra over and over.

Hoyt didn't know how long he lay there, only that when he opened his eyes his fist was clenched on his chest;

the other hand dug into the carpet. And when he lifted the fist, he realized it was clutched around a pill bottle. *Oblivion.* He quickly unscrewed the lid and poured out four pills, knowing one pain pill had no hope of touching his kind of agony.

Hoyt lay there until his body began to ease. He climbed to his window, threw it open, and fell across the bed. The pill bottle was tucked safely in his pocket. If he had to choose between feeling everything or nothing, right now it was no decision at all.

Before you go...

From the author: I hope you enjoyed Reckless River. I want to thank you for joining the Men of Mercy on their adventure. I would like to invite you to post a *review* of the book on Amazon or Goodreads.

–Lindsay Cross

* * *

For updates about new releases, as well as exclusive promotions and giveaways, sign up for Lindsay Cross's insider mailing list here and **be entered monthly to win a $50 amazon gift card.**

www.lindsaycross.com

email: **lindsaycross@lindsaycross.com**
Facebook: Lindsay.cross.author
twitter: @lindsaycross101

RAVAGED RIVER
MEN OF MERCY, BOOK 4

Special forces operative Hoyt Crowe wasn't just damaged... he was broken. After suffering brutal torture in captivity, his once lively spirit is shattered. Now his greatest adversary isn't some unknown terrorist in a foreign country, it's himself.

Hayden James watched Hoyt slide into a private purgatory of post-traumatic stress disorder, taking her heart with him. No longer warm and loving, he is cold. Hardened. A shell of his former self.

When an old enemy threatens Hayden's life, Hoyt must find the strength to slay his inner demons or lose the woman he loves forever.

REDEMPTION RIVER
MEN OF MERCY, BOOK 1
RESURRECTION RIVER
MEN OF MERCY BOOK 2
RECKLESS RIVER
MEN OF MERCY BOOK 3
DAVID: MEN OF MERCY NOVELLA
RAYLAN: MEN OF MERCY NOVELLA
RAVAGED RIVER
MEN OF MERCY, BOOK 6

Lindsay Cross is the award-winning author of the Men of Mercy series. She is the fun loving mom of two beautiful daughters and one precocious Great Dane. Lindsay is happily married to the man of her dreams – a soldier and veteran. During one of her husband's deployments from home, writing became her escape and motivation.

An avid reader since childhood, reading and writing is in her blood. After years of reading, she discovered her true passion – writing. Her alpha military men are damaged, drop-dead gorgeous and determined to win the heart of the woman of their dreams.

FOR YOUR **FREE COPY** OF DAVID, A MEN OF MERCY NOVELLA, SIGN UP FOR MY NEWSLETTER AT WWW.LINDSAYCROSS.COM